infamous

CHRONICLES of NICK

infamous

SHERRILYN KENYON

St. Martin's Griffin ≈ New York

INFAMOUS. Copyright © 2012 by Sherrilyn Kenyon. All rights reserved. Printed in the United States of America. For information, address St. Martin's Press, 175 Fifth Avenue, New York, NY 10010.

www.stmartins.com

ISBN 978-1-250-00282-2 (hardcover)
ISBN 978-1-250-00816-9 (e-book)

First Edition: March 2012

10 9 8 7 6 5 4 3 2 1

For my boys, who always inspire me
and who fill my life with love and laughter.

For my husband, for all the wonderful things you do.

To Monique, Matthew, John, AMT, Holly, and all
the wonderful SMP staff
who help make dreams come true.

For Kim, Lisa, Tish, Loretta, Jacs, and all my friends
who keep me sane.

And to everyone who is old enough to know better,
but young enough to do it anyway.

Most of all, to you, the reader.
Thanks for taking this journey with me and Nick.
We hope you enjoy it and that you return for
the next one.

infamous

PROLOGUE

It wasn't every day you learned that you were the son of a ferocious demon and that your destiny was to end the world. Or that the guy you thought was your whacked-out uncle was actually you from the future trying to prevent not only your death, but that of basically everyone else. . . .

Literally.

All in all, being that he was only fourteen years old, Nick Gautier was handling it pretty well.

Yeah, not really. Stunned into complete silence, which very seldom happened, Nick couldn't breathe as brutal reality sucker-punched him. Hard. Mercilessly.

Right where it hurt most. Well, not *physically* there. But mentally it felt like his gonads had been stomped straight into the ground. His head swam from nausea.

Trying to get a handle on everything, he clutched at the broken stones on the stoop where he sat outside his new apartment building on Bourbon Street. Ambrose—the future him—stood to his left, towering over him with a pitiless sneer.

How was it possible that he was Ambrose?

Or more to the point, Ambrose was what he would become. . . .

How could *he,* an average kid roaming the backstreets of New Orleans, be the ultimate evil? He didn't feel particularly evil. Most days, he didn't feel anything except stressed out by school, or tired of his mom nagging at him about everything from the clothes he wore, to the length of his hair, to how late he stayed up. Some days, it felt like she was looking for a reason to be ticked off at him.

Boy, if she knew *this* about him, he'd never hear the end of it. She'd probably ground him until he was

at least three or four thousand years old. Yeah, it sounded ludicrous even to him, until he looked at Ambrose standing all bad ass and tough at his left.

Ambrose is me from the future. . . .

He glanced around the section of Bourbon Street where his new apartment was located. Everything looked the same. The broken sidewalks that made up the French Quarter. The cars parked in a line on both sides of the street. The row of shotgun houses that led to stores and restaurants . . .

But nothing was the same.

Most of all, *he* would never be the same again.

I am a demon.

"No, no, no," Nick repeated as he tried to come up with some other explanation. One that made a little more sense and that didn't leave him as a tool for the darkest forces in the universe.

Unfortunately, there wasn't one. Not that any of *this* made sense. It was all pretty farcical when you thought about it.

Him. Nicholas Ambrosius Gautier—smart-mouthed, streetwise kid. Typical teenager. Gaming guru. Anime and manga obsessed otaku. Socially awkward around any girl his age.

Total evil.

Dang, his principal had been right all along. . . .

He really was demonspawn. Too bad Peters had gotten eaten by zombies before he found out the real truth of Nick's parentage. Old fart would have been proud to be proven right.

Nick really was destined for a life of total destruction.

Even though he wanted to, he couldn't deny it. Ambrose had the same exact blue eyes and dark brown hair he had. The same sneer that he often wore when things ticked him off—the one that got him grounded every time his mom saw it. More than that, Ambrose had the identical scar on his palm that Nick had been given when Xenon cut his hand for blood. A scar that hadn't been on Ambrose's hand the last time he'd seen him.

I'm in a flippin' Twilight Zone *episode.*

He had to be. Nothing else made sense.

So where was his voice-over, telling the audience

how he'd screwed up and taken a wrong turn down some suburban street or some such crud? *C'mon, Rod Serling. Don't let me down. I need you to come in and tell me that I'm in a nightmare. Tell me about this new dimension of sight and sound.*

But there was no reprieve. Not from this skewed reality.

And not from the fact that he was the hated and hunted son of a demon . . .

"I'm evil." He tried to accept that and still he couldn't. If it were true, how could he go to Mass all the time with his mom? Shouldn't he burst into flames when holy water touched him? Feel a burning sensation or something when he took communion? For that matter, he'd been an altar boy for years.

But he'd never once experienced the slightest bit of discomfort from any of that. The worst thing that had ever happened to him in church was when the priest had fallen asleep during his last confession—which said it all about how boring his life had been prior to all of this.

Yeah, okay, and then there was the time when he'd

tripped going down the center aisle and spilled in-cense all over the place. But that hadn't been a result of his birthright, unless you counted clumsiness and the fact his thrift store shoes had been too big for his feet.

"I am evil," Nick repeated one more time.

Ambrose shifted his weight to one leg as his dark scowl intensified. "No, Nick. *We're* evil. We were bred to be soldiers for the darkest of powers." He said that so lackadaisically—Like, *Hey, the sun's shining. Look, the neighbor's dog is in your trash again. Dude, you're wearing one ugly shirt.*

Oh, and by the way, you're a demon in human form.

Yeah . . .

Much like the tacky Hawaiian shirt Nick was wearing, it just didn't fit.

"Then why are you trying to help me?" he asked Ambrose.

Ambrose snorted. "I ask myself that every day, and I have no answer. Part of me wants to tell you to just embrace your birthright and go with it. To let the evil have its way and carry you to the Nether Realm for your enemies to use as they see fit. God knows, fighting it never gave me any peace or comfort. Not once. Just a giant sized ulcer. You want the honest truth? Caring about others has made my entire life suck from beginning to end. When you don't care about anyone or anything, nothing can hurt you. When you do . . ."

Your enemies had you by your stones. He'd already learned that lesson.

Still . . .

"You haven't answered my question."

Ambrose sighed. "Because I don't have an answer, kid. Contrary to what you think, we're all mice lost in a maze. No one really knows what they're doing. You go left for whatever reason, but you don't know if it's the right direction or not until you're either electrocuted or you get the cheese. By the time you find out which it is, it's too late to turn back. You're either dead or you're fed. There's no third option."

"I have to say then, that I prefer fed over dead."

Ambrose laughed bitterly. "So do I. Some days, anyway." He glanced skyward as if looking for divine guidance of some kind. "I seriously hope I'm not about to make another mistake." He rubbed his hand against his forehead as if he had a pain there, then leveled a piercing stare at Nick. "Fine. I'll tell you the truth. All of it. For better or worse. Let's put the cards on the table and see how we screw things up this time, shall we?"

Nick wasn't sure if that was a good thing or not. But either way, he wanted to know exactly what was going on and what he was up against.

Ambrose faced him. "This isn't my first rodeo, but it is most definitely the last. You, Nick, are the only hope I have of getting it right. I've tried three times before this and each one was worse on the outcome than the last. When I started tampering with our lives, I had more humanity in me. I've all but lost it now. My last attempt burned out something inside me, and I'll be honest, it scares me. And I don't scare. Ever. Not after everything I've been through. But the degree to which I don't care anymore—about anything—is a frightful thing. At times, I want it all to end. Because when it does, *my* pain will stop and I'll have some degree of peace. Finally. It'll seriously suck for everyone else. But like I said, I'm to the point where I really don't care anymore. I'm holding on to my humanity by the thinnest thread imaginable, and any day now, I expect it to break. God help us all when it does."

A chill went down Nick's spine. He didn't want the bleak, lonely future Ambrose described. Most of all, he didn't want to become Ambrose. While he was jaded and suspicious by nature, there was still a part of him that honestly believed people were good and decent. Most of them, anyway.

He glared at Ambrose as he absorbed those words. "Then why should I listen to anything you tell me? For all I know, you're setting me up so that you can have your peace and end the world. . . . And what do you mean you've tried three times? How?"

"I forgot how ADD I once was." Ambrose shook his head. "No wonder Kyrian was so sharp with me so many times." He took a deep breath before he answered Nick's question. "I've mentored three different Nicks before you. Four if you count my original childhood."

"Ooooriginal?" He dragged the word out as that thought played through his mind. Did that mean . . . ?

Ambrose let out another bitter laugh. "My life was slightly different from yours. Not much. Little things. But it's those little things that can make a huge difference in what happens to us later."

Yep, it was exactly what he'd suspected. And that truthfully terrified him.

Never underestimate a man's ability to screw up the best laid plans—that was one of his friend's favorite sayings.

"Such as?" Nick asked.

"The first attempt I made at correcting the past, I had Nick tell our mother about the Dark-Hunter world as soon as he was dragged into it." He winced as if the memory was unbearable. "I really thought that was the perfect solution. I did. All these years, I kept telling myself that if only she'd known about the paranormal, she'd have been wary of it and not—" He broke off to curse under his breath. Then he turned back to Nick. "But she couldn't handle it or believe it . . . It was a total disaster. Because of our father, she thought it was a mental defect— schizophrenia to be precise. That first Nick ended up medicated in an asylum with no one to protect him from our enemies. I'm still scarred by what was done to him. Worse, without us living at home, Mom never stopped working at her club and she was shot dead during a robbery."

Nick wanted to vomit at the mere thought. "Are you serious?"

Ambrose nodded. "There's nothing like watching multiple outcomes play out before your eyes and then live in your memory. I now understand why Savitar sits on his island, away from everything."

Who? Nick had never heard of such a person. "Savitar?"

"A being you'll meet one day. For now, it's not important. Just remember, you can't talk to your mother about *any* of this. She doesn't want to know, and she'll never accept the fact that she had the son of a demon."

Who could blame her for that? He personally couldn't think of any woman who would welcome that news. *Hey, hon, guess what? Your son that you nurtured in your body for nine months and then sacrificed your life and dignity to raise is destined to end the world. Aren't you proud?*

Yeah, that just didn't work.

All right then, he wouldn't tell his mother about himself, his father or his Dark-Hunter boss Kyrian. Truthfully, he'd been tempted to let her know why Kyrian was *different*, why he worked so late at night and wasn't around in the daytime. But every time he'd thought about it, his gut had kept him silent.

Score one for the gut. Too bad his brain wasn't as smart.

For the very reason Ambrose had named, he'd been afraid of how she'd react. There were times when he felt like his mother was looking for a reason to have him committed or institutionalized. Like she feared him becoming his father so much that she was itching for some sign to confirm that he was every bit as violent and awful, and lock him up before it was too late and he hurt someone.

"What happened with the other attempts?"

"Next we were sucked into the Nether Realm at age seventeen where . . ." His voice broke off and he visibly cringed as if that memory was even worse than the one before. "Whatever you do, kid, stay away from Azmodea. Don't believe any demon who tells you lies about how great it is. Because for you, it's not, and I can't stress the *not* part enough. Whatever you do, avoid creatures named Azura and Noir. Only slavery waits for you there. A slavery so brutal, you can't even conceive of it. And it would give even Quentin Tarantino nightmares."

That was an impressive thought and he took Ambrose's warning to heart. "Never heard of that place, but will add it to my 'under no circumstances' list." Like eating broccoli, doing laundry, or feeding Mark's "dog" that was actually a thirteen foot gator with a nasty attitude and a taste for Cajun. "And the Nick after that?"

He let out a slow breath. "Suffice it to say, it didn't go well either."

"How so?"

Ambrose gave him an arch stare. "I'm you, Nick.

Trust me when I say you don't want to go there, and let's leave it at that. There are some memories no one needs to have. And I'd give anything to purge it."

"Yeah, but if you know me, then you know—"

"Nick!"

Gah, he hated that exasperated tone adults used.

Fine. Whatever. He wouldn't press the issue. There were plenty more questions he had. And he dreaded the next one, but he had to know. "And with me?" *I.e. how's it going in comparison to the others?*

Please don't add me to the nightmare list. He wanted life to get better, not worse.

"It's different this time, too. But in unique ways. Some things are the same and others . . ."

"Name some," Nick prodded when he didn't continue.

Ambrose paused in his pacing before Nick's stoop. "You already know about the Dark-Hunters and Squires. I didn't find out about them until *I* graduated high school. You met Simi at fourteen. In my original past, I met her just before I became a Dark-Hunter."

Nick sucked his breath in at that unexpected bomb. "*I* become a Dark-Hunter like Kyrian?"

Ambrose nodded.

That wasn't good. Thoughts whirled through his mind. Dark-Hunters were immortal warriors who protected mankind from the preternatural evil that preyed on them. While each DH came from a vastly different culture and time, the one thing that united them all was that something horrific had happened to them. Something so bad that they sold their souls to the goddess Artemis for an Act of Vengeance against the one who hurt them.

Nick wasn't sure he wanted to know what would happen to him that was so awful that he'd do such a thing, especially if he couldn't see it coming.

Or stop it.

"Did *you* get shot the night you met Kyrian?"

Ambrose nodded. "Nothing about that event changed. It played out for you, the same way it played out for me and the others. For some reason that is lynchpin event and it never alters. It's what happens after that, that goes in varying directions."

Nick let that rattle around in his head. What would be worse than being shot by a friend? *I mean yeah, I want revenge on Alan and Tyree for that, but not so much I'd sell my soul to get it.*

So most likely, he wasn't the one who died. Who else would be in his life in just a few years that he'd care that much about them?

Girlfriend?

Wife? Would he be married by then?

Possible, he supposed. His wife's betrayal was what had made Kyrian a Dark-Hunter. Talon became a Dark-Hunter after his wife died and his sister was killed.

Who do I lose?

Not wanting to think about that right now, he returned to quizzing Ambrose. "What else is different?"

"You've already met Tabitha Devereaux—" A smile played at the edge of his lips that made Nick wonder what caused it. "I didn't meet her until I was out of school and working for Kyrian. But the change that concerns us most is that my father died when I was ten."

Nick frowned. "My dad's still in prison. And alive as far as I've been told."

"Yeah. This is the first time that's happened. Damned if I know why. He should be dead by now. Because he's not, it's allowing enemies to find you sooner than they should be able to."

Nick definitely didn't like the sound of that. "What do you mean?"

"What I mean is there are currently two Malachais using their powers here in New Orleans—you and our father—and there should only be one in existence at a time. Once a new Malachai is born and reaches puberty, the other dies—usually violently so—"

"Are you telling me that if I ever have a kid, it's going to grow up and kill me?"

A cruel smile twisted Ambrose's lips. "You can have them. But it's like playing Russian roulette. If they don't inherit your powers, the human part can't handle your Malachai demon blood and they die before they're ten. The one who reaches ten and lives . . . that's the one who will replace you."

That explained so much about his father's attitude toward him. No wonder he hated him so. "Meaning I'll die around their tenth birthday?"

Ambrose sarcastically touched his nose to let Nick know that he was correct. "That's the way it's always worked in the past. One of the beautiful things about us . . . Until we use our powers, we are invisible to almost all other gods and preternatural creatures. If they try to see our future, they see one that looks human. Kids, grandkids, the whole package. They have no way of knowing who and what we are until we evolve and flex our powers. But the one thing that has always held true—there can only be one Malachai demon with full powers at a time."

"Why?"

"It was a bargain made after the Primus Bellum— the first major war of the gods. Both sides were required to put their soldiers down."

Nick grimaced at what he was sure was a euphemism. "You mean kill them?"

Ambrose nodded. "But the commander of each side was spared. One Malachai. One Sephiroth. They exist in balance and so long as the truce holds, there can be no more than the one."

"So what changed?"

"No idea. With our luck, by coming to the past as a Malachai, I screwed the pooch to the point it'll never walk again. It's the only thing I can think of. But since you didn't have powers yet, I didn't think it would be a problem. Whatever the cause, something is out of synch here, and no one knows what it is. All we know for sure is that your power is concentrated with Adarian's. So long as your father lives, there's a cosmic bounty on your head so steep it's staggering."

"Why?" Nick asked.

"Whoever kills you, gets to take your powers as a bonus. It's why you're in the worst sort of danger imaginable. No one, except you, can kill Adarian, so no one will try for him."

Which meant it was open season on Nick.

"If I die, can't my father have another child?"

"You don't have to die for it. He can have another kid at any point—but only one of you can have the Malachai powers and only one of you will live to adulthood—that's the theory, anyway. However, death isn't the worst fear you should have, kid. There are many things a lot worse, and those things are after you right now. You can't trust anyone . . . except me. I'm the only one who truly has your back."

"You said earlier that I could trust Kyrian."

"You can. He's a good man, but he's not powerful enough to fight what's coming for you. No one is, except *you*."

That reignited Nick's temper as he remembered the fact that Ambrose had left him alone to face one demon already when the jerk could have helped him. "And you're not going to help me?"

"I can't."

"Yeah, right. Correct me if I'm wrong, but aren't you already screwing with cosmic law by being here?"

"This isn't about cosmic law. It's about survival. *Our* mutual survival, and saving the people we both love more than ourselves."

"Then help me."

"I am."

Nick was aghast at his simple answer. Sitting on

the bench wasn't helpful. He needed a teammate, not a water boy. "By doing nothing?"

"Exactly. If I use my powers here to fight, that will be three Malachais using power in a single location. Even *you* know what that means."

Yeah, triangulation. With three points, anything could be located.

Ambrose gave him a droll stare. "You don't want me to do that. Really."

True, but that meant he was going this alone and he wasn't learning things fast enough. Most of all, it meant he had a giant target on his back. "Man, this is so screwed up."

"Welcome to our life," Ambrose said bitterly.

"Yeah, well, no offense, you can take it and put it where the sun don't shine." Nick sneered in disgust as he digested everything Ambrose was telling him. "And how do I know you're not lying anyway? You say to trust you, but trust is earned, not demanded, and I don't think enough of you to give it to you."

Ambrose grabbed him by the front of his shirt and yanked him up from the stoop. "Listen to me, you little punk," he snarled in Nick's face. "I hate you. You understand? I hate you with a passion that burns brighter than the hottest star in the universe. If I could, I'd tear your throat out and end everything right here and now. But the one thing I know is if we die, something a lot worse than us will take our place and the tiny handful of people I still love will suffer unimaginable agony. *That* I cannot allow to happen. Even if it means stomaching you for a little longer. We, who were born to end the world, are the only hope there is for saving it."

Nick tried to break free, but it was impossible. "That doesn't make any sense."

Ambrose shoved him back. "Tell me about it. But that's where we are. I can guide you and advise you. That's it. I can tell you where and how I screwed up and what the other Nicks did wrong, but you will have to live this life and—"

"I'm so confused. How can you remember everything? Do my actions not affect you?"

Ambrose laughed. "My powers are infinite and beyond your comprehension. Some days, they're even beyond mine. But this particular one that allows me to come back to the past and talk to you, I borrowed. And I had to bargain hard for it. The demon gave me three chances to set the past right. When I failed and he came for me, I killed him and took his blood. That's what's allowing me to help you now. Once I'm out of his blood—which is why I can't always come back to save your ass—you'll be totally on your own and I won't have any memory of ever tampering with the past. Whatever *you* do will be my final memory and the rest will be gone forever."

"Dude, that's so messed up. You drink blood?"

Ambrose gave him an irritated grimace. "Is that all you got out of what I just said?"

"No, but that's so disturbing. How can you drink someone's blood?" Nick shivered in revulsion. "Gah, I can't believe I'd ever be that gross."

"Son, you'll do a lot more than that before all is said and done."

Nick made gagging noises.

Ambrose cursed. His expression said he was imagining Nick's neck in his hands and Nick's eyes bulging as he choked the life out of him. "I can't believe my fate is in *your* hands."

Now that was just rude and it thoroughly riled him. "Yeah, well, from what you just said, it's not like you did any better yourself. *I* can't believe *your* ugly butt is what I have to look forward to becoming. Talk about a letdown. You know, I had plans. I was going to be a lawyer. Do some good in the world. Not become," he gestured at Ambrose, "some self-absorbed dickweed."

His expression turned even colder. "If I were self-absorbed, I wouldn't be here. But it's easy for you to judge me. You haven't been betrayed. . . . Yet."

"Not true. I was shot by my best friends."

"Alan, Tyree, and crew . . . that wasn't betrayal, kid. Deep inside you knew who and what they were. What you were in for when you threw in with them. What to expect. You can't fault a snake for biting you when it's the very nature of the beast to do so."

Ambrose narrowed his gaze on him. "No, Nick. I'm talking *real* betrayal. The kind you don't see coming. The kind that tackles you to the ground and kicks your teeth in, and forever ruins your life. The kind that stays with you for decades after it's over. By the time you graduate, you'll consider what Alan did to you a favor. It got you off the street at a time when you were headed in the wrong direction, and it made your mother's dreams come true."

His mother.

A bad feeling went through Nick as everything came together in his mind. As another realization groin kicked him. While Ambrose looked tired, he wasn't *that* old. Probably not even as old as his friend Mark, and definitely not as old as his mother, who was only twenty-eight.

In less than ten years, I'll become a Dark-Hunter. . . .

There was only one thing he could think of that would make him do something so drastic in that amount of time.

"Mom dies, doesn't she? That's why you became a Dark-Hunter, isn't it?"

In that instant, Ambrose's eyes changed from blue to the same black color as Kyrian's. The wind blew his long coat out from his legs and swept his hair back from his face. A double bow and arrow—the mark of a Dark-Hunter—appeared on his cheek and his fangs flashed in the fading daylight.

Dark-Hunters die in sunlight.

But not Ambrose . . .

How could he be outside and on the street when he shouldn't be able to? How was he able to hide his Dark-Hunter traits?

The wind sent a chill down Nick's spine that he felt all the way to his soul.

"Because of *you*," Ambrose sneered that word, "and your stupidity, your mother, Bubba, Mark, and . . . others close to you die horribly. That is the landscape we're trying to repaint. And if you fail them this time, it's over. For all of us."

CHAPTER 1

If banging your head against a brick wall burned a hundred and fifty calories an hour as they said it did, then Nick should be emaciated. 'Cause he'd been banging it so hard these last two days that he should have a concussion by now.

"Mom, please . . ."

"I said no and I meant it. You're too young to date."

Fifteen? Really? Since when was fifteen too young to date? If he didn't know better, he'd swear she was from the Dark Ages. Heck, for that matter, Kyrian was more open-minded and he really was from the Stone Age, or Iron Age, or one of those boring ages that they tried to force feed him in school.

That man had actually dated in a chariot. . . .

Nick had to stop himself from rolling his eyes— that was like throwing gas on a roaring fire while wearing kerosene soaked clothing when his mom was in this mood.

I'm old enough to death match demons and zombies, stop the apocalypse, deal with Death on a daily basis, and hold down two jobs, but I can't meet my girl for a movie. . . .

Yeah, that made all the sense in the world.

He sighed irritably. "I'm a year older than you were when you had *me*."

She narrowed those beady little blue eyes at him and lifted her chin to glare up at him. He still wasn't used to looking down at his mom, who barely reached mid-chest on him these days.

The fact that someone so incredibly tiny could cow him with nothing more than an arched brow didn't sit well with him. But regardless of arguments and differences of opinion, he loved his mother and wouldn't do anything to hurt her or her feelings.

Which was how she cowed him with a single glance. . . .

I'm such a wimp.

"Precisely my point, Nicky. You see what kind of trouble you could get into? Are you ready to be a father at fifteen? No, I don't think you are. You can't even remember to take out the trash without me reminding you three times a day. Which, for your information, is the amount of times a day a child demands food."

It wasn't that he needed reminding so much as the fact that he hated doing it and kept hoping she'd forget about it.

Better not mention that. It'd get him into more trouble. So he went in to attack her first argument. "Technically, if I got a girl pregnant right now, I'd be sixteen when the baby was born."

Pulling her blonde hair back into a ponytail, she glared at him. "Not funny, Nick. How dare you make a joke about this. I am *not* amused."

"Well, personally, I think you've done a great job with me, Ma. And that was with no help whatsoever. I don't know why you're complaining."

She put her hands on her hips and glared furiously. "And you're trying to distract me with flattery. It won't work. You can't date until you drive, and that's that."

There was another sore topic for him. "I keep begging you to teach me."

"Not in my brand spanking new car. It's the only new car I've ever owned and it's the only one we have. If you wreck it, we won't have a way to evacuate during hurricane season."

Nick growled low in his throat. He had more than enough money in savings to buy a car, but because of his age, he couldn't sign for one, and his mother refused. *That money's for college, not a car you don't need. There ain't no place you need to go that your feet or a streetcar can't carry you to.*

Ugh! His mother frustrated him on so many levels.

He gave her a sullen pout. "So basically, I'll never learn to drive, and therefore will never date."

She smiled proudly before she turned around to get her shoes from her bedroom. "Now you got the picture, Boo."

He mocked her words. Until she snapped around to face him as if she knew what he was doing.

Nick gave her his most charming grin. "C'mon, Ma. Everyone else in my class is dating. Even Madaug."

"And if—"

"Everyone jumped off the Pontchartrain would you join them?" he asked in falsetto before she had a chance.

Yeah, that got him another hostile glare. "Don't mock me, boy."

"Sorry."

She jerked her shoes on. "No, you're not. But if you do that again, you will be." She straightened. "Now, I'm off to work. I'll be home around midnight. Are you going to the Halloween haunted house your school's sponsoring?"

Nick snorted. "Oh yeah, Mom. Just what I want to do. Wet my pants in front of my classmates and scream like a girl. It's another attempt of yours to make sure I never have a date as long as I live, isn't it?"

He could tell by the way her lips twitched that she didn't want to be amused. In the end, she lost the fight and laughed. "You're terrible." Kissing his cheek, she ruffled his hair. "Be a good boy and I'll see you in a little bit."

She opened the door, then shrieked.

Nick braced himself, ready to fight whatever was out there.

Until his mother stepped back, laughing. "Goodness, Mr. Grim, you scared at least ten years off my life. Nick didn't tell me his tutor was coming over tonight." She cast a chiding look at Nick who was as surprised by Grim's appearance as she was. But since they were dealing with Death, he didn't respond. As always, Death came unexpectedly. . . . whenever *he* wanted. "Next time, Boo, warn me about potential company." Smiling, she stepped past Grim. "You two have a good night. Sorry I have to rush off, but I'm late for work."

Grim shut the door behind her. To Nick, he looked like any other young man in his late teens, early twenties, with tousled dark blond hair and gray eyes, dressed in a black hoodie that had a skull and crossbones on the back. But the Grim Reaper could project to others any form he wanted them to see and so Nick's mother interpreted him as someone in his early thirties. Someone who was respectable.

She would literally die to know she'd just let the Grim Reaper into her house.

Laughing, Grim turned to face Nick. "Your mother

is so oblivious it kills me. I just love that about her. Most people, even though they can't see my real form, have some reservations in my presence. But not your mom. She honestly believes me to be human. Priceless."

"Yeah." And that was one of the things that concerned him most about her. She lacked any kind of ability to sense the preternatural. "She still thinks Kyrian's a drug dealer. You wouldn't believe how much grief she gives me about working for him."

Death curled his lip. "Don't mention your boss to me. People who cheat Death piss me off. I hate that whole thing Artemis does with bringing the dead back. Really, there shouldn't be a loophole."

Nick clamped down on mentioning the fact that one day, he'd be another one who would cheat Grim. That day should prove interesting, given their relationship. "How does Artemis do that, anyway?"

Grim scoffed. "Like I'm dumb enough to tell a Malachai? Do I have 'stupid' tattooed on my forehead?"

Knowing better than to answer that sarcastic jab—only a fool lipped off to Death, Nick scratched at the back of his neck.

Grim, who was extremely OCD and couldn't stand foreign germs, tucked his hands into his pockets and closed the distance between them. "So how's my least favorite pupil?"

"Not dead yet."

"Unfortunately, I know." Grim released a heavy sigh. "Pity that. I keep waiting for something to get ahold of you and not let go, but no such luck. . . . Yet."

"Love you, too, Grim. I so look forward to our get-togethers."

"I'm sure you covet them as much as I do."

Yeah, it ranked up there with root canals and losing limbs. Without commenting, Nick went to get his box of "toys" for their lesson, but Grim stopped him.

"We're taking a break from the divination for a while. I think you've mastered most of it."

Nick would argue that since the last time he'd tried to use his pendulum, it'd swung up at him and almost put out his eye. The bridge of his nose was still tender from it and that'd been a week ago.

As for the rest, it came and went with no rhyme or

reason. But he was always up for learning something new. "What are we doing, then?"

"Silkspeech."

Nick arched his eyebrow at a term he didn't understand. "I'm going to learn to talk to fabric. Wow. Awesome power there, Grim. Just what I always wanted to do. Can't wait to get started. Point me to a comforter."

Grim let out an aggravated growl at Nick's sarcasm. "It pains me so that I can't kill you."

"Yeah, well, what can I say? Not everyone gets to rankle Death and live. I relish my role in your world."

Grim mumbled something under his breath that sounded vaguely like a threat. "Silkspeech is the power of influence and control."

Finally, a power worth having. "Influence?"

"The ability to sway other people to believe what you want them to believe or to do what you want them to."

"Like mind control?"

"Yes and no. Mind control won't work on those who are really hardheaded. You know. . . . Creatures like you."

Well, if it only worked some of the time—"Then what good is it?"

"Fine." Grim headed for the door. "If you don't want to learn it."

"Wait, wait, wait. I didn't say that. I want to influence others." Especially if it could change his mom's attitude about dating, driving, chores . . .

Yeah, it had a lot of possibilities. With luck, he might not ever have to take out trash again!

Grim turned around slowly. "Word to the wise, short stack, when you do use this power, you have to be careful. Like all the others, it can sometimes come with a devastating side effect."

"Like what?"

"It could cause someone to kill themself. Alter their fate. Impact you in ways you won't know about until it's too late."

Oh goodie. Another power he couldn't count on. Just what he wanted.

At this rate, he wasn't sure why he was being trained. It was like giving nuts to a squirrel who had no teeth.

Nick let out a heavy sigh. "All these powers and the only one that actually works is the ability to call for help—and that one only so long as Caleb isn't in the shower or with a woman. Why can't one . . . just one power work the way it's supposed to?"

Grim's expression was wicked and cold. "Technically, they do. The problem is every human is different and they react to stimuli in ways unique to them. *That's* what you can't count on and it's what makes your powers appear to misfire. Before you use them, you have to take time to know your target."

Nick frowned. "I don't understand."

"Yes, you do. It's instinctive in you, and it's why you gravitate toward some people and run from others." Grim picked up one of the porcelain dolls Nick's mom collected and studied it as he talked. "Let's take the term 'redneck.' Some people think of it as a badge of honor. Others as the ultimate insult." He returned the doll to its shelf. "Originally, the word had an entirely different association and meaning. Back in the day, rednecks were union coal men from Pennsylvania, West Virginia, and eastern Kentucky- a far cry from the Deep South where most people mistakenly believe all rednecks live. They were from all races and creeds, and proudly wore a red bandana around their neck as a way of identifying themselves to others, and as a mark of solidarity of the working man standing up against the big corporations who exploited them. In short, they were folk heroes and admired."

Nick widened his eyes. When Grim and Kyrian talked about history, it was interesting. When his teacher did it, it put him to sleep. "Really?"

Grim nodded. "It took decades before it was twisted into a derogatory term. Happens a lot with language. The word 'war' once meant to be cautious, as in 'warning.' 'Precocious' originally meant 'stupid.' But I digress. The point is, Slim, people have triggers. Words or images that cause a surge of negative emotion to run rampant through them. If I were to call your friend Bubba a redneck, he'd laugh and agree. If I were to call your friend Mark that, he'd be extremely offended and probably, to his detriment, try to punch me. Whenever you attempt silkspeech, you have to understand how it might adversely affect your target. If you accidentally hit on that person's trigger, then you could end up with a violent response instead of a positive one. Or vice versa."

Nick nodded as he followed Grim's teaching. It was something he'd been doing for years, especially with jerks and bullies like Stone at school. "So what you're saying is I have to learn what buttons to push."

"Exactly."

"That's basic psychology, Grim. How's that supposed to be a power?"

His eyes flashed red, then black. "You'll be able to do it without saying a word to them. One thought from you and you'll be able to push those buttons."

Oh, now that was cool. "So I'll be like Obi Wan Kenobi with my Jedi mind tricks." He held his hands up and fanned them around like he was conjuring the Force. "'These are not the droids you're looking for.'"

Grim let out a long breath in frustration before he glanced up at the ceiling. "It's like trying to train an ADD cat in a mouse factory."

"Hey, now. I'm focused." Especially compared to how he was in a real classroom.

Grim scoffed. "I only have about thirty percent of your attention twenty percent of the time. The rest of your brain is off on gaming strategies, scantily clad women, and all the things you intend to do once you're grown and out on your own."

Okay, Death had a point. But what was wrong with

that? Nick felt like he had a noose around his neck. Physically and mentally, he was grown, and yet everyone still treated him like a kid. A fact that was really beginning to annoy him. At his age, his mother had been out on her own with a baby. Kyrian had been a veteran Greek soldier, fighting against Roman occupation. And who knew what all Grim had been in to at his age.

For all of his mom's acting like he was mentally defective and couldn't tie his own shoes, he'd been taking care of *her* most of his life. Helping pay bills. Doing chores. Watching out for her. Helping Menyara with her car.

Over the last year, he'd been shot and had battled preternatural enemies from every corner. The only people who didn't treat him like a five-year-old were Kyrian and Acheron.

And Grim.

If you want respect from others, you have to give it. His mother's words came back to haunt him. Sobering, he gave a curt nod to Grim. "All right. You have my undivided attention."

"That'll last three seconds," Grim said under his

breath. "Honestly, if I didn't know better, I'd swear you're not the Malachai. It mystifies me that something as worthless as you could have any power whatsoever. You were born white trash and that's all you'll ever be." He raked Nick with a scathing sneer. "You're nothing."

Rage darkened Nick's gaze. Blood rushed through his veins so fast that his entire body heated up to the level of molten lava. "I ain't *nothing*, boy. You about to find out just what I *can* do."

Grim laughed. "That's it. I finally do have your attention, and you've just learned the first lesson of influence. You use your divination and clairvoyance to strike the nerves of the person you're trying to manipulate. Even someone with a will as strong as yours can be influenced. Not with your mind, rather with your mouth or actions. I can't control you, but I can set you off and manipulate you to have the emotional or physical response I want you to. *That* is one power no one is immune to."

Nick scowled as he tried to understand all the nuances of Grim's lesson. "You didn't mean what you said?"

"Oh, I meant it. But I used your triggers to get the

response I wanted. However, what I did wasn't subtle. It's the subtle you have to master, and that is what will make you truly dangerous. The best influence is always the one that goes undetected. The one that your target thinks was their idea."

"It sounds impossible."

"You would think, but it's not. People are very simple, and you'll be amazed at how easy they are to sway, no matter who they are or where they come from."

And Nick didn't like how easy it'd been for Grim to rile him. Kyrian, Menyara and his mom were right. He was way too hotheaded for his own good. "Is there any way to detect it when someone is trying to use it on me?"

Grim nodded.

"Then teach me, Great Master. For I don't want to be nobody's bitch."

A dark light shined inside Grim's spooky eyes. "Aw, Nicky-baby, therein is the problem. Sooner or later, we're all somebody's bitch. And there's a power heading for you right now that is going to test every part of you. One you're not going to see coming until it pins you to the wall and guts you. Oh happy day for me, eh?"

CHAPTER 2

Nick grimaced as Stone Blakemore drove his over-developed muscular shoulder into Nick's in the hallway of his high school. Pain exploded down his arm, making him want to pummel the beast with his two-hundred-pound backpack until Stone begged him for mercy.

"Watch where you're going, trailer park!" Stone snapped as he shoved at Nick and kept walking toward his locker. Stone's pack of ubiquitous idiots followed in his wake, laughing about it. Yeah, okay, 'cause running into a guy in the hallway was such a hoot. Oh to have the intellect of a Cro-Mag so that something as innocuous as picking belly lint could be amusing. . . .

Nick turned to answer that insult with one of his own, but that thought fled as Nekoda appeared in front of him from out of the crowd. Dressed in a tight cream sweater and jeans with her brown hair pulled into pigtails, she took his breath away and instantly vaporized all thoughts of Stone.

Forget his powers, hers were much more impressive. She could turn a guy's brain into mush with nothing more than a single smile. One touch and he was completely helpless before her. Her mere presence could suck out every part of his intelligence and leave him a drooling loser, trailing after her, desperate to do anything she asked of him . . . even carry her shiny pink purse.

"Hi, handsome. Where were you last night?"

Not where he'd wanted to be. That was for sure. He'd have much rather been holding hands with her in a dark movie theater than listening to Grim tell him what an idiot moron he was.

Man, he could stare into Kody's green eyes forever, especially when she looked at him like she was doing right now. Like he mattered to her. "My mom wouldn't let me go. Sorry."

She frowned. "Why?"

Shifting his backpack to the shoulder Stone hadn't bruised, Nick sighed. "She considers anything I do with you to be dating, which she thinks I'm too young to do." Then under his breath, he mumbled, "Don't get me started."

Her scowl deepened. "I don't understand. We've done plenty of things together. Why would she object to a movie?"

He gave her a sheepish grin. "She doesn't really know about those other things. I didn't exactly tell her I was meeting *you* for them."

She tsked at him. "Lies of omission are still lies, Nick."

"I know, Kode. I do." But telling your mom that you were being pursued by demons out to kill you and that this hot girl in your school was helping to fight them off wasn't something he wanted to do. Especially not after Ambrose's dire warning months ago. "Don't nag at me, okay? I'm over it for the day."

Her concerned expression went a long way in making him feel better. "Did something attack you this morning?"

Nekoda and Caleb were the only two people in his high school who knew who and what he really was. While Caleb was his demonic bodyguard sent to keep him from dying prematurely, Nick still wasn't sure what Kody was. She wouldn't say and he had yet to guess.

Talk about lies of omission. . . .

But the two of them had bled for him. So until they did something against him, he trusted them implicitly.

"The mother beast sank her fangs into my hide for everything from forgetting to take out the trash last night to not brushing my hair enough this morning." He didn't bother mentioning the toilet-seat-was-left-up-again and pick-your-underwear-up-off-the-floor lecture. No need to horrify his girlfriend with anything that personal. "I'm still smarting from it."

Her smile made his stomach jump. "Gotcha." She tugged at the lapels of his hideously orange Hawaiian shirt that had oversized bottles of Tabasco sauce all over it. Another thing his mother insisted he wear because she had this mistaken belief it looked respectable and . . . brace yourself . . . "rich." "New shirt, huh?"

He growled in response.

Laughing, Kody rose up on her tiptoes to lay a quick kiss on his cheek, in spite of the "no public displays of affection" laws that governed St. Richards. "Consider this a nag-free zone, and you rock the tacky shirt look in a way no one else can. Trust me. Only you could be *that* hot in something that foul. But you better hurry or you'll be late for homeroom again."

The bell rang a heartbeat later.

Nick cursed his luck as he dashed down the hall with Kody leading the way to their classroom. Just inside the door of their drab tan early morning prison cell, Kody pulled up short, causing him to skid to a halt.

Ms. Richardson, the meanest troll this side of the Nether Realm, clucked her shrewish tongue at them. With a sneer on her ugly face, she tapped at the cheap watch on her wrist. "I see you're both late again. This is what? Your third tardy, Mr. Gautier? You know what that means."

Oh yeah. After-school detention. And even better, more quality time spent with Richardson. Just the thing he wanted to add to his Christmas list—right after a vicious attack of intestinal misery.

Why couldn't a demon come for him now and gut him? Suck him into some grisly hellmouth . . . *That* he'd actually welcome. Heck, after the morning he'd had, he might not even fight it.

Closing his eyes, he summoned his silkspeech powers for a solo try. "But the bell hasn't rung yet."

Richardson froze for a full second. Then she blinked. "I'll see *you* at three o'clock."

Crap. It hadn't worked. Big surprise there. And it offered further proof that Richardson wasn't human.

Irritated, he took the slip of paper from her hand while she glared at Nekoda.

"And you, Ms. Kennedy. One more and you'll be joining Mr. Gautier's after-school detention."

"It's pronounced 'Go-shay,'" Nick said, correcting her "Gah-tee-aaa." He hated whenever people mispronounced his name.

"Of course it is." Could her tone be any more snide? "How could I forget that backwoods Cajun is a corruption and affront to the beautiful French language."

And she despised Cajuns with a passion. Something she let everyone know, which begged the question of why the woman lived in New Orleans, home of the Cajuns. One of his ancestors must have run over her cat or something when she was a kid . . . nine hundred years ago by the looks of her.

At least that was probably the last time that thing she wore for a dress was in fashion.

In spite of the fact he knew he'd pay for it later, Nick gave her his most charming grin. "*Quoi d'autre?, cher.*" What else, dear? "*Laissez les bons temps rouler!*" Let the good times roll. The motto of New Orleans and his own personal credo.

He winked at her. Richardson was now fuming at him as he went to his seat behind Caleb, who was rolling his eyes at Nick.

Nick set his heavy backpack down on the floor, and couldn't resist one last taunt. "Ain't no *Bouki* here, *cher.* Me and my *bele* gonna pass a good time at lunch. It don madda to *moi.* I done brought me a *boucanée* gator po' boy and some *fraîche* beignets for eats. Yum!"

The hideous grimace on her face was something

she must have copied from a gargoyle. "That'll be enough, Mr. Go-chay. Or I'll add another day to your detention."

Don't do it. Sit down and shut up, Caleb said in his head.

But Nick couldn't stop himself. "Go-shay," he corrected her pronunciation again.

"What was that?" Richardson asked haughtily. "Oh, I know." She narrowed her mousy eyes on him through her dark-tinted glasses. "The sound of another detention day added. I'm so glad I'll have someone to clean my room for me tomorrow afternoon, too."

Oh, he wanted to shove that smug smile down her throat.

Grinding his teeth, he sat down.

I told you. Didn't I tell you?

He glared at Caleb.

Kody patted his shoulder before she went to her seat on the opposite side of the room. Stone turned around in his desk to mock Nick with silent laughter.

One day, you crotch-sniffing freak, I'm going to have the powers to send a shock bolt at you and watch as you lose control of your form. Yeah, that would be hilarious. Stone lying naked in the hallway, flashing back and forth from human to wolf form. And with any luck it'd make Richardson have a coronary.

Talk about a twofer . . .

Nick returned Stone's glare. Though he physically appeared to be fifteen, Stone was a werewolf who, in actuality, was in his late twenties. Since Stone's people didn't age the way humans did, they were kept at home a lot longer before being sent to school, which was supposed to teach them how to interact with humans. But even with those extra years of home training, Stone wasn't any more mature than a human teen.

Wait. What was he saying? Stone functioned on the level of a socially stunted five-year-old.

And Stone, because of his father's money and the fact that he played on the football, basketball, *and* baseball teams, thought he was above everyone, and that all should bow down to him. In particular, he and the other animals he ran with had singled out Nick as the omega wolf to be picked on and belittled. In part because Nick, until he'd started working for

Kyrian, had been a poor scholarship student. However lately, Stone's animosity stemmed from the fact that his on-again off-again girlfriend, Casey Woods, had been making advances at Nick.

But Nick had never been Stone's willing victim, and it was not in his genetic code to back down from anyone or anything. As a result, their fights were the stuff of legends among the student body and faculty.

As Richardson started calling roll, the door opened to admit two unfamiliar students with their principal, Mr. Head. Taking them to Richardson's desk, the principal spoke in a low tone to her while the boy and girl swept nervous glances over the room.

"Must be new meat," Stone whispered loudly to his friend Mason.

Mason nodded. "He don't look like much, but the girl's edible."

"Mason!" Casey snapped as she turned around in her seat to grimace at him. "Stop it! You're so gross. Both of you." She paused to pass a hot look at Nick, who did his best to not react to it or let Kody see it.

Too late. He got that what-are-you-doing-Nick stare

from Kody right before she shot a girl-I'm-going-to-pull-you-bald-headed-if-you-don't-leave-my-boy-alone sneer to Casey.

Casey rolled her eyes at Kody before she flounced around in her seat and tossed her hair over her shoulder.

Oooo, not something he'd advise her doing, since he'd seen Nekoda handle a sword. His girl had no qualms about beheading things she saw as a threat.

Too bad Casey didn't know that.

He still didn't know what game Casey was playing with him. As the head cheerleader, she'd been Stone's girl off and on for the last three years. But for the last year, every time Nick turned around, she was in his face, making passes at him.

"Class!" Richardson clapped her hands together to get their attention. "We have two new students. A brother and sister transferring in. Joey and Jill Becker." She pushed her glasses back up on her crooked nose. "Take your seats, children."

Joey grabbed the seat up front by Richardson's desk—poor dude. He'd soon learn. Jill took her time skimming the room before she smiled at Nick and made her way to the empty desk on his left.

Kody turned to give him an arch stare.

Nick held his hands up in surrender. *I'm innocent,* he sent his thought to her.

The look on her face said she didn't believe him.

How do I get into these things? More important, how could he get out of them?

He certainly couldn't help it if his hotness attracted the opposite sex. Yeah, okay, that was a joke. He didn't know what was in the water lately, but no man wearing his hideously orange shirt, and possessing his teen clumsiness caused by his ever lengthening body could ever seriously attract anything but flies and mosquitoes.

Jill held her hand out to him. "Hi, I'm Jill."

Feeling the daggers Kody was shooting at him, Nick reluctantly shook her hand. "Nick." Then he quickly let go.

"You wouldn't mind showing me to my next class, would you, Nick?"

Help me. . . . Where, oh where art thou, hellmouth?

Why have you forsaken me in my hour of desperation?
Open quick and I'll throw myself in.

Caleb turned to face her. "I'll be happy to show you. I'm Caleb, by the way."

"Mr. Malphas?" Richardson snapped irritably. "Do you have something to share with the class?"

Caleb grinned at the condescending shrew. "No, Ms. Richardson. I was merely offering to help our new student not get lost or be late to her next class."

"While that is nice of you, you need to listen for your name."

"Yes, ma'am."

Gah, that had to irritate Caleb. Thousands of years old, he was more powerful than anyone Nick had ever met, except for Acheron. He had no doubt the demon could fry Richardson in her seat.

And to think, he'd once been jealous of Caleb's Hollywood-slick good looks, perfect body, great wardrobe, and money. Until he'd learned the truth about him. Now Nick knew there wasn't enough money in the universe to compensate Caleb for what he'd been through, and for having to put up with Nick's cranky butt all the time. While the demon wasn't big on sharing anything about himself or his past, there was no missing the haunted shadows that darkened Caleb's eyes whenever he thought no one was looking.

It made Nick wonder if his own scars were that visible whenever he let his guard slip.

Not soon enough, the bell rang, liberating them from Richardson's whiny drone. Thank goodness he didn't have her for English anymore. Last year had been the longest of his life.

Nick had just slung his backpack over his shoulder when Jill planted herself firmly in front of him. He passed a nervous glance to Caleb, then to Kody, who seemed less than pleased by the attention Jill was giving him.

"My first period is in room 214. Can you help me find it?"

Nick stepped back so that Caleb could slide in.

"I'd be more than thrilled to show you," Caleb said in his deepest drawl.

Jill frowned. "I'd rather Nick guide me, if you don't mind."

The expression on Caleb's face was priceless. With his fashionably cut, black hair and dark good looks, he wasn't used to taking second to anyone when it came to a female's attention.

Kody wrapped her arm around Nick's and brushed her hand through his dark brown hair. "I'm sure Caleb doesn't mind in the least. However, I do have a bit of a problem with it. I'm Kody. Nick's girlfriend. Nice meeting you." She all but hauled him out of the room.

Because of her tight grip on his arm and his unwillingness to hurt her, Nick was still stumbling in the hallway as they made their way to first period. "Easy, Kody. I wasn't doing anything wrong."

She loosened her hold. "I know you weren't. While you are absolutely gorgeous, in spite of what you think, it's that demon glamour you have that attracts every female you meet."

Further proof Richardson wasn't female.

"The older you get and the more you access your powers, the stronger it becomes. I wish we could find something to turn it off."

"Yeah, but doesn't Caleb have it, too?"

"Unfortunately, no. He's a different type of beastie. His kind were bred to fight, not serve."

"Serve" was a polite term for demon slavery. Something his father had been bound by for thousands of years until he'd either convinced or tricked, or probably both, his master's servant into freeing him. No one was sure how Adarian had broken free of the Nether Realm, since everyone who'd made the mistake of asking him that had been gutted.

As for Caleb, even though he wasn't a "servant" class demon, he was now enslaved to Nick, but again, Nick had no idea how or why. Caleb wasn't into sharing any more than his father was.

Nick paused in the hallway next to Kody's locker so that she could drop off her sweater. "You still haven't told me how it is you know so much about me and my powers."

"I know." She bent down to unlock the door.

Yeah . . . after a year, he should be used to her dodging his questions about her, her powers and her ability to know him so well.

Nick jerked to attention as he saw a shadow run

across the wall, then vanish into a crack above the bathroom door. "Did you see that?"

Kody stood up immediately. "What?"

Nick turned his head and used his powers to try and sense whatever had been there. But he didn't pick up on anything. "Must have been my imagination."

Spinning her lock, Kody narrowed her eyes. "Last time you said that, we almost got slaughtered by a mortent."

True, and he still had that tight feeling in his gut that usually signaled some form of demon species was nearby.

His gaze went to a flash of pink approaching them. It was Brynna Addams—one of the first friends Nick had made at St. Richards and an all-around sweetheart.

Smiling, she touched Kody on the arm. "Hey hon, I was wondering if I could borrow you after school? LaShonda and I got drafted to do the decorations for the Fall Out Dance, and I could really use some help." She turned her pitiful begging look to Nick. "You, too, Gautier. Want to help a sister out?"

"I would love to, but I have to work today. Kyrian

has some returns I have to make, and a pickup from Liza's."

Brynna pouted before she turned back to Nekoda. "Please, Kody?"

She hesitated, then nodded. "Sure."

Squealing, Brynna hugged her. "You're the best!" She dashed off, vanishing into the crowd.

Nick laughed. "Thank goodness she grabbed *you*. I don't want to be in the dog house anymore."

"You're still not in the clear, buddy."

Nick sighed. "Story of my life."

The warning bell sounded.

"You better go," Kody said. "I don't want to see you get another detention."

"*You*? At this rate, I should just make a bed on the floor of Richardson's room. Tell me again why *she* couldn't have gotten eaten by a zombie?" Nick fell silent as he contemplated a way to facilitate that happening. It wasn't too late. "I wonder if Madaug has any more copies of that game laying around."

Kody paled. "Don't even joke about that. Now go."

Saluting her, he turned and headed toward his first

period, where Caleb was waiting at their computer lab table.

Either Caleb or Kody was with him in every class— something they'd both insisted on. After what had happened last year with the coach who'd sold his soul for victory—literally—and who had then blackmailed Nick into helping him get items he could use to kill students, the two of them were paranoid something would grab Nick in the middle of the day if one of them wasn't nearby.

Nick's home was considered a safe zone since they'd set up protection symbols and sealed the apartment. However, the school was a public building with hundreds of people in it—including some known preternaturals who were supposed to be there, and who posed no threat to him. There was no way to make it completely safe without banning those students, too.

Nick sat down at the same time Caleb shot to his feet. "Something wrong?"

Caleb narrowed his eyes as he made a slow circle around his stool, scanning every corner of the room. "There's something here. Can you feel it?"

"I thought I saw a shadow in the hallway a few minutes ago."

Caleb's eyes flashed orange.

Nick glanced around to make sure no one else had seen him do that. "Yo, D, the freak eye thing? Dead giveaway, man. Sit down before the wings pop out, and we both end up in a real science lab, under the microscope."

"Malphas?" their teacher snapped. "You have trouble finding your seat?"

Caleb turned at Mr. Tendyk's question. "No, sir." He sat down beside Nick.

The bell rang.

After closing the door and dimming the classroom lights, Tendyk turned on the overhead projector that displayed his desktop for everyone in the class to see. Nick sucked his breath in sharply while the rest of the room erupted into chaos.

Instead of the boring icons they were used to staring at on a vomit green background, Tendyk's desktop wallpaper was a montage of Brynna Addams naked, doing extremely lewd things.

Tendyk almost broke his computer as he fumbled to

turn it off. "Who's responsible for this?" he demanded angrily.

Utter silence rang out.

Until Stone laughed again. "From the looks of it, I'd say Brynna Addams. Who knew *that* was hidden underneath all those high buttoned shirts and sweaters?"

Laughing, Mason high-fived him.

Pandemonium returned as everyone had a foul or gross comment to make. Everyone except Nick and Caleb. Nick was too horrified by how Brynna would react once she found out about it. And he was sure some snotwit would beeline right to her with the news. There was nothing the goobs in his school loved more than to be the bearer of really bad news, especially to the person it related to. It was like they enjoyed seeing the misery it caused, firsthand.

He turned to Caleb. "That wasn't Brynna, was it?"

Caleb shook his head. "That was someone's idea of a sick joke."

Speaking of sick, Nick felt ill over it. His stomach heaved in sympathetic agony for her. "Can you tell who?"

He did that weird head cock move as if he were listening to a song only he could hear. "No idea. But it was done for sheer malice."

"Brynna will die when she finds out."

"I know." A tic started in Caleb's jaw. "Can you feel the hatred behind it?"

"Now that you mention it . . . is that what the icky tickling is down my spine?"

Caleb nodded.

Nick sighed heavily. Well at least he knew what was causing *that* symptom. "Is it demonic?"

"No. This is human evil. Demon hatred comes with a distinctive odor to it."

"Yeah, well, this stinks, too." Nick was repulsed by whoever had done something so vicious to someone so kind. Why would anyone hurt Brynna so? In all the years he'd known her, he'd never heard Brynna say a mean thing about anyone.

Not even him.

"All of you!" Tendyk snapped. "Line up in the hallway and be silent. Stone, I want you to go to the office and tell Mr. Head that I need him down here, pronto."

Laughing, Stone went to obey.

Nick reached for his backpack.

"Leave it, Gautier," Tendyk snapped. "No one is to take anything out of here."

Nick hesitated. His grimoire and pendulum were in his backpack, along with his Malachai dagger. If his bag was searched and they happened upon those . . .

It would get ugly, especially since his grimoire was written in blood. Granted, it was *his* blood. But adults didn't seem discriminating when it came to kids bleeding on things during school hours.

I've got it covered, Caleb said in his mind.

Releasing a relieved breath, Nick headed outside with everyone else.

Caleb crossed his arms over his chest as they lined up against the wall of bright red steel lockers. "You know what the only thing worse than an evil demon is?"

"My mother when she's really ticked off at me, especially when it's justified."

Caleb snorted. "No, Nick. Human cruelty. All the

centuries I've lived, I've never understood it. Instead of banding together, your kind seems ever determined to tear each other down. And for what? Jealousy? I just don't get it."

And coming from a demon, that pretty much said it all. "You're not seriously telling me that demons are never cruel?"

"Some are. But you know who they are, and you see them coming. You can smell them from days away. Humans, on the other hand, are insidious. You don't see it coming until they've stabbed you in the back and through the heart."

Nick scowled at his implication. "What are you saying, Cay?"

"I can't tell who did this, but I can tell why they did it. This was meant to shame Brynna and hurt her to the deepest level."

And as those words left Caleb's lips, Nick became aware of the conversations around him.

"I told you Brynna was a slut. My mother said her mama was one, too."

"I always knew her goody-two-shoes persona was an act."

"Man, I wish I'd known she'd do that. You think she's busy Saturday night?"

Nick cringed at their ugliness. "It wasn't Brynna," he said defensively.

Mason scoffed at him. "You're an idiot, Gautier."

"Yeah," another student concurred, "didn't you see *that* in there?"

"With farm animals, too! Oh my God, I'm so disturbed."

"You are? Imagine how that horse felt."

They all burst out laughing.

Nick started to respond, but Caleb stopped him.

"Let it go."

That was easier said than done. "Brynna's my friend."

Before Caleb could comment, the principal stalked past them and into the room. Nick stood on his tip-toes so that he could see Tendyk show the principal the horrific montage through the window in the classroom door.

His pocket started vibrating. Nick pulled out his Nokia 9000 and flipped it open to see he had a new e-mail. As he tried to access it, his phone blew up with texts about Brynna and the photographs. Apparently, their classroom wasn't the only one spammed with that filth.

An instant later, a door down the hallway opened. Brynna ran out, sobbing hysterically. Laughter from her classroom rang in the hall and mixed with the laughter of the jerks around him. Laughter that was only drowned out by a few dickweeds making offers to her.

His heart aching, Nick started to go after her and calm her down.

Caleb caught his arm in a tight grip. "I can't stress enough to you that you need to stay out of this."

"Why?"

"Use your powers, Nick. Look at what's about to happen."

Nick glanced around until he found something shiny enough to use for scrying . . . the silver on the water fountain. It wasn't very big, but it was enough that he could focus his powers with it.

And there in that small, two-inch strip, he glimpsed the horror that was about to become Brynna's life over this single act of cruelty.

In that moment, he completely disagreed with Caleb. "She needs a friend."

"Yes, she does. But right now, the administration is looking for someone to blame for this. You walk in there too soon and this will be hung around *your* neck. Trust me."

That would be his luck, too.

Even so, Nick would deny it if not for the fact that Caleb had a lot more life experience to draw from. You didn't argue colors with Picasso. Car facts with Richard Petty. And you definitely didn't question human behavior with Caleb.

Standing down, Nick felt that strange sensation again. While Caleb had assured him this was human in origin, he wasn't so sure.

There was something else here. Something dark. Cold.

Lethal.

And it wasn't Caleb.

CHAPTER 3

A darian froze as he felt a sensation he hadn't experienced in thousands of years. For a full minute, he didn't move as he tried to pinpoint it. If he didn't know better, he'd swear it belonged to Noir's primary guardian. But he'd made sure when he escaped the dark lord's Nether Realm that the only creature who could find him would be punished to the point he'd never be able to track him down.

No, it couldn't be Seth. Seth was still being tortured. Noir would never take a chance on sending Seth after him.

This was something else.

Where are you . . . ?

More to the point, *What are you?*

He felt the creature pulling back before he could locate its exact position. Had it detected him? That was always his biggest concern. While he couldn't be defeated openly, everyone was susceptible to a sneak attack, especially when they didn't know what was stalking them.

"Malachai! You have a visitor."

His gut tightened. Was the visitor the one he'd sensed? Or was it someone or something else? His senses and powers on full alert, he allowed the guard to cuff him so that he could be escorted to the visitation center.

As one of the most ferocious and feared inmates in Angola, he was always heavily guarded and never allowed near civilians without being fully shackled. Something he found hysterical since the only thing that kept him here was himself. There were no walls built by man that he couldn't tear down with a whisper. No chain forged he couldn't melt.

But he chose to live here for several reasons. The

primary one being that all of this concentrated human malice cloaked his presence from those who were searching for him. The inmates' negativity and hostility also fed his powers. With so many willing victims and predators on tap, his juices never thinned. He always had someone feeding him.

To a demon, this was paradise.

The guard opened the door and stood back so that Adarian could enter the small cubicle. As he sat down, the lights dimmed and he was allowed to see his visitor on the other side of the glass.

Adarian glared at the blond man who was drumming his fingers idly against the tabletop. "What are *you* doing here?"

"You told me to keep you posted." That gravelly tone was spoken at a level that no human could hear. Only a demon.

And while he'd wanted updates on his son, he'd assumed they'd come through Caleb or in his cell at night. Not out in the open like this. The last thing he needed was for someone to identify the creature in front of him.

"Then speak and be quick about it."

His visitor arched a brow at Adarian. Shifting slightly in his chair, he caused a portion of his black button-down shirt to fall open, revealing a grisly skull tattoo in the center of his chest. His black eyes flashed with anger. "You don't order me around, Adarian. I'm not one of your slaves. I'm your master."

"No," Adarian corrected. "You're my partner."

"*You* bargained with me," he reminded Adarian.

"True, and you accepted, thereby making us equals. You help me. I help you. That exchange of services makes us partners."

Grim didn't appear to care for that in the least. But then Death thought himself above everyone and everything.

One day, he would learn the truth. No one was above dying.

Not even Death.

Grim growled in the back of his throat. "I now know where your son gets his most irritating qualities."

Adarian didn't comment on that. "How goes his training?"

"Slowly. He lacks focus. Not to mention, whoever blocked his powers did a great job of it. Unlocking them isn't as easy as it should be. Some of that is because he hasn't been really hurt. Yet. His mother has wrapped him in a layer of love so thick, it's hard to breach. The kid needs tragedy in his life. Without that, it's impossible to push his hatred and make him act on it. He needs someone to hate with a burning passion."

Adarian curled his lip. He couldn't afford for his son to be slow. The sooner Nick learned how to hate, the sooner he'd learn to kill, and the quicker Adarian would be able to leave this place and have the freedom he'd craved since the moment of his birth.

Unlike his son, he'd always known who and what he was. His mother had purposefully conceived him to destroy his own father and to buy her freedom from the dark primal gods she served. From the moment of his birth, he'd been breastfed venom and succored on bitter hatred for everyone and everything. As soon as his powers had manifested and he'd killed his father, his mother had sold him to Noir to be enslaved and used by the sadistic god who'd wanted to destroy his enemies and take over the human realm.

Adarian still had nightmares over *that* quaint experience. If he'd ever possessed a shred of decency or humanity, his time spent in Azmodea had destroyed it.

And those gory centuries spent there were why he'd gutted his mother the instant he'd escaped Noir's custody. Why he would never allow himself to be enslaved again. Not to anyone.

Even Grim.

But Grim wanted to see the Apocalypse he'd been created for. And like Adarian, Grim didn't want to be in a subservient role when he delivered it. He wanted to lead. Adarian could respect that.

However, he didn't really care about Grim. He wasn't capable of caring.

At least that was the lie he told himself.

"You want your Apocalypse, I want my revenge. Train my boy and deliver his powers to me. I need them."

Grim nodded. "If you would allow me to kill his mother—"

"No!" Adarian growled. "You harm her and I will rain down a hell on you that you can't even imagine."

Grim's eyes snapped fire from the fury he kept repressed because he knew better than to show it to Adarian. Not even Grim would get away with that. "Fine. But you better remember what I've done to work this little miracle for you. I want a piece of Nick when all is said and done."

"You can have it. Now go and don't let me see you here again." Adarian got up and left the room. His original plan had been to use his son to rebuild his army. But this last year, as Nick's powers had grown, he'd felt his own start to wane—something he couldn't allow anyone to know.

There couldn't be two Malachais in existence. It was forbidden. But if he could unlock Nick's powers and have Death kill his son before Adarian lost all of his, he could feed on Nick's heart and absorb his powers, too. It would give him the strength of two Malachais.

Then no one would ever be able to defeat him. He wouldn't have to fear Noir or anything ever again.

That was what he lived for. Then he'd be able to find the ones who'd cursed him to this existence and end that curse once and for all.

But first, Nick had to die.

After finally being liberated from his detention, Nick wanted to hunt down whoever had humiliated Brynna and beat them until they begged for mercy. Never in his life had he been angrier.

His stomach knotted, he headed into the gym to meet up with Kody, Madaug, Caleb, and LaShonda. The son of two scientists, Madaug was one of the smartest people Nick had ever met. The kid knew something about everything. And like Nick, he felt invisible unless one of their resident bullies needed someone to kick or shove into a locker. Just under six feet tall, Madaug had dark blond curly hair and bright blue eyes. He always wore glasses, and preferred hoodies over all other attire.

LaShonda was one of the prettiest girls in the school. Barely an inch shorter than Madaug, she had a pair of hazel brown eyes that practically glowed. And her dark brown hair was ever changing. This week, she wore it straightened and to her shoulders. She'd been one of Brynna's best friends since second grade and the two of them were almost always together.

"Are we it?" Nick asked, dropping his backpack next to Caleb's.

LaShonda's eyes sparkled furiously. "Everyone else banged out. They didn't want to be on a committee with a slut like Brynna." She curled her lip. "I take that back, but I won't repeat what some of the guys said. Gah, people disgust me."

"It's ridiculous so don't get me started." Nick let out a long breath, then frowned at Madaug. "Boy genius? Any chance you can shed some light on who planted that crap against her?"

"I wish, but they deleted it from Tendyk's computer immediately and reformatted the harddrive before writing over it. Since it's legally considered child porn, they were afraid of a lawsuit. Head is hoping he can scare someone into a confession."

"Yeah, 'cause that works so well on hoodlums," LaShonda huffed. "I don't know about you guys, but without Brynna, I really don't want to do this. Screw the dance. Let the jerks show up to an empty gym. It's what they deserve. I just want to go home and make sure she's okay. I've been trying to call her, but she won't pick up."

Kody folded her arms over her chest. "I think we all want to check on her."

Nick agreed. "I've been over it a thousand times in my head and I can't figure out who or why anyone would do this to her. Shon? You have any ideas?"

"None. It's not like she goes around collecting enemies, you know? We're talking about Brynna, here. Has there ever been a nicer person created? Ever?"

Nick would say his mother, but he didn't want them to mock him for it.

LaShonda checked her phone. "Why don't we call in a rain check and do this on Monday? Hopefully, Bryn will be back by then."

Nick nodded. "Sounds like a plan. Are you going over to Brynna's from here?"

"Yeah."

"Call me and let me know how she's doing."

LaShonda patted him on the arm. "Will do. I'll see you guys later."

Madaug shrugged his backpack over his shoulder. "I wish I could have seen the photos."

Caleb arched his brow at the comment.

"Not for *that* reason," Madaug snapped as he realized what Caleb was thinking. "I don't want to see her in any kind of graphic portrayal, but I know the pictures had to be Photoshopped. If I had a copy, I could prove it."

Nick scoffed. "Given how foul they were, you're better off not seeing them. I'm still traumatized."

Madaug pushed his glasses back up on the bridge of his nose. "You know, I tried to invent eye-bleach when I was a kid. Didn't work out, though. But I haven't given up. One day, I will find a way to erase recent memories before they move into permanent storage."

From anyone else, that would be a joke.

From Madaug . . .

You could put it in the bank.

Madaug retrieved his hoodie. "I'll see y'all tomorrow."

Nick didn't speak until he was alone with Kody and Caleb. "Is there really no way to do some of the voodoo whodoo mojo things you two do to find out who was behind it?"

Caleb snorted. "Nice rhyme there, Dr. Suess. And sorry. There's nothing I have to trace it."

Kody dittoed Caleb's sympathy and his comment.

Nick checked his watch. "Fine. I need to head over to Kyrian's for work anyway."

Caleb retrieved his backpack. "I'll walk you over."

Nick hated the thought of being walked home like he was incompetent. "Not your prom date, Cay. Don't want to be, neither."

"Have no fear. You're too hairy for my tastes, Gautier. And no offense, you're not pretty or sexy enough to change them."

Nick gaped. "Now that was just hurtful and mean. Why you want to hurt me in my tender place like that, *cher*? Don't let this calm exterior fool you. I got feelings, too."

Kody laughed at them. "I swear, there are times when it seems you two are the ones dating, and I feel like the third wheel."

"Ah, baby," Nick said with a grin. "You know better. You're the only girl for me. Caleb is no competition whatsoever for you."

Caleb shoved Nick's backpack at him. "Get out of here before *I* hurt you."

Laughing, Nick opened the door that led to the back hallway, then froze as he saw a small group of students gathered around graffiti someone had painted across several lockers.

Spencer Sexton is gay! If that wasn't bad enough, there were photos of Spencer necking with another guy taped all around the words.

What the . . .

"Students!" Mr. Head snapped as he came rushing toward them. "Get out of here. Now! Disperse!"

As Nick left the building, Spencer grabbed him and hauled him to the side, away from the cameras and any possible faculty sightings. Even though he was only fifteen, Spencer was already over six feet tall, with enough muscle on his body that most people thought he was a lot older.

Caleb started to follow after them, but Nick motioned to him that it was all right. He could handle Spencer without help, and he had a pretty good idea what Spencer wanted with him. And the last thing Spencer would want for this was an audience.

"Who did you tell?" Spencer growled in his ear.

"Nobody."

He glared at Nick. "You're the only one who knows about me, Gautier." Something Nick had discovered purely by accident one night when he'd stumbled across Spencer on a date with another guy in the back row of the almost empty movie theater.

"I told you I'd take it to my grave, Spencer, and I meant it. I haven't breathed a word of it to anyone. Ever. Not even in my sleep. Are you sure your boyfriend didn't spill it?"

He saw the doubt in Spencer's eyes. But he didn't know if that was for him or the boyfriend.

"On my life, Spence, I wouldn't do this to you. I wouldn't. I know what it's like to be picked on for things you can't help. I'm not about to do that to someone else."

Spencer finally let go of him. He raked a trembling hand through his hair. The anguish in his eyes made Nick feel for him. "Those photos aren't me. Where did they get them?"

"I don't know." Nick glanced over to Kody and Caleb who were close enough to watch them, but not enough to overhear their conversation. "Someone's trying to mess with people's lives for some reason. We know what they did to Brynna is a lie. Maybe that's what they're doing to you, too. Maybe they have no idea that you're really gay." But those rumors had been circling about Spencer since grade school. While everyone pretty much suspected the truth, no one had proof of it. Spencer even had a girlfriend he'd been 'dating' for over a year now. The last thing Spencer wanted was to be bullied or attacked for being different.

Nick couldn't blame him for that and he definitely wouldn't judge him for it, either.

Caleb and Kody approached them slowly.

"You okay, Spencer?" Kody asked.

His eyes watering, Spencer shook his head. "No. I feel like I've been publicly violated. But I'm going to find out who did this, and when I do . . ." He turned his steely gaze to Nick. "You'll be real glad you're not them."

"Already am."

"Sexton!" Mr. Head shouted from the door. "I need you here, immediately."

Sighing, Spencer headed over.

Nick jumped as his phone went off again. Pulling it out of his pocket, he saw a new text message from an unknown number.

Want more dirt on our classmates? Visit my site: theothersideofStRichards.com

"Got you, you worthless pig-dog." Nick actually smiled.

Kody frowned. "Got who?"

Nick held his phone up in triumph. "Whoever is doing this just made the mistake of texting me with their stupidity. I'm going to Bubba's. Y'all coming?"

Kody inclined her head. "Right behind you."

"You lead."

Gripping his phone, Nick walked the few blocks over to Royal Street where Bubba's store, The Triple B, was located. The only combination gun and computer store in the world—that Nick knew about anyway—it had the largest selection of guns and computers in the state of Louisiana. Which said it all about the owner. Bubba was a different breed, unlike anyone Nick had ever known. He danced to his own tune and didn't care who saw him do it, either.

Bubba was also a walking enigma. Most people dismissed him as a total rube, but that would be like trying to define the ocean as simply wet. While Bubba did have a thick Tennessee mountain drawl, he'd graduated with honors at the top of his class from MIT. He had several Ph.D.s, including a doctor of science degree in theoretical nuclear and particle physics. Nick didn't even know for sure what that was, other than impressive.

The man also knew more about horror movies than anyone with a real life should. In fact, Bubba was forever wearing a black horror T-shirt of some kind, and it was usually accompanied by a red flannel shirt. Even in the summer heat.

Though to be fair to Bubba, the server farm Bubba ran at The Triple B had to be kept around fifty degrees year round. And since that was where Bubba spent much of his day, Nick could understand wanting something a little warmer than a T-shirt.

Still, that was why the good Lord had given them hoodies. Too bad Bubba couldn't find that section of a clothing store.

But as Nick entered, he drew up short as he caught sight of Bubba behind the glass counter in an expensive black suit with a blue dress shirt and blue striped tie. Even more shocking, Bubba had on a pair of glasses, and his thick beard had turned into a fashionable goatee

Holy hand grenades. The man almost looked normal. He was still humongously tall with an aura of I'll-kick-your-butt-if-you-laugh-at-me, but . . .

Please, don't tell me you finally blew up Mark . . .

"Someone die?" Nick asked.

Bubba gave him a droll stare. "I'm about to leave to pick my mama up from the airport, and I know she's going to want to stop by church as soon as we get into town, so that she can thank God she didn't crash."

That only confused Nick more. "I've seen you in church . . . a lot . . . and you've never been dressed like *that* before."

"That's 'cause my mama wasn't there. If I went into a church in jeans with her, she'd beat me senseless. The woman still won't wear pants to Mass. She says it's disrespectful to the priest and to God." He held his hand up. "Don't ask. I've tried talking sense into her, but she don't listen to me."

Nick was baffled by how anyone could cow the mighty Bubba of all people. The man was epic. Larger than life. Most of all . . . "Yeah, but you're old."

Bubba arched a brow at him as if he was offended by Nick's words. "I'm not *that* old. I've barely cracked past thirty. And in mama years, it don't matter, boy. Hell, she still cuts my meat up for me at Thanksgiving before she gives me my plate. I'm lucky she's not still spooning me Gerber in a high chair."

Caleb and Nick laughed at the ludicrous image.

Kody made a sound of irritation. "Well, I think it's sweet."

Bubba inclined his head respectfully to her. "Thank you, Miss Kody. Now what can I do for y'all?"

Nick stepped forward to hand Bubba his phone. "There's someone messing with the kids at school, posting awful stuff about them, and whoever it is, just texted me this Web site. Can you help us find out who it is?"

Bubba grumbled in the back of his throat. "I would. You know that. But I can't be late to pick up Mama. She'll end up adopting half the staff at the airport if I leave her there unattended. Mark!" He shouted out so unexpectedly that all three of them jumped.

A few seconds later, Fingerman snatched at the curtain that separated the front of the store from the back room. In his midtwenties, Mark had shaggy brown hair and bright green eyes. Dressed in a baggy tan T-shirt that had seen better days, he looked like he hadn't shaved in a couple of days.

Ah, that was where Bubba's beard had gone.

Mark had been working for Bubba off and on for years. But more than that, the two of them were best friends, and Mark was every bit as crazy as Bubba.

Wait, on second thought, he was even crazier. Bubba didn't make a habit of dousing himself in duck urine to ward off zombies. Thank goodness Mark wasn't wearing it today, 'cause that stuff stank with a big capital S.

"Dang it all, Bubba, how many times do I have to tell you not to do that? You scare the crap out of me with that booming voice of yours. It carries and breaks the sound barrier. One day, you're gonna cause me to leave a pile of it in the back room and I'm not gonna clean it up. You cause it. You clean it."

Bubba mumbled something that sounded like Latin.

"I'm not a wimp," Mark said defensively. "And I'm not your dog. Don't bark at me, boy. One day you gonna make me bite."

Nick cleared his throat to remind the two of them that they weren't alone. "Uh, guys? My phone?

Malicious lunatic at school? Your mom at the airport?"

That snapped Bubba's attention to where Nick wanted it. He handed the phone to Mark. "I need you to trace the IP on this and find out who registered the domain."

"Yeah, all right. I can do that."

"I know you can. That's why I called you out here."

Mark clenched his jaw in a way that let Nick know he was having to force himself not to comment. After a few seconds, he gestured toward the door. "Don't you need to go get your mama? It's a long trip from Bucksnort to New Orleans, and God love the good-hearted woman, she never met a stranger a day in her life."

"I'm going." Bubba opened his jacket to check the pocket and make sure he had his wallet. He patted his pants, then frowned.

Mark picked his keys up from the counter and held them out.

With a sigh of relief, Bubba took them from him. "Thanks."

Inclining his head, Mark didn't say anything until after Bubba had left the store. "I swear, I love his mama, but I hate whenever she comes to town. That boy gets so beside himself he can't think straight."

Caleb snorted. "I didn't know he ever thought straight."

Mark laughed at that. "True. All right, y'all, come on back and I'll trace this for you."

They walked around the counter and through the curtains. Kody took a seat at the long, tall worktable that was strewn with various computer parts. When she reached for a motherboard, Mark grabbed her hand. "Make sure you ground yourself before you touch anything." He stressed the last word.

She frowned. "Ground myself? I'm not floating, am I?" From anyone else that would sound like a joke, but since Kody could actually fly . . .

Mark placed her hand on the metal computer casing. "Static electricity is your worst enemy in computers, and when pumping gas."

Caleb and Nick exchanged an amused grin. Knowing Mark, this had to be good. After all, Mark was the only one Nick knew who could set fire to his jeep by simply answering his cell phone.

"Pumping gas?" Nick asked.

"Yeah, I once blew up my uncle's motorcycle by accident and set fire to my favorite pair of jeans. 'Course it'd been even more wrong had I done it intentionally. Anyway, I slid off the vinyl seat and touched the nozzle without grounding myself. The spark ignited the fumes and that was all she wrote. You'd be amazed how many people a year blow themselves up. Believe it or not, I'm not the only one . . . Not exactly sure how that makes me feel, though. Glad I'm not the only one, but still . . . "

Mark sat down at the bench and pulled the keyboard toward him. "Did you know there's been over two hundred reported cases of people who ignited themselves and their cars because they didn't ground themselves before touching the nozzle? It's true. Most are women who started pumping, gas, that is, then got back in the car, and when they got back out to touch the nozzle, ka-boom. I have to say that I am not proud to be one of the very few men who have done it. Kind of embarrassing, but if I can keep one of you from learning my lesson, then it's worth a little humiliation. I'm just glad Bubba wasn't there to see it and mock me for it."

Nick laughed. "That's what I love most about you, Mark."

"What?"

"Your whole purpose in life seems to be to serve as a warning to others on what not to do."

Laughing with him, Mark started typing. "Sad, but true, kid. Sad, but true. Now let's see what we can find."

They waited quietly while Mark worked.

Nick's phone started ringing. Without missing a single keystroke, Mark handed it to him. Now *that* was impressive. But then, Mark was the master of one hand speed typing. Something he'd perfected while keeping one hand buried in a potato chip bag while he worked or surfed.

Pressing the answer button, Nick held his phone to his ear. "Hello?"

"Are you dead?"

Nick hesitated at the sound of Kyrian's deeply

accented voice. "No, but that tone sounds like my death might be imminent. Why?"

"You know what time it is?"

Nick glanced to the clock on the wall and cringed. It was after five. "Sorry, boss. I got distracted."

"Yeah, and you didn't call your mother and she called me worried sick about you."

Nick scowled. "Why didn't she call *me*?"

"She tried and you didn't answer. Then she tried again and it rolled straight to voicemail. She now thinks you're dead in a ditch."

Great. Detention *and* grounded. Just what he wanted. "I'll give her a call."

"And . . ."

"I should have called you and told you I'd be late to work. I'm really sorry, Kyrian. I am. I had something come up at school, and I've been working on it since I got out of detention. I just let time get away from me. It won't happen again, boss, I promise."

"It's fine, Nick. But only because this isn't a habit with you. That's why we got worried. You're always so good about keeping in touch that when we lose you, it rattles us."

Nick cringed at that. He couldn't stand to upset his mother. "Sorry. I'll head on over and—"

"Don't worry about it. I don't have anything that can't wait until tomorrow. Go see your mom so that she'll know you're all right."

"Okay. You sure you don't need me to do anything?"

"Did you check with Kell about the status on my replacement sword?"

"I did, and I tracked it down. It'll be delivered tomorrow morning. They accidentally sent it to Cleveland. I also dropped off your dry cleaning on my way to school, and will pick it up tomorrow afternoon. During lunch, I scheduled an appointment for the Lamborghini to be serviced on Friday, and I got Mr. Poitiers to agree to pick it up and drop it off for you. I e-mailed Acheron about Halloween, and he said to tell you and Talon that there will be two new additions moved in for it. Someone named Gallagher and Wulf. They'll arrive on the twenty-eighth. I've already e-mailed Talon about it and was going to tell you when I got over there. Lastly, I called Liza and she will have Rosa's birthday present from you wrapped and ready. I'll grab it on my way home and make sure Rosa gets it tomorrow along with the card you have in your top desk drawer. Anything else you need?"

"No. You are on top of it and I appreciate it. I really am impressed with you, Nick. You're a good kid."

Nick's face ignited. He wasn't used to praise from anyone and it always embarrassed him to get it. "I'm just trying to do my job, boss." But it was more than that. Nick owed Kyrian a debt that couldn't be repaid. The man had saved his life after Nick had been shot last year. Not only had Kyrian kept Nick's friend from killing him, he'd taken Nick to the hospital and paid for them to patch him up.

It was that debt that had led to Nick working part time for him so that he could repay the hospital bill.

"All right," Kyrian said kindly. "I'll see you tomorrow."

"Okay. If you need anything else . . ."

Kyrian laughed. "Bye, Nick."

Nick hung up, then dialed his mother at work. Since she didn't have a cell phone of her own, he had to call in on the restaurant line.

"Sanctuary on Ursulines. How may I help you?"

He'd know that sweet drawl that was tinged with a hint of a French accent anywhere. It belonged to a tall, beautiful blonde woman who was all legs and all curves. "Hi, Aimee, it's Nick. Can my mom come to the phone for a second?"

"Boy . . ." she stressed that word in a way that made him inwardly cringe, "your hide is so tanned, I could make shoe leather out of it. Hang on and let me get her."

Nick dreaded what he knew was coming.

Sure enough, he heard the tears in his mother's voice. "Nicky, baby? Are you okay?"

I'm such a jerk. How could he have forgotten to call her? She'd been bad to worry about him before he'd been shot. Since that night when he'd almost died, she was barely one step short of insane when it came to his well-being.

"I am so sorry, Mom. I didn't mean to worry you."

"But are you all right?"

"I am."

Those two words cured the tears. It also sent her reeling into a realm of anger that instantly knotted his gut. "How dare you scare me like that! Have you any idea how worried I've been? Why didn't you answer your phone? Where have you been? Why aren't you at work? I swear, if you're hanging out with those hoodlums again, I'm going to ground you until you're in an old-age home. You hear me? Why aren't you answering me, Nick, huh?"

"'Cause you always yell at me when I interrupt you."

"Are you sassing me?"

"No, ma'am." That would be all kinds of stupid, especially in her current mood.

She let out a sound of ultimate peeve. "You're grounded for a week. You hear me?"

"But Mom—"

"Don't you 'but Mom' me. I've had it with your irresponsibility. And you think you're mature enough to drive and date? Really, Nick? You can't even remember to dial a phone or take trash to the curb or lower a toilet seat or pick your underwear up from the floor, and you think you can handle operating a car in New Orleans' traffic? I don't think so. You've got a long way to go to become the man you think you are. You hear me?"

He really, really hated those last three words that she said every other sentence whenever she yelled at him. He clenched his teeth to keep from arguing.

"Now I have to go and get back to work. I don't know where you are, but you have fifteen minutes to walk through the doors here. If you're further away than that, you're grounded for a month. You hear me?"

"Yes, ma'am."

"Clock's ticking, buster. You better run for it." She hung up on him.

Sighing, Nick looked at Kody, then Caleb.

"We heard," Mark said. "Pretty sure the folks in Slidell heard, too. You better get on."

"I'm going." He held his phone out to Mark.

"I got everything I need. I'll call you once I get it all tracked."

"All right. Thanks."

"You want us to come with you?" Kody asked.

Yeah, that was *all* he needed. There was no telling what insanity his mom would come up with if she knew he'd been with Kody when he should have been at work. "No, she already thinks I'm goofing off instead of working. If she sees you guys, she'll really be hot. I'll catch y'all later."

Nick grabbed his backpack from the floor, shrugged it over his sore shoulder, and ran up the street toward Ursulines as fast as he could. Luckily Bubba's store wasn't all that far from Sanctuary. But he didn't want to push it. The sooner he got there, the happier his mom would be.

He didn't slow down until he reached the doors of the three-story red brick building that housed one of the most famed bar and grills in New Orleans. There was a huge bear of a man at the door to greet all new-comers. Most wouldn't think anything about it, but Nick knew whoever was on door duty was there to assess the threat level of any preternatural clientele entering the building. And for reasons no one would explain, the doorman always had them cue *Sweet Home Alabama* on the jukebox whenever Acheron showed up. There was much about Sanctuary Nick still had to learn.

With long blond hair and beefy arms, the doorman was fierce and intimidating. Until he recognized Nick and gave him a wide, cocky grin.

Nick let out a relieved breath. Oh good, it was Dev. One of four identical quadruplets, Dev was always easygoing and fun to be around. While Dev's brothers, Cherif and Quinn, were nice enough, Remi was the one who scared him. If Nick had to face his mom in this mood, he was glad Dev was on duty. He was the one being who might keep his mom from killing him.

"Hey, Dev."

Dev clicked his tongue. "Nicky, Nicky, Nicky . . . I don't envy you, *mon fils*. Your mama gonna take a bite of your hide and mount it to the wall."

If the knot in his stomach drew any tighter, he'd have diamonds in the toilet later. "Yeah, I don't envy me either. Want to trade?"

Dev laughed. "You'd think that, but no. Believe me, you don't want to see my *maman* when she's angry. You, *Maman* likes. Me, not so much most days. Trust me, she has a bear of a temper."

Nick snorted at Dev's play on words. Dev was poking fun at the fact that he and his family were shapeshifters whose alternate form was that of a bear.

Shaking his head at Dev, he went inside. It took a minute for his eyes to adjust to the dark interior.

Dev's sister Aimee was at the bar, picking up drinks.

"Now where were you, mister?"

He jumped at his mom's angry tone in his ear. How had she snuck up on him? Dang, he could rent her out as a ninja.

"At school. I had detention." *Go ahead, Nick. Throw gas on that fire . . . .*

"For what?" she growled.

"Being late."

She narrowed her blue eyes at him. "And why were you late?"

"Stone slammed me—"

She flung out her hand to signal him to shut-up. "Don't even start that. You take responsibility for your own actions. You hear me? Now why were you late?"

He ground his teeth as he forced himself not to show any kind of anger toward her. But he was really getting tired of being treated like an idiot who couldn't tie his own shoes. "I didn't get to class until after the bell rang." There, that was the truth.

"Nicholas Ambrosius . . . do not test me. Not today. I am not in the mood for *your* crap."

You hear me, he mocked silently in his head. 'Cause he wasn't quite stupid enough to do that out loud.

He forced himself to speak in a calm tone. "I don't know what to tell you, Mom. I screwed up by not calling and I'm sorry. It was a bad day at school and two of my friends are under fire. I was just trying to help them, and I wasn't thinking about myself."

She frowned. "What do you mean 'under fire'?"

"Someone started attacking them publicly and posting awful pictures of them and insults for everyone to see."

Anger darkened her gaze as he struck the nerves in her that Grim had mentioned. The one thing his mother couldn't stand was for anyone to gossip or speculate about someone else. She'd had too much of that done to her when she'd ended up pregnant with him. "Who?"

"You don't know Spencer, but Brynna was the other one they attacked."

"Addams?" she asked incredulously.

He nodded.

Now his mother looked as sick as he'd felt. "Why would anyone attack Brynna?"

"I don't know. That's what I was trying to find out. She ran out of school crying earlier, and I just wanted to help her, you know?"

Finally his mother hugged him. "All right, Boo. You're forgiven, but still grounded."

Of course he was.

She gently pushed him toward the small booth where he normally did his homework. "I'll bring you some food. You get your homework started."

Not happy about this at all, Nick obeyed before he got into more trouble. He sat down and started rummaging through his backpack. As he pulled out his math book, he saw that shadow flit across the wall again.

Turning his head, he tried to pinpoint it. But it was gone so fast, he wasn't sure he could trust his eyesight in the dim room.

Suddenly, his grimoire heated up beneath his hand. With a hiss, he snatched his hand back. He blew cool air across his palm to help with the stinging while he opened the book with his other hand.

"All right, what are you trying to tell me?" He pulled out his pendulum and pricked his fingertip. Reciting the spell to activate it, he squeezed three drops of blood onto the page. For a second, it didn't react. Then the blood rolled across the page until it formed words.

> *Horror. Terror. Nightmares. Dreams.*
> *Some things are never what they seem.*
> *Discord. Strife. Shame and Pain.*
> *Into all lives, they will rain.*
> *But none of them will cut so deep . . .*
> *As the enemy you did not see.*

He was still trying to decipher it when his gaze was drawn to the napkin holder. There in the shiny metal, he glimpsed the future to come.

It was Brynna, and she was hanging by her neck in her bedroom.

CHAPTER 4

Nick jumped up and fumbled for his phone. He had to get ahold of Brynna before she let her hurt feelings overtake her common sense. Life was hard for everyone, but pain was transitory and it would eventually leave. He knew that better than most since he'd been spoon-fed a steady diet of shame, humiliation and agony since the moment of his birth.

Death was forever. There was no undo button on it. Not unless you knew how to summon Artemis, and even then, there was no guarantee she'd take you.

His hand shaking from his panic, he dialed Brynna's number and waited.

She didn't answer.

As he was hanging up, his mom returned with a hamburger and fries. Her brows drew together in a worried frown. "What's wrong?"

"Ma-m-mom, I got to go."

The fury returned to make her eyes snap blue fire at him. "Sit your butt down, boy. You're on restriction."

"I know. But—"

"No buts," she snapped. "Sit down and do your homework. Now!"

He shook his head. "You're going to have to ground me again. I've got to go check on Brynna. I got a really bad feeling, and she's not answering her phone. I have to make sure she's okay."

She took a step back and eyed him suspiciously. "Is that really what you're doing?"

"Cross my heart, Mom." He made a small cross in the center of his chest. Something he only did when he meant it.

"All right. Go on and check on her, then. I won't hold that against you. You want to take the burger with you?"

Nick grabbed it from her tray, then kissed her

cheek. "Can I leave my books here? I'll be back as soon as I make sure she's not doing something stupid."

"Sure."

Taking a bite of his burger, he headed for the door.

"Hey, Nick?"

He paused to look back at his mother and swallowed his food. "Yes, ma'am?"

"You're a great kid. Much better than I deserve. I just wanted you to know that while I'm hard on you, I do see how wonderful you are. You do me real proud and I mean that."

Her words warmed him. "Thanks, Ma. I love you, too." Smiling at her, he rushed out to get to the streetcar so that he could bust tail to make it to Brynna's house as fast as possible. *This would be so much easier if I had a car. . . .*

Or if Ambrose or Death would teach him how to teleport. Now there was a power he'd love to have. Of course with his luck, he'd teleport someplace bad like the Arctic Circle while in his underwear.

Or buck naked into his school's gym during a pep rally. Yeah, that'd be a lot worse than freezing his nether regions on an iceberg. He'd much rather have penguins point and laugh at him than the girls in his class.

He came around the corner of the French Market at a dead run. For once luck was with him. The streetcar came in right as he reached the platform.

And he made the best time ever getting to Brynna's house. A huge, dark gray antebellum mansion, it dwarfed his entire apartment building. Even though it made him uncomfortable to be around a place this nice and elegant, he'd always liked coming here. Whenever Brynna's mom was in town, she usually had fresh cookies or cupcakes sitting in a glass case on their kitchen island. And her dad had never once looked at him as if he was trash or made a comment over the fact that Nick didn't belong around his daughter. All of the Addamses were as nice as they could be. Something he deeply appreciated.

Nick opened the wrought-iron gate and sprinted across the small front yard and up the steps to the front door. He rang the bell.

A few seconds later, Brynna's little brother, Jack, opened the door and stared up at him. "Yeah?"

"Is Brynna home?"

Jack shrugged. "Don't know. Don't care."

I am so glad I'm an only child. . . . Nick sighed and tried again. "Is your dad around?"

"He's running errands. Be back later."

"Can I come in and see if Brynna's in her room?"

Jack narrowed his gaze on Nick. "Ain't no boy not related to us supposed to be up in her room. Ever."

"I won't go in it. You can come with me and make sure I stay in the hallway. Please? I won't be here long. I just want to make sure she's all right."

"Yeah, okay. I heard her crying earlier. Figured it was something stupid. She cries all the time, anyway. When she's happy. When she's mad. When she's sad. Whenever she breaks a nail or has to take medicine. Girls are so weird. I try not to pay attention to them." Jack stepped back so that Nick could enter the house.

Nick headed for the stairs. "Where's her room?"

"First one on the left." But Jack didn't follow him up. Instead, he drifted past the stairs, toward their kitchen.

Taking the stairs two at a time, Nick didn't pause

until he got to her door. *Please be okay. Please . . .* Terrified of what he might find, he knocked. "Hey, Bryn? It's me, Nick. You in there?"

"Go away." There was no missing the tears in her voice.

"I can't. Not until I know you're all right." Nick leaned his head against the white wood and wished he could make it better for her. He hated for anyone to be this torn up, and for what? Meanness? Jealousy? Really? Why would anyone with a soul do this to someone else? Could they truly feel satisfaction or derive happiness from stabbing someone else so ferociously?

"I know you're hurting, Bryn. Believe me, I know how it feels to get your emotional teeth kicked down your throat so far that it makes you choke on the last shred of your dignity. I do. Just when you think you can hold your head up and everything will be okay, in walks your mom with this tacky, awful bright orange fish shirt that she makes you wear to school so that everyone can poke fun at it and call you names. That sick feeling in your gut that tells you, you can't take it anymore. That life sucks hard and it won't ever get better. That you're walking on the tightrope, trying to hang on with your toes 'cause you got no safety net, and you're barely one sneeze away from being a stain on the floor. But you're not alone, Brynna. You're not. You've got a lot of people who care about you. People who love you and who would be devastated if something ever happened to you."

She opened the door. Her dark hair was rumpled and her eyes bloodshot and swollen. With her mascara smeared around her eyes and down her cheeks, she looked so miserable that it wrung his heart. "I'm not as strong as you are, Nick."

"No. You're stronger than me."

Shaking her head, she hiccupped.

Nick wiped at the tears on her face. "You know, I was having this really crappy day a couple of years ago. It was so bad that I honestly thought about throwing myself off the Pontchartrain bridge. I was so sick of being kicked and mocked for things I couldn't help or change. Told how worthless and disgusting I was. How stupid and trashy. And as I sat in the cafeteria at a table by myself because I was a social outcast and didn't have enough money for lunch, this beautiful girl came over and sat down beside me. She split her turkey sandwich and homemade cookies with me and bought me a bag of chips and a milk. Do you remember what she said to me?"

Tears flowed down her face. "No."

"'No one can make you feel inferior without your permission.'"

"Eleanor Roosevelt."

Nick nodded. "You said to me, 'Don't let them hurt you, Nick. One of you is worth ten of them. And one day, we're going to be grown and everything will be different. They'll matter even less to you then than they do now. So don't even waste a single thought on them and their cruelty. Besides, they wouldn't be attacking you if they didn't think of you as a threat to them. People only go after the ones they're jealous of or scared of.' And I asked you that day why anyone would *ever* be jealous of something like me."

Brynna sniffed. "Because there's a light inside you

that shines so bright it's hard to look at. You are kind and funny, and you're the smartest boy I've ever met. Most of all, you see potential and opportunity where others see obstacles."

"Yeah," Nick said, his throat tight as he remembered all the times when all he'd needed was a kind smile from someone. Anyone. And Brynna had been that one person that day when he'd felt battered beyond his endurance. "Those words etched themselves into my soul, and I think about them a lot when Stone and them get started on me. While other people have kicked me, coming and going, you never did. You are an angel, Brynna. Don't let the haters win. They wouldn't have attacked you had they not felt inferior to you. So you hold your head up and you dare them to come after you. And know that when you do, you're not facing them alone. You've got me, LaShonda, Kody, and dozens of other people who will take on the devil himself for you."

She threw herself into his arms and sobbed against his neck. "I love you, Nick. You've always been such a good friend to me."

Patting her on the back, he knew she meant that the same way he did. As friends. "I love you, too. Now if we want to be really evil, let's sic Tad on them."

She laughed at the mention of her older brother, who'd graduated early and gone on to college up in Baton Rouge. "He would beat them senseless, wouldn't he?"

"You know it, and he's the one person outside of Bubba and Mark who could track them down and then some."

"Hey, Brynna? You here?"

Wiping at the tears on her cheeks, she drew a ragged breath. "Up here, Daddy."

Nick put a little distance between them as her father climbed the stairs. When he reached the landing and caught sight of Nick outside Brynna's bedroom, he stopped dead in his tracks.

Now Nick had always known that Mr. Addams was a large man, and by large he meant really tall and muscular. But right now with that furious glower on his face, Nick could swear that her father grew about nine inches taller and his muscles expanded to the size of Rambo's. And he was pretty sure that crazy light in her father's eyes came from an image of him gutting Nick where he stood.

Holding his hands up in surrender, Nick took another step away from her. "I did not step one foot inside her room, sir. I swear it on my mother's life. We've been out here the whole time."

Brynna wiped at her nose. "I had a really bad day at school, Daddy, and Nick came by to check on me and cheer me up."

Relaxing, her father closed the distance between them. "I got a call about it from Mr. Head. It's why I came on home."

Nick edged himself closer to the stairs. "And now that I know you're not alone, Bryn, I'm going to head back home. If you need anything at all or someone to talk to, any time day or night, call me."

Brynna frowned. "Did you really come all this way just to check on me?"

Nick shrugged sheepishly. "I don't know anyone else who lives out this way."

Her smile warmed him. "Thank you so much, Nick."

"No problem." He inclined his head to her before he went to the stairs.

Mr. Addams followed him down to let him out the door.

Nick paused in the foyer and looked up to make sure Brynna wasn't on the landing before he spoke to her father. "Mr. Addams, I don't know what the principal told you, but I am seriously worried about Brynna. I was in the class that saw . . . those lies about her, and it was pretty gruesome what they did. And I know how mean some of the kids at school can be. You might want to keep her home a few days and watch over her. Please make sure she's not left alone. I know her mom's in Seattle and girls like to talk to girls. If she needs someone, I can volunteer my mom. She had a bad situation in high school, too. And she survived it. I know she thinks the world of Brynna and would be more than happy to help her anyway she can. She's working tonight at Sanctuary, but she'll be home all day tomorrow."

Her father smiled at him. "Thanks, Nick. I really appreciate it."

Nodding, Nick left. But he didn't go too far. He stopped by the fountain that they had in the middle of the yard and stared into the water. It took a few minutes for his powers to kick in. When they did, he saw Brynna still crying in her room as she hugged one of the stuffed animals she kept on her bed. He saw her upset and angry. However, the image of her killing herself was gone.

Breathing in relief, he headed back to the streetcar while his thoughts ran through everything that had happened.

Caleb had assured him that this perverse maliciousness was human-spawned, but he couldn't shake the feeling that something else was behind it. It just didn't feel right. Yeah, people were cruel. They were nasty. He'd seen the worst of humanity. Had looked into the eyes of a friend as that friend beat him to the brink of death and then ruthlessly shot him on the street.

More times than he could count, Nick had sneered at the hypocrites around him and bathed in their condemnation.

Still . . .

He heard something whispering in his ear in a language he couldn't understand.

Nick froze as he tried to comprehend it. Was it the voice of the ether spirits that Caleb listened to? The ones who carried information and wisdom?

Ambrose had told him that he would one day be able to access the universe—see all things hidden. Know the unknowable. It'd sounded far-fetched, but the one thing he'd learned over these last few months was that absurdity was the true natural order. Trying to find sense in the world was like trying to unlock the key to the universe using a Tinkertoy.

In a way, he missed living in ignorance. Those days of supreme comfort he'd had back when the world had made sense, and any problem he had could be cured by his mother pulling him into her lap and kissing his boo-boos. Back then, he'd dreamed of being a teenager. He'd told himself that once he had a job, he'd be a man.

But he didn't feel like a man.

Well, some days he did. Some days, he felt as ancient

as Acheron, who was over eleven thousand years old. Other times, he still wanted to run to his mom and have her make it all better.

He was at such a strange time in his life. Caught between childhood and being his own man. His mom had leaned on him so hard at times that he felt like he was the parent. Like they'd raised each other.

And at the same time, he couldn't imagine being his age and having a toddler to take care of. It was a wonder his mom was sane. Not to mention the fact that he'd been a sick little kid. For the first two years of his life, he'd been in and out of hospitals for all kinds of weird things.

Because you were demonkyn. He knew that now. His human part had been fighting his father's DNA. And the demon in him had been trying to kill the human half.

How had his mother met such a creature as his father? It was something she refused to talk about. Nor would she speak ill of him.

For better or worse, he is your father, Nick. Family is family, no matter what.

And his mother was whacked for that thought. He'd only met his father a couple of times in his life, during visitations at the prison. His only real memory of the man had come from when he was ten and his father had lived with them for three whole months after someone had been dumb enough to parole him.

Like some bad Hollywood cliché, his father had laid up drunk and knocked them around until one of his former inmate buddies had convinced him to rob a bank. During the robbery, his father had brutally slaughtered four people he claimed were demons trying to kill him. At the time that'd seemed stupid.

Now, not so much. It probably had been demons out to get him.

Instead of going for an insanity defense or fighting the conviction, his father had pled guilty and been sent right back to Angola. About a year later, just shy of Nick's eleventh birthday, there had been a huge riot where his father had been wounded. He'd also killed a guard. Something that guaranteed he'd never be paroled again.

Let's hear it for family.

But Nick didn't believe blood ties created family, or

that his father's whacked out DNA had to define the person he was to become. In his world, family was something you chose to have. It was the people you loved who loved you back—those you could call in the middle of the night who would rush to your side without complaint. They were the only ones who mattered. The ones who counted. As far as he was concerned, his family was his mom, Menyara, Kyrian, Rosa, Liza, Bubba, and Mark. And Acheron was the weird uncle no one was sure about. Caleb was that acerbic cousin you liked, but you didn't know why.

And Kody lived in a place in his heart that was uniquely hers.

Maybe he felt that way because, other than his mother, he'd never really known blood kin. He'd never once met his grandparents. The closest he'd come to that was seeing them in passing at the mall during Christmas years ago. His mom had ducked into a store and Menyara had told him who they were, and why his mother was so upset, and didn't want to be seen. Now, he couldn't even remember what they'd looked like. He wouldn't know them if they stepped on him.

"Nick?"

He paused on his way back to the streetcar as he heard his name, but couldn't place the voice. Turning around, he didn't see anyone near him.

Just don't be more mortent demons out to attack me while I'm alone. Caleb would kill him for being so stupid.

"Nick!" A car moved and then he saw Jill running toward him, waving.

What was it about Jill that made him so uncomfortable? And it wasn't the same kind of nervousness he had with Kody. He was twitchy with Kody because when she was around all he could think about was how good her lips tasted. And his body would go white-hot with horomonal overload until he could barely think of anything else.

He wasn't attracted to Jill at all. So what about her was fueling his aversion?

Give her a chance, Nick. She'd been nervous on her first day . . . Just like you'd been.

True. Not to mention, he'd had more than his share of off days since then. He shouldn't hold one of hers against her.

"Hey, Jill," he said as she stopped in front of him.

She grinned broadly. "I didn't know you lived out this way."

"I don't. I came by to see Brynna."

Her face blanched. "The girl who made all those awful photos with animals?"

"No," he snapped. "The girl someone lied about. Those pictures were doctored."

She actually got huffy with him. "That's not what *I* heard about her."

Keep talking, babe, and you're really going to alienate me. And seriously tick him off. "Yeah, well, you're hearing it now. I was there and can tell you that they were forged. It was obvious. Brynna has never done anything like that, and wouldn't."

She smiled. "If you say so. I don't know her well enough to comment."

"Then you don't know her well enough to carry a rumor that is completely untrue."

Jill went silent for a few seconds. "That's a really good point. I never thought of it that way."

"Yeah, well, I don't like gossip." He'd had too much

of it spread about him and his mom. "As my mother always says, great minds discuss ideas. Average minds discuss events. Small minds discuss people. And life's too short to worry about what other people do or don't do. Tend your own backyard, not theirs, because yours is the one you have to live in."

"Wow, that's deep. Are you, like, one of the scholarship kids?"

He hated that question. In theory, scoring high enough to get a scholarship should be a mark of honor. But somehow it'd been twisted around by his classmates to mean that anyone who had a scholarship couldn't afford to go to school at St. Richards and had no business there because they weren't worthy.

"Yeah, I'm one of the scholarship kids."

"That's so cool. Me and my brother got in last year, but we weren't able to get one of the scholarships. We tried twice, though."

Now he felt awful. "I'm sorry, Jill."

Her smile returned. "It's okay. The church was real good to us. They were taking up a collection to help my parents with tuition when this really nice old couple volunteered to sponsor us. They're paying for everything . . . right down to the pens and book bags. They even took us shopping to get new school clothes."

"That's decent of them. They must be really great people." His mom would never have allowed someone else to pay for Nick's school, never mind his clothes. She was fierce in her beliefs that you take nothing from no one. What you had, you earned, or you did without until you could afford it.

No one owes you a living, Nick, and they definitely don't owe you respect. Just because they have excess doesn't mean we're entitled to it. Life isn't about what you can take from someone. It's about what you can earn.

As Kyrian would say, he who dies with the most toys wins and the spoils always go to the victor. So win big.

But then his mom was also the first one to donate to charity any time the nuns called for toys or food or such for the underprivileged. He'd never quite understood that, especially since most of those "underprivileged" people were a lot better off than they were. However, he had too deep a sense of self-preservation to ask her about the dichotomy in her rationale. She could get real testy if she thought someone was calling her a hypocrite.

"They are the best," Jill continued. "Mr. Gautier is a banker and Mrs. Gautier's a lawyer with an office downtown. You don't know them, do you? I was wondering since you had the same last name and all."

"I don't. But then Gautier and its variants are fairly common in Louisiana and southern Mississippi. There are four other kids at St. Richards with the same last name. I guess if you go far enough back, we're all related, but I don't have any living relatives that I know of."

"Really?"

"Yeah, my parents are both only children." Something he'd learned from Ambrose after he'd confessed that he wasn't really Nick's uncle. Ambrose didn't want anyone else stepping forward and claiming to be a long-lost relative of Adarian's. The last thing he wanted was for Nick to put his trust into the wrong person.

"That's so sad. I've got almost two dozen cousins

and a little sister in addition to my brother Joey. What about your grandparents? Surely they weren't only children, too."

"I don't know anything about my grandparents. My dad's parents died a long time before I was born and my mother never talks about hers."

"I'm sorry, Nick."

He shrugged nonchalantly. "Nothing to be sorry about. It just is. You can't miss what you don't know."

She smiled again. "I like talking to you. You're really smart and you have a great way of looking at things. It's unique and makes me think."

Every warning bell he possessed rang out. Flattery and insults both brought out the same reaction in him—*What do you want?* In his experience the people who flattered him to his face were the first ones who stabbed him whenever he turned his back. He hated it. Maybe he was judging her wrongly, but he'd been burned enough to be very wary of people's motives.

He heard the sound of the arms about to lower over the street. "My streetcar's coming. I need to get back to the Quarter."

"Oh, okay. It was good talking to you. I'll see you in school tomorrow."

"Yeah. Later." Nick ran to the platform, grateful to have an excuse to get away from Jill. He had no idea why she bothered him so, but . . .

He didn't trust her and he didn't believe in wasting time around people he didn't trust. While they might be all right, it wasn't worth the gamble. He'd rather be doing his homework, which said it all.

It didn't take that long to get back to Sanctuary. His mom was busy with customers so he headed straight to his corner booth and resumed pulling his books out.

A few minutes later, he was tugging at his hair as he tried to understand his chemistry assignment when something white appeared next to him. Arching a brow, he looked over to see a double fudge sundae.

His jaw dropped as he looked past the three cherries to see his mom smiling at him. "Should I be scared? I get a burger *and* a sundae, and it's not my birthday? Who are you, strange woman, and what have you done with my mother?"

Laughing, she rolled her eyes—something that

would have gotten *him* grounded for a week. "Mr. Addams called me and told me what you did for Brynna. I don't have any hero cookies, so you get a hero sundae instead." She added whipped cream to the top, then set the bottle down next to him. "I love you, Nick."

"Ditto." He grabbed the spoon and dug in before she changed her mind or he did something else that got him into trouble and made her take it back.

With a shake of her head, his mom started away, then stopped to frown.

Nick glanced up, and did a double take as he saw Kody a few steps away. His mom didn't look as pleased to see her as he was.

"Hi, Mrs. Gautier," Kody said with a genuine smile. "Um, this isn't a date, and I know Nick's on restriction. Nick had no idea I was coming, but I knew he was here, and I wanted to ask him about the algebra homework we have. That is, if it's okay with you?"

His mom relaxed. "I'm sorry, sweetie, you didn't have to explain. I wasn't frowning at you. I just . . . ever have a weird déjà vu moment? When I saw you in the light . . . it was so strange. Like I'd seen you before, but you weren't you. Anyway, I'm being silly and it's nothing against you. You want me to bring you something?"

Kody looked past his mom, to his sundae. "Any chance you might share that?"

"Only with you."

She met his mother's gaze. "May I have another spoon?"

His mom pulled one out of her apron pocket. "I'll grab you some milk and water to drink, too."

"Thank you, Mrs. Gautier."

Kody sat down next to him while his mother headed toward the bar. She kissed his cheek before taking a bite of his sundae. Ah, the sneaky woman. She knew that little peck bought her instant distraction and guaranteed her that he would be incapable of speech for the next few minutes.

"Mark can't find squat on who registered the domain. Whoever it is went through a company and all that's showing up is that company's information. Worse, the company is based in Canada."

Which meant, with Mark's luck, if he hacked it, it would cause an international war. "That sucks."

"That's what Madaug said. Still, Mark said he could and would eventually hack it, but it might take a few days. After you left, we got on the site and . . ." She closed her eyes and winced.

"What?"

"It's awful, Nick. The site is mostly lists. Most stuck-up. Most obnoxious. Most likely to run an old lady over. Ugliest, et cetera." She took another bite before she continued. "It also has personal information posted like who's gay. Who was caught mooning the crowd or flashing themselves at Mardi Gras. Who's a virgin. Who's slept with the most people. Those who have been treated for eating disorders and drug addictions, or STDs. Students who are cutters and alcoholics." She hesitated before she added, "Who's been arrested."

Nick went cold. "Am I on it?"

She hesitated before she spoke. "Did you really shoplift?"

Righteous indignation and anger burned through

him. "No! I had a sucker in my pocket when I went in and the store owner didn't believe me. He called the cops, saying I'd stolen it from his store. But I didn't. I swear it. My teacher had given it to me for scoring highest on a class test."

She put a comforting hand on his arm. "I believe you, Nick. I do. It also lists what everyone's parents do for a living. Whose parents are alcoholics or drug addicts."

So much for the sundae. He no longer had any kind of appetite. He could hear the implication in her tone.

The students whose parents had been to jail, or in his case, had taken up permanent residency there.

"It tells everyone my dad's a felon, doesn't it?"

She nodded. "And it still lists your mom as a strip-per."

In that moment, he fully understood his father's need to kill people 'cause if he could be locked in a room for five seconds with the person behind this, he'd tear their head off, and laugh like a loon while he did it "Anything else about me?"

"They claim you cheated on your entrance exam, and that the only reason you weren't thrown out for it is because your mother traded favors to the administrator to keep him from turning you in."

Fury tore through him. "I swear, I'll—"

Kody placed her finger over his lips to keep him from ranting. "Madaug is hacking into the site even as we speak to delete it all. For everyone."

That helped, but it didn't change one thing. "Yeah, but how many people have seen it?"

"Do you really care?"

He wanted to lie and say no, but he thought too much of her to do that. "Yes, Kody. I do care. There are some things that you just don't want other people to know about you. Things that they don't need to know. I would think if anyone should understand that, it's you. Case in point, even after a year, I don't know who or what you really are. Your real age. Anything. Who are *your* parents? Did the site say anything about you at all?"

She scoffed. "I'm on the most obnoxious list, worst dressed, and the she-enhances-her-attributes list. The parent thing is only what I have listed on my school record. It says my father's a judge and my mother an accountant."

"Is that true?"

"Depends on the definition you use."

Nick snorted. "You're never going to tell me anything about you, are you?"

Sadness furrowed her brow. "I hope I never have to tell you."

There was a note of foreboding if he ever heard one. What was she? Another angel of death like Grim? Or something a lot worse?

Was there anything worse than Grim?

He really hoped not. "Will you at least tell me if you're a demon?"

She swallowed her bite of sundae. "Definitely *not* a demon. You'd be able to see my real form if I were."

That was news to him. "Really?"

"Really. The perspicacity you developed is honed enough that you will always see a demon no matter the form it's taking. It might only be a flash that lasts no longer than a single heartbeat, but they can't hide from you. Unless . . . they're possessing someone."

Possession was never a good thing. "I don't understand."

"Demons have two very scary cloaking powers.

The mid and upper-level ones can assume any disguise they want. Kind of like Caleb appears to everyone as a teenager while he's really thousands of years old."

Yeah, Nick had seen his real form and he was . . .

U-g-l-y. But scary enough to run Freddy Krueger out of the dream realm.

Kody continued her explanation. "The lower demons and those who haven't mastered their powers yet can take possession of someone. That takes a lot less energy and talent."

"Really? I would have thought that was harder."

"Some people are remarkably weak-willed and make very easy targets for all creatures. The best protection? Know yourself and have your own thoughts, right or wrong. Never let someone else think for you or you'll find yourself a sheep in the slaughter mill."

Nick forced himself to smile and act naturally as his mom returned with Nekoda's milk and water. He waited for her to dash over to a table before he resumed their conversation.

"Like in *The Exorcist*?"

"Yes. The human has to do something that opens a conduit for the demon. Usually the demon uses a power called silkspeech or influence to get their target to do something they shouldn't. The moment the doorway's opened, the demon slips in and takes control of their body. The human has no idea they're even possessed."

He knew this scenario a little better than he wanted to. "They become Madaug's zombies."

"Pretty much, but they don't have a bokor or outside master controlling them. The demon can only control them so long as it's inside their body. That's why you won't be able to detect them."

"Ever?"

"Depends. The Malachai has some exceptional abilities. So normally I'd say never. In your case . . . who knows? I wouldn't put any ability past your father, and you have the potential to be even more powerful than he is."

"How so?" Nick asked.

"Honestly, we're not sure. It's one of those things where we can see into the future, but you have some very distinct and exceptionally diverse paths you could follow and until you choose, we don't really know what will happen to you, or what you'll do."

Nick frowned at that. "We? Who's the rest of the group?"

"Speaking in the royal sense of the word."

Uh-huh. Nick wasn't so sure she was being honest about that. He was dying to know who 'they' were, but he'd been around Kody long enough to know she wouldn't divulge anything.

"But we can alter my future, right?"

"That's the plan," she said wistfully. "If you give in to the demon side of yourself, you will destroy every-one around you. You won't be capable of love or com-passion." Her words sent a shiver down his spine as he remembered the way Ambrose had attacked him. She was right. The last thing he wanted was to become *that* version of his future.

"What mangy, nasty rat died on top of your head, and why would you keep it there?"

Nick frowned at the angry tone from two booths over. He looked up to see Wren, one of the busboys, trying to clean an unoccupied table that was filled with dishes, while a man with a small group in the booth next to it harassed him. Tall and lean with blond dreadlocks that fell over his face, obscuring most of his features, and all of his turquoise eyes, Wren didn't appear much older than Nick. Extremely antisocial- as in Wren took it to a whole new level uniquely his own- he seldom spoke to anyone. Rather, he functioned like a ghost, moving ninja-style through the restaurant and doing his job without comment or complaint.

What the moron antagonizing him didn't know was that Wren was a tigard. Half white tiger and half snow leopard. And like a mighty shinobi, he could strike fast and hard with very lethal accuracy.

Nick held his breath for the bloodshed he was sure was imminent.

"Hey, freak! I'm talking to *you*," the customer in the booth behind Wren called out. The man looked to be in his early twenties and beefy enough to back his animosity. *If* Wren were human. "Are you deaf as well as dumb and grungy?"

His cronies in the booth with him laughed while Wren ignored them. Without so much as twitching an eyebrow, he pulled the empty glasses into his plastic tub and stacked up the small plates.

"Ted," the overly siliconed woman beside him whimpered in a strident, nasal tone that begged for her to take lessons from Wren's silence, "have mercy on the poor retard. He is just a busboy, after all. It's actually nice of them to hire someone who is obviously mentally defective. Everyone should hire the handicapped."

Nick looked around for his mom who would take the woman's head off for saying that. He'd been smacked in the back his head by her enough to know better than to say something so vicious. Those lightning fast, out of the blue head whacks also explained a lot of his own mental damage.

"Yeah," Ted snarled in response, "but that hair is stinking up the place and I'm trying to eat here." He lobbed a ketchup soaked french fry at Wren. It landed on his white uniform sleeve and slid down it, leaving a long red stain.

Wren went ramrod stiff.

In that moment, Nick saw the tigard in Wren. The way he held himself low and rigid reminded Nick of a cat in the wild targeting its prey before striking.

The tiger lies low not from fear, but for aim. . . .

Wren blinked, then seemed to calm himself. He wiped down the table, picked up his tub, and moved on.

At least he tried to.

As he walked past the booth, the man shoved him. Wren stumbled and almost dropped the dishes. But at the last minute, true to his tigard genes, he caught his balance and kept the dishes from spilling out of his tub.

"That's it, boy," Ted sneered. "Run home to your mama."

Wren met Nick's gaze and the pain those words wrought infuriated him. He couldn't stand to see anyone abused. It didn't matter that he knew Wren could take care of himself. He wasn't going to tolerate this and do nothing to stop it.

Climbing over Nekoda, he went to check on his friend. But no sooner had he stood up than the bully shoved Wren again.

Aw, buddy, it's on . . . Nick pushed the man back toward his booth. "You need to sit down, shut-up and leave him alone."

The man raked a sneer over him. "That's some ego you got there, punk." He laughed over his shoulder, at his friends. "You like a Chihuahua that thinks it's a Doberman." Facing Nick, he sobered and narrowed his eyes with deadly intent on Nick. "Now, you're the one that needs to sit down and mind your own business before I shut your mouth for you."

"Nick, let it go," Kody said from behind him.

The man looked past Nick to where she sat in the booth. "Man, that's one fine piece of—"

"You better lay off my girl and watch your language around her."

The man laughed. "Punk, you're toast. I know karate and am a third-degree black belt." He punched at Nick.

Then Nick did what he did best. . . .

CHAPTER 5

Nick launched himself at the man and latched on to him with everything he had. Grunting, the man tried to flip him off his back, then he slammed Nick against the wall, trapping Nick between his steroid enhanced form and the brick. Ted used his body to slam Nick there repeatedly. Nick tightened his hold around the Ted's neck, trying to find the carotid and cut off his blood flow there like Bubba had shown him.

You don't gotta be strong, Nick. A little bit of pressure in the right place and you can own anyone.

Still, the man did everything he could to get Nick off him.

"That's right. Uh-huh. Uh-huh," Nick said arrogantly. "You might know karate, boy, but I know gorilla, and I'm a level-forty champion in it. Let's hear it for Diddy Kong! Ew! Ew! Ew! Ew! Ew!" He mimicked the sound of a gorilla as he held on for dear life.

Her eyes filled with an equal mixture of humor and horror, Nekoda kept one hand over her mouth while Wren burst out laughing so hard he had to set his dishpan down before he dropped it.

"Oh my God, Nick! Nick! What are you doing? You don't even know that man." His mother came running over to them. "Get off that man's back. Now!"

Nick hesitated. "Not sure that's a good idea, Mama. He might kill me if I do."

"You damn straight, punk! I'm gonna kick your—"

"You ain't kicking nothing here, boy."

The man finally stopped trying to buck him off his back as Dev or Remi or one of the quads grabbed Ted by his shirt front and held him still in one beefy paw of a hand. "Slide down, Nick. I've got it from here."

It wasn't until Nick's feet were back on the ground and he saw the bow-and-arrow tattoo on Dev's biceps that he knew which quad had saved him. "Thanks, Dev."

"No problem. Now let me take out the trash and I'll be right back to help clean up the mess he made."

Nick gulped as he met his mother's furious glower. *Dude, don't leave me.* Cherise Gautier might be a tiny little slip of a woman, but she scared the snot out of him. Especially when she eyed him like she could go through him, like she was doing right this very second.

His butt was already doused in gas. She was about to throw it into the fire pit and roast marshmallows over his carcass.

"Mama, I can explain."

"No. I don't think you can. I *know* you can't." She let out a sound of supreme exasperation. "You don't fight, Nick. Not for any reason. You know this. How many times do I have to tell you before you learn to listen? Huh? I raised you better. You're not an animal to just grab someone and start pounding on them for no reason. What were you thinking? I'll tell you what you were thinking. Nothing. Nothing at all. And I expect better from you than that. You're at an age now where they'll send you to jail for fighting. Do you understand me, boy? Jail. Prison. Just like your daddy."

She leaned in to whisper harshly. Except her idea of whispering was loud and clear, even over the music playing. "And at my job, no less. Are you trying to get me fired again? You are, aren't you? You're not going to be happy until we're living on the street, eating out of Dumpsters and I have to prostitute myself to feed you. You are grounded until you graduate. You hear me? You're never getting a car or a license. *Ever.* You're too hotheaded for one. You have no business driving a car when you can't even sit and do your homework without flipping out and attacking an innocent stranger! What? Someone's going to cut you off in traffic or blow their horn at you. Are you going to drag them out of their car and beat them on the street for it? Are you? You're just like your father. Violent to your core. You don't know how to stop yourself. You take everything too far and you overreact without thinking it through or taking a minute to consider the consequences. You're going to get yourself killed one day because you can't see past one second of what's going on."

With every word she spat at him, and she kept going, and going . . . and going, he felt like he was being
slapped and stomped. Like he was the lowest scum-
sucking parasite ever born.

Dev let out a sharp whistle behind her.

Jumping in startled alarm, she turned around to
see him.

"Cherise, settle down. You're giving the poor kid a
concussion with that verbal beating. It's all okay."

She glared harshly at Nick. "No, Dev, it's not. He
knows better. And—"

"Cherise," Dev said again, cutting her off. "I was on
my way over here to do something a lot more extreme
than what he did to that jerk."

She scowled. "How do you mean?"

"Nick was protecting me," Wren said in a tone so
soft it was barely audible.

Dev nodded. "That dick was insulting Wren and
Kody, and when he went for Wren's back and attacked
him, Nick stopped it. Besides, Nick wasn't beating on
him, Cherise." Dev started laughing. Hard. Which
really didn't help Nick's deflated ego in the least. "Your

boy was hanging on for dear life—like a scared kitten on a wild bronco."

Oh yeah, just emasculate me on the floor, Dev. Thanks.

Dev kept on laughing. "Damn, to have had that one on camera. We could have made some serious money. It was hilarious. . . . 'I know gorilla.' Priceless, Nick. Just priceless." Dev laughed until he was coughing from it.

Nick wanted to crawl under something. The only thing that kept him from feeling any worse was that Kody had seen him fight for real and knew he normally did a little better than this. Jumping on someone's back was only used when he went up against someone who outweighed him by a couple of hundred pounds.

And that was just in the man's arm weight.

"Thank you, Nick," Wren said, inclining his head to him. Wren's pet monkey, Marvin, stuck his head out of Wren's apron pocket where he must have been sleeping and chattered at Nick as if in approval.

Dev clapped him on the shoulder so hard, Nick stumbled. "You got some serious stones on you, boy. You grow some more, and fill out, and we'll hire you

for bouncing." Dev kept snickering. "Gorilla," he mut-
tered again as he wandered back toward the door. "I
gotta tell Aimee that one."

Now that they were alone, except for Kody, who
slid back into the booth in an attempt to be invisible,
his mom swallowed.

"I'm sorry, baby."

But Nick was still too raw to listen. She had ver-
bally slapped him—again—in front of everyone, and
he was tired of being publicly humiliated for doing a
good deed. "No, Ma. You're not. You do this to me all
the time. You make up your mind without bothering
to find out any of the facts. You always assume I'm in
the wrong, no matter what it is. When I was accused
of stealing, you wouldn't even listen to me tell you
what had happened. And even when I forced you to
hear it, you called me a liar in front of the man and
the cops. You refused to stand up for me. You looked
at me then, like you did just now—like I'm your worst
disappointment and you're sorry you kept me. Like
I'm nothing. I was just a baby, Ma, and you let them
take me all the way to the police station in a squad

car. You said it would be good for me to see what happens to criminals—that maybe I'd think twice before I stole something else. I was a scared little kid, Mama. Most of all, I was innocent. I don't mean to be rude or disrespectful, but I'm a real good kid. All I think about, morning, noon, and night, is taking care of *you*. Of not letting *you* down like everyone else has done. I do exactly what you tell me to. I keep my grades up and I work thirty hours a week before *and* after school. No matter how tired I am or what time it is, I walk you home every time you have to work at night. And I think I've earned a little benefit of the doubt from you once in a while. But it don't matter how much I do that's right. In your eyes, when it counts most, I'm always wrong."

Tears choked him, but he wasn't about to let them show. He was stronger than that. "You know all those fights I've gotten into at school, Mama? The ones you have repeatedly reamed me out over? They weren't for me. I ain't never had a fight because someone insulted *me*. I'm tough. I can take it. God, I'm so used to it that it flows over me like water over a duck. What I was defending in those fights was *your* reputation when they insulted *you*."

He could handle the cruelty from his classmates. The brutality from the demons sent to kill him. He could take his teachers and principal thinking he was the worst sort of scum-trash.

What he couldn't stand was how quick his mother misjudged him when he went out of his way to do things to please her.

He locked his jaw, trying to keep the tears from falling. That was all he needed.

Cry in front of his girl like he was some kind of baby who couldn't handle his emotions.

Nick shook his head. "I don't know what else to do to prove to you that I ain't Adarian Malachai. To make you see the real me and not this misconceived notion you have of a pain in your butt, sent here to shame and humiliate you. I don't know what's worse. The fact that you have no confidence in your ability to raise a decent person or the fact that you expect me to turn psycho for no reason. It's not my fault Adarian's my father. I didn't pick him, and I'm sorry that I'll never be anything but your personal disappointment." His heart pounding, he turned around and headed for the door.

"Where are you going, Nick?" his mom called after him.

"According to you and everybody else, Mama," he snarled, "I'm going straight to hell, and there's nothing I can do to stop it."

Nick stopped as he reached the table Wren was currently cleaning. He pulled out a small handful of bills and set them down with the others that had been left in the empty bread basket.

Wren frowned at him. "What's that for?"

Nick jerked his chin toward the booth where the man had been sitting. "You work too hard not to get what you're entitled to. Since I cost you the tip, it's only fair I make it up to you." And with that, he left.

Putting his hands in his pockets, Nick headed down Royal, toward Bubba's. He'd go home in a few minutes. But right now, he wanted to be with someone who didn't accuse him of things when he didn't deserve it. For all of his faults, Bubba had always trusted him and treated him like a man, and not some brain or genetically defective kid.

"Nick?"

He paused as he heard Kody's voice. Part of him wanted to ignore her, but it wasn't her fault his mom had laid into him in front of her. So he stood there with his head hung low, wishing he was anywhere else in the world than right here. Right now.

Yeah, one day he might have infinite powers capable of destroying the entire universe. But today, he was just another loser mandork, embarrassed to the core of his being.

Kody moved to stand directly in front of him. Bending her knees, she came up to capture his lips with hers. Nick closed his eyes and inhaled the sweetest scent he'd ever known.

She cupped his face as she kissed him, and he forgot all about his anger and hurt. After a few seconds, she wrapped her arms around him and held him close as she buried her face against his neck—something that sent chills all over him and made his blood race.

He held her against him and pressed his cheek against the top of her head. "Thank you, Kody."

"I didn't do anything."

Yes, she did. She cared. And that meant more to him than anything else.

Clearing his throat, he draped his arm around her shoulders and started back down the street toward Bubba's.

"Your mother loves you, Nick."

"I know. But she doesn't trust me."

"She worries about you."

"I worry about me, too, but I don't go around accusing me of . . . stuff I know not to do. I don't understand why she can't see *me*." He clenched his teeth. "I don't get it. I just don't. You know, she actually asked me back when I played football why I wasn't friends with Stone Blakemore. 'He's such a nice boy, Nicky,'" he mocked in a falsetto. "'You can see all the good breeding in him. He's such a gentleman. You could learn a lot hanging out with him and his friends.'" He curled his lip. "Stone, Kody. Stone. The boy who carries his only two brain cells in his jock strap, and who isn't happy unless he's picking on someone or mocking them." The boy who called Kody a whore every time he saw Nick.

"Your mom always sees the good in people."

But not in me.

And that was what always kicked him hardest. Stone, the idiot bully, was perfect. He, the ever dutiful son, was defective. . . .

The injustice stung so deep that it left a bleeding wound inside his soul. What would he have to do to make his mother realize that he wasn't . . .

What?

A demon?

Something born to destroy everything?

A tool for evil?

Capable of murder?

His stomach churned even more as he realized that he was exactly all of that. And more. *You're destined to destroy everyone you love.*

Maybe his mother saw more than he thought she did.

"Is she right, Kody?" he asked, needing to know

the truth about himself. "Am I really going to flip out one day and become my father?"

She pulled him to a stop. "We all have choices, Nick. Even if it's nothing more than the choice between lesser evils. No one can take away your free will. Not even the gods. It's the one gift that can never be returned, stolen, or revoked. We can blame others for our bad decisions. We can say that we had no choice. But it's always a lie. No one puts your hand on the gun but you. Only you can decide if you pick it up or leave it alone."

"What about silkspeech?"

"That's the power of influence, Nick. It's not mind control. If the person is strong in their convictions, they can't be controlled. You cannot compel a pacifist to murder."

He wasn't sure he believed that. "You don't think that with the right motivation, you can make someone do anything?"

"What I think is if someone held a gun to your head and threatened to kill you, your mother would do anything they asked to keep you safe. But that is her freewill decision that she, alone, makes. You see what I'm saying? She could choose to let you die. We know she won't, of course she won't, but that's because of the decisions she makes every day to put your life above hers. You can motivate someone to action, but in the end, they are the one who makes the ultimate and last decision to either do or do not."

His little Yoda sage made sense.

She reached up to cup his cheek in her hand. "I don't know if you'll turn evil. Only *you* can decide which side of this fight you're going to support. But I believe in you. I do. Otherwise, I wouldn't be here. And I definitely wouldn't be protecting you. All of us have darkness inside us, and at times it possesses and seduces us in ways we never thought possible. Gives us promises that if we give in to it, it'll make things better. I've not always done the right thing for the right reason, either. And I'm ashamed of some things I've done. We all are. Mistakes don't have to define us. They're how we learn and grow. They show us who and what we don't want to be. It's why they're mistakes. And you, my love, are such a stubborn, stubborn boy, I can only imagine how much more obstinate you'll be as a full grown man. I honestly can't imagine you doing anything you don't want to. So, no, I don't believe for a second that you'll simply snap a wheel and turn evil. And I can't imagine you *ever* being like your father. No matter what."

He took her hand into his and kissed her knuckles. "I don't know what I'd do without you, Kody."

"Remember that the next time Jill or Casey talks to you."

He smiled at her. "I always do."

She gave him a quick hug, then let him go so that they could check in with Mark.

Nick opened the door to The Triple B and let Kody enter the store first. The moment they were inside, he paused as he heard Bubba and Mark arguing on the other side of the curtain.

"Get your hands—"

"Did I not tell—"

"You don't know—"

"I know. You're—"

"Stop. Just stop. You—"

"Me, stop You're—"

There was an attractive lady on the other side of

the glass cabinet, leaning against it with one hand propped against her cheek, looking oddly bored and amused all at the same time. An impressive feat really. With dark auburn hair that was cut in a chic style, and an elegant navy blazer, she straightened up and smiled as she caught sight of them. "Hi, y'all," she said in a thick Tennessee drawl that was identical to Bubba's and Mark's. "How y'all doing?"

Contrary to misinformation and bad Hollywood attempts—some from people who ought to know better—not all Southern accents were the same. You could easily peg where someone came from by the sound of their accent and the words they used. And nowhere outside of New York City was it more obvious what ward or district you originated from, how educated your parents were, and how much money they had, than here in New Orleans. Even the name of the city itself was pronounced completely different depending on what street you grew up on.

Literally.

Nick's Cajun accent wasn't nearly as thick as his mother's, unless he wanted it to be. And the Cajun version of French was all their own. While they could understand the French and the French could usually understand them, the Cajun way of pronouncing things and altering French grammar could send purists into fits.

Menyara's Creole accent was as thick as his mother's jar of refrigerated roux, and he loved the sound of it.

He wasn't quite as pleased with his own. No matter how hard he tried to hide his accent, it always came out in certain words like "praline," "etouffee," "pecan," and any time he lost his temper. You could easily tell how mad he was by how Cajun he sounded. And if he started spewing all Cajun words, duck.

"Can I help y'all with something?"

Nick smiled as he approached her. "You must be Bubba's mama, Dr. Burdette. It's an honor to meet you, ma'am. I'm Nick Gautier and this is Kody Kennedy."

At the mention of his name, her demeanor changed completely. She went ramrod stiff and arched an irritated brow at him. "Nicholas Gautier, as I live and breathe. Now there's a name I know well. Explain to me, boy, why you want to go and shoot me in my head when you don't even know me. What'd I ever do to you?"

Nick sputtered as he tried to come up with an explanation for how he'd shot through her portrait that Bubba kept hung on his wall. "I-I didn't mean to. It was an accident. I swear it."

She started laughing, then chucked him lightly on the shoulder. "I'm just joshing with you, Nick. Calm down, son. I don't want to have to put down newspapers 'cause you wet the floor in a panic like my old hunting dog used to do every time Michael blew something up in the house. He had that poor old thing a nervous wreck until the day the Lord took her. I am absolutely not offended . . . much, that you blew my head off. But that's all right, I was raised in the middle of four brothers, and with Michael for a son, I'm used to having to dodge bullets. Literally, most days."

Without pausing or breaking a sweat, she went right into another segue. "Did he ever tell you about the time he was supposed to be napping and instead, he climbed up on his daddy's gun cabinet, trying to get to the AC vent—whatever he was going to do up there, I don't even want to know—I never asked. Anyway, poor boy slipped, hit the lock somehow, and popped it off. Next thing you know, his daddy's 410, of all things, falls out and misfires. I was out in the yard with a friend, oblivious to my son's stupidity, until a bullet whizzed right between us and shattered my birdhouse. By the time I got in the living room, Michael was trying to hide the gun behind the couch. Like I wouldn't notice the busted cabinet hanging open and the gun missing out of its slot. Not to mention it was longer than the couch. Point being, don't think anything about it, Nick. I am not offended," she repeated.

Whoever said Southerners talked slow had never been around one raised in a big family. Here he'd always thought Bubba talked fast, but he had nothing on his mother.

"Hey, Michael!" she called out, finally interrupting Mark and Bubba's fight. "You got visitors out here to see you. Stop arguing with your girlfriend and come on now." Laughing, she winked at Nick. "The way them two carry on, I keep waiting to get a wedding invitation for them to take their nuptials. I ain't never seen anything like it in my life, and especially not between two straight men. At least not to where it didn't end up in a fist fight after a couple of minutes."

"Michael is Bubba?" He felt stupid for asking, but . . .

His mother screwed her face up. "Oh, I hate that name he uses. Do I look like I'd name my son Bubba?" The way she said the name it sounded like the ultimate insult. "That I would gaze down upon my precious bundle that I had succored for months inside my own body and given all my devotion to and say, 'Dear Lord, thank you for this wonderful gift. Let me call him Bubba, so that he can grow up and be mocked before he even opens his mouth.' Did he ever tell you how he got that dang nickname?"

"No, ma'am. I didn't even know it was a nickname. I thought his nickname was Cheese."

"Oh, and don't even get me started on *that* topic. Cheese? Really, Michael? For *that* I sent you to the best private school in town." She shook her head as if to clear it. "Nah, they named him Bubba when he was in tenth grade and had gone up to Ohio State for a summer football camp program. Those snotty brats started calling my baby Bubba because of his accent that they constantly mocked him over. And instead of stomping them into the ground like he should have, he started using Bubba as a joke."

"Mama," Bubba said as he came out of the back. "I can't beat up everyone in the world for being stupid. Have you seen how many of them are out there? I work retail. Trust me. The world's eat up with it. And aren't you the one who's always saying, 'you can't fix stupid, son, so don't try?' Besides, I got better things to do with my time than fight every idiot I come into contact with."

She snorted. "Please. It wouldn't be much of a fight. Have you looked at yourself, boy?

Nick gaped at her words. He couldn't believe she'd encourage Bubba to fight when all he did was get dogged out by his mother for even thinking about fighting.

The universe had a sick sense of humor.

Dr. Burdette shook her head, then met Nick's gaze. "I don't know where he gets his gargantuan size from. My entire side of the family is mutantly short. Heck, I'm taller than two of my brothers. They are truly concentrated evil which is why they're meaner than all get out. And while his daddy is average, his daddy *is* average. Genes make no sense to me."

Bubba snorted. "You know, Mama, I don't find that comforting given the fact that you're one of the top pediatric surgeons in the country, and have written several defining works on genetic links to diseases." He glanced at Nick and Kody. "It's kind of like the time she baked me cookies when I was a kid, and then came up to my room to offer them to me while I was getting dressed for Halloween."

"Oh Lord, not that again," his mother said under her breath.

Nick was so confused. "What's wrong with cookies?" His mom tried to bake, but it was not her forte. They were always burnt on the outside and still raw dough on the inside.

Bubba snorted. "Nick, I'm telling you this for your

own good. If a woman, even your own mother, comes up and offers you cookies while she's wearing a black apron with a skull and crossbones on it . . . decline. Just saying."

His mother laughed. "It was during Halloween. Good grief. Who knew I'd scar you for life by offering you a snickerdoodle? I can just hear that conversation with your therapist now. 'Oh, Doctor, it was so awful. There I sat as a little innocent child, playing my video games on my little baby tummy, when all of a sudden, my mean, awful mama, who'd just come off a thirty-six-hour shift at the hospital, who had driven two and a half hours to get home so that she could finish sewing up my Gene Simmons costume for trick-or-treating after my daddy had accidentally sewed the sleeve shut, and bake me some mummy dogs and snickerdoodles, offered me one.'" She held the back of her hand to her forehead. "'Oh the humanity, Doctor. Oh the humanity I have seen. You just don't know my pain. You. Just. Don't. Know.'"

She gave Kody and Nick a droll stare. "I'll bet if you tried to give him a snickerdoodle today, he'd scream like a girl and run for cover." She paused and narrowed her eyes. Then a wide smile broke across her face. "I know what I'm making for dinner." She grinned at Bubba. "You got any cinnamon in your kitchen, Bugaboo? Or is it all half-empty cereal boxes and Snickers like normal?"

"I got a loaf of bread and some peanut butter, too."

She rolled her eyes. "Oh I'm so sorry, honey. I didn't mean to insult you." Her voice shook with laughter and sarcasm.

Nick laughed. "I like your mama, Bubba. She's a lot of fun."

"That's 'cause she's not busting *your* chops. As my dad would say, she's like a head injury. Only funny when it happens to somebody else."

He wouldn't argue that. No one was immune from the blistering tongue of maternal criticism. But Nick wanted to return to something Bubba's mom had mentioned that he hadn't known about Bubba. Something he just couldn't wrap his mind around. "Did you really play football?"

Bubba shrugged nonchalantly. "For a little while."

"Little while, my pink patootie." His mama turned her attention back to Nick and Kody. "Let me tell you about my baby boy, Nick. He was a first-string line-backer. One of the best you ever saw. When he wasn't blowing stuff up around the house conducting bizarre experiments," she glanced sideways at Bubba, "like the time he tried to launch the TV into space for the aliens to see—"

"Mama, I was four years old, let it go already. Dang . . . Do something stupid around your mama, one time, when you're four years old and you never live it down."

She ignored his interruption. ". . . He had a football in his hands and was leaving everybody in his wake. No one could catch him. The people who knew better than to mock him used to call him Battleground Bull-dozer Burdette or Trip B for short. He had a full-blown football *and* academic scholarship to MIT, where he was one of their most valued players all four years he was there. He had offers to go pro and I don't mean one or two teams. He was the number-one draft pick and was promised everything you can imagine if he'd sign. He could have played for any NFL team, anywhere."

Nick was completely stunned. He'd had no idea. Bubba never really talked about his past, and the fact that he was a football star . . . .

That absolutely shamed Nick's Peewee Bowl Championship wins he was so proud of. "Why didn't you go pro?"

A deep sadness creased Bubba's brow. "I had a lot of reasons that made sense to me back then." He swallowed hard. "It doesn't matter anyway. . . . I'd have probably had a massive injury on the field that would have cut my career short. As they say, all good things come to an end. Now, moving out of the past 'cause there ain't no reason to be there, let's talk about this cybernut on the loose at your school. You guys got a major problem."

"Yeah, we know."

"No, Nick, you don't." He crooked his finger for him to follow into the back of the shop.

Nick headed in and as soon as he saw the monitor where Mark was working, he froze. There were all kinds of photos on the site about his classmates. Some pretty graphic. Some gross. And some were just wrong. "What the . . ."

Mark let out a long breath. "If this weren't cruel, I'd be impressed by the skill level. Someone spent a lot of time and they've done some incredible PI work on a whole lot of people."

"But what concerns us most is this link." Bubba took the mouse from Mark's hand and clicked on the word "Sources." "They've named everyone who gave them information on someone else."

Nick ground his teeth as he read over the list and saw his own name listed as an informer. "They're absolutely lying. I never told anyone anything about Spencer. Nothing. Not even my mama." In that moment, he wanted to find the site owner and back over them with his poor driving skills. "What's under 'Cyblog'?"

Mark clicked on it. "The social ramblings of a jealous lunatic—keeping in mind that the man who is making this accusation against the site owner sleeps in duck urine and rather than go to a bar to troll for dates, spends his nights in the gator-infested swamp searching for zombies with Bubba. Believe me, I know crazy when I see it."

Shaking his head, Nick didn't comment on that as he read the rantings against his classmates. Mark moved his hand so that Nick could take possession of the mouse.

There was a photo of some of the cheerleaders, including Casey, from the haunted house his school was sponsoring. Under the photo—*These are some of the nauseating fleas I have to stomach in class. Couldn't you just puke? Look at them, the only thing smaller than their IQs is their skirts. Vo-mit.*

Nick let out a low whistle. "I'm not sure I want to know what's under the 'Classmates' link."

Mark crossed his arms over his chest. "No, you probably don't. It's basically pages they've set up with doctored photos of your classmates in sexually explicit acts, or naked."

Nick decided to take his word for it. Until Madaug perfected his eye bleach formula, he didn't need to see something that would disgust him. "And you can't find anything on the person who did this?"

"Nada, buddy. Nil. Nothing."

This was so bad.

Bubba put a comforting hand on Nick's shoulder. "Don't worry. We'll keep working on it. We're going to find out who's responsible."

"Thanks, Bubba." Sickened by the kind of callous individual who could do this to someone who'd never harmed him or her, Nick faced Kody. "I'm going home before I get into any more trouble, and wait for my mom to get off work."

"Okay. Call me if you need anything."

Most people would hear that and think she meant for him to use a phone. But he had several ways to contact her that didn't require anything more than his thoughts

He kissed her on the cheek before he left out the back door of the building. If ever his powers would work correctly for him, now would be the time.

Unfortunately, the only thing he could see about the future was his coming restriction that would hang over his head until graduation.

At least it didn't take long to make it home. He went

inside and locked the door, then cursed as he remembered he'd left his backpack at Sanctuary. He wouldn't be able to finish his homework until late tonight.

You could go get it.

Yeah, and chance another severe tongue-lashing from the mothership? No, thank you.

Grumbling at his own stupidity, he went to his room. He kicked off his shoes, then threw himself across his bed and reached for the radio. He needed some loud, make-the-neighbors-hate-my-guts music to improve his dismal outlook.

But as he reached for the controls, a chill went down his spine.

Unsure of what it meant, he scanned the room and . . .

Every protection sign he had on his walls—signs that were never visible to the naked eye unless something inhuman was trying to get to him—was lit up like Christmas in the Quarter. His walls literally glowed bloodred . . .

Crap! He was under attack.

CHAPTER 6

Nick rolled off the bed and grabbed his baseball bat from the corner . . . yeah, okay, stupid weapon against the paranormal, but it was better than nothing.

In spite of all the symbols and Caleb's assurances that nothing could breach the sanctity of his room, a mist appeared in the corner closest to the window.

Nick tightened his grip on the wood. Just as he was about to put out the cosmic call for help and go all Louisville Slugger on his intruder, the creature materialized. Tall, shapely, and evil to the core of her soul, she stood on the other side of his bed in a short ruffled skirt, a black leather bustier, and purple leggings. Her red and black hair was pulled into pigtails that were held in place by spiked bands that matched the collar around her neck.

"Good grief, Simi, you scared me senseless." Nick let out an audible sound of relief as he let the bat slide out of his hands and back to the floor. "What are you doing here?"

She blew out a hard breath that made her bangs fly up as she pouted in irritation. She was even tapping her burgundy Docs on the floor. "Akri done gone off with that dumb old heifer goddess again, and the Simi done got bored sleeping all the time and started twitching, and making Akri jumpy, which makes the old cow-faced heifer grumpy. Which personally, the Simi thinks is great. Anything the Simi can do to rankle the heifer, the better. One day, the Simi gonna eat that heifer, too. No matter what Akri say. Yum. Yum. Or actually, probably more tummy ache than yummy full. But anyways, 'cause the Simi was doing the St. Vitus dance of stir-crazy impatience and thereby Akri was doing the St. Vitus Dance by default, Akri say the Simi could come and visit them bear people to get some good eats. Soooo, the Simi decided to come see her favorite blue-eyed demon boy and since he always being grounded for being stupid, Simi said, hmmm . . . let's go check his room, 'cause that's where he normally is when he's grounded. And here you are. And now so am I. Hi, akri-Nick."

Nick rubbed his hand across his face as he tried to make sense of her prattle. But that was the thing about Simi. She seldom made sense. "I'm sorry your dad ditched you for his girlfriend again." He seemed to do that to her every few months.

Simi shrugged. "It's okay. Akri more miserable than the Simi is. And he say he come get me as soon as he can. Until then . . ." She pulled a white bib out of her coffin-shaped purse and tied it around her neck. "You wanna come get eats, too? You the only one the Simi knows who can eat as much as she does."

"I would love to, Simi, but . . ."

"Akri-Nick grounded."

He nodded. "Sorry."

She sighed heavily. "Don't be sorry. The Simi'll eat some for you. Now cheer up. It all be okay."

"I hope so, Simi." He really did.

"Trust the Simi. She ain't never wrong." She made a kissing noise at him before she vanished.

It wasn't until then that he remembered something.

Simi *never* set off the alarms in his home.

Caleb? He used his thoughts to summon his protector.

What? Wow, Caleb sounded put out.

I have a situation here. My walls are glowing and I don't know why. He'd barely finished that last word before Caleb appeared in front of him.

Without a word, Caleb turned a slow circle as he scanned the room from floor to ceiling.

Nick frowned as he watched him. "What is it?"

"Not sure." Caleb's eyes glowed, then glazed over. He spoke in demon tongue with that thick, gravely voice that was made for scaring the life out of people. "They're coming for you, Nick."

"Who?"

"Noir. One of his demons found Adarian somehow. I have to go warn your father."

Nick scowled. "I don't understand."

"And I don't have time to explain," he growled. "Nekoda! Come, sit on Nick until I return."

She flashed into the room beside Nick. "I won't go anywhere."

"I'll be back." Caleb vanished.

Nick wasn't sure he liked this at all. "What's going on?" he asked, hoping she'd be more forthcoming than Caleb.

"I'm not sure. There's something probing your perimeter."

Lovely. Just what he needed. More demons who wanted him dead. "Who is Noir, by the way?"

For once she actually answered his question. "One of the six primal gods. And he's the one who owns the Malachai."

Now he fully understood the bone-deep chill. His master was trying to summon him home. "Why hasn't one of you told me this before now?"

"We were hoping we wouldn't have to. That we could keep you protected from him."

"Why?"

"Because you and your father are what fuel him. He gets the majority of his power from the Malachai. Every time you think of him or say his name, you give him a charge. Do you understand?"

Yeah, he did and he hated it. "Even if I'm sleeping and I dream of him, I can charge him?"

"Even if you're sleeping. That's why we didn't tell you. And why scare you when there's nothing you can do about it anyway?"

For a full minute, he hyperventilated over the thought of being dragged into a hell realm and kept there like a pet. "Where is this . . . primal god?"

"At the moment, trapped in what's called the Nether Realm, or more correctly Azmodea."

The place Ambrose had told him not to go to. "How did he get trapped there?"

"Your father escaped him. And through his demons, Noir has been pursuing him ever since the moment he broke free. But for all of his other faults, Adarian is extremely crafty and has managed to avoid capture. Definitely not an easy thing to do."

"So the war with the Malachai and Sephiroth—"

"Sephirii. Sephiroth is singular. Malachai is plural too."

"So I would be correctly called a Malachoth?"

She snorted. "No. You're always *the* Malachai, because unlike the Sephiroth, you are an amalgamation of evil. The sum of it all as it were, which is why your name always takes the plural form."

Wonderful. He was the son of all evil. Just what a guy wanted to hear. *'Hey, kid? You have pimples. Hair in uncomfortable places. Strange body odors you never had before. A body growing so fast it leaves you completely uncoordinated. You're socially awkward.*

'And if that's not enough fun for you, you're going to morph into the evil Power Ranger and destroy the world.'

Nice . . . .

"You really know how to cheer a brother up, girl. Thanks. I always wanted to be called the sum of all evil. Makes me so proud I got up this morning."

Kody shrugged. "Sorry."

"So tell me more about he who can't be mentioned by me."

She sat down on the edge of his bed and he did his best not to let that take his mind to places that could only get him into some real normal boy trouble for once.

No female other than his mom had ever been near his bed before.

Down, boy. This wasn't the time to be thinking about *that*.

Yeah, but you have a really hot woman on your mattress. . . .

And that just didn't happen to him every day. Demon attacks, yes. Daily humiliation? Double check.

Hot babe on bed?

Never.

Unaware of the havoc she caused him, she toyed with the fringe on his blanket. "It's really complicated, Nick." She bit her lip, which really didn't help the heat in his blood. "At one time, there were six gods who had dominion over the elements of the earth. Three who embodied the positive elements and three who were the negative. On the positive side—Verlyn, who was in charge of vegetation and fertility. He was an earth god and he fed everyone. Cam was the goddess of white and gold. The sun goddess. Her gift was love and light. Then there was Rezar. So beautiful that no one could even look at him without being filled with such lust it would cause them to spontaneously combust. He was the god of fire and passion. Those three were the divine guardians of humanity and the ones who created the Chthonians . . . beings taken from all sentient life forms on earth. The Chthonians were charged with making sure that none of the gods abused their power."

"Kind of like a divine police force?"

Kody nodded. "And in all things, there is perfect balance. The gods of negativity are Braith who is essentially a war goddess. Though her color is gray, she is not ambivalent about her place in the dark order. She stands firmly with Noir and Azura against the light gods. She's the goddess of metals, and was the one who taught mankind how to forge weapons out of the earth's raw materials so that they could fight each other. Azura is the goddess of water. Seemingly harmless, she lures you in and then drowns you horribly. And lastly . . ."

"He whose name I cannot say or think."

She nodded. " Noir is all things dark and deadly. And the way the story goes, the gods of light, after Braith had taught mankind how to fight and they saw what the future would hold for man and the other sentient creatures, got together and created the Sephirii. They were to be the protectors of man and the consorts of the primal gods."

Now that was an interesting word. Did she mean what he thought she meant? "Consorts?"

"Lovers."

Yes, she did. Nick sputtered indignantly. "Ah now, that ain't right. Why couldn't I be one of *them*?" He'd much rather be a divine consort than the instrument of all evil. Definitely sounded like more fun.

Kody patted his hand. "Well, hon, you'd be dead now if you were."

"No, you said there was *one* left. One Malachai and one Sephiroth."

Her face paled. "Trust me, Nick, you don't want to

be Jared. His existence is nothing but pain and utter misery."

"Oh . . . never mind." He had enough of that in his own life. If Jared's was worse, he'd gladly take evil tool status. "Please continue." Nick sat down on his bed, but made sure to put a good amount of distance between them. "You left off with the consorts."

"Noir, Braith and Azura were livid that the light gods had dared create an army to be used against them, so they forged their own to maintain the balance."

That writing went all over the wall. Up, down, sideways and back. "And eventually, they all had it out."

"Yeah," she breathed. "That's the problem with stockpiling weapons. Sooner or later, someone always pulls the trigger."

Stacking his pillows against his headboard, he leaned back and didn't mention to her that whenever she spoke about the primal gods, a strange light surrounded her. "You're related to one of those primal gods, aren't you?"

She averted her gaze. "What do you want me to say?"

"I'd like the truth, for once."

Still, she refused to look at him. "I can't give you that, Nick. Not where I'm concerned."

"And that really bothers me, Kody. What if I did that to you?"

"It would bother me, too. But I would try to trust you and to understand why you were bound to keep secrets."

He scoffed. "You say that because you're the one holding the cards and I'm the one wondering if you really are here to protect me . . . or," he paused on what concerned him most. People betrayed. Alan had taught him that when he stood over him and cold-bloodedly shot him for refusing to commit a felony. Kyrian's wife, the woman he had given up an entire kingdom and his inheritance to wed, had ruthlessly handed him over to his enemy to be tortured and executed.

And he would become a Dark-Hunter in a few years because someone would bring about the death of his mother.

Was Kody the one?

"Are you here to ultimately harm me," he finished, putting it on the table for her to confirm or deny.

Either way, she could be lying and he'd have no way to know for sure. *We're all rats in a maze. Truth isn't known until we're fed . . .*

Or dead.

This time, she locked gazes with him. "Have I done *anything* to make you mistrust me?"

Not technically.

Nick tucked his arms behind his head as he eyed her. "Aren't you the one who told me that omitting a fact is as good as lying?"

She shook her head at him. "Now I know why you want to go to law school. You'd make a great litigator."

Yeah, but he didn't really like arguing or confrontations. Not that he'd ever back down from a fight. *That* wasn't in him. Still, he'd rather avoid conflict than seek it out.

If only other people would be kind enough to let him do that. Some days, it seemed like the entire world was on a quest to shove him as hard as it could, and not let him walk away.

"I want to go to law school, Kody, because I don't like being pushed around. People use a lawsuit as the ultimate threat against other people. I want to be in the position to glare at them and say 'come get some' whenever they try it with me."

She smiled at him. "You are ever, at your core, a warrior."

And knowing he was the Malachai, it made sense. That was what his people had been created for. But why then, would he rather have peace than war?

"Why do you think my mother chose my father?"

Kody frowned. "What do you mean?"

Nick allowed his thoughts to drift to the one question his mother refused to answer. "I've always wondered why my mom, especially as young as she was, would do what she did with a loser like my dad. Why did she sleep with him? I just don't get it. As beautiful as she is, she could have had anyone. Or better yet, no one until after she graduated high school. Or best of all, not until she got married." It was his mother, after all. That's what mom's were supposed to do, and then only when they wanted kids.

As for himself, while his body was more than willing—a lot and especially anytime an attractive woman was near him—he had no intention of taking that chance while he was still a kid. He knew exactly how hard it was for a teenager to raise a child, and he had enough responsibility on his shoulders. The one thing his mother had drilled into him—*You bring an innocent baby into this world, you do whatever you have to take care of it and provide for it.*

For that reason, he wasn't about to sleep with *anyone* until he was mentally and most of all, financially, ready for the possible outcome of having a wife and baby to support.

"Do you really want the truth?" Kody asked.

"I certainly prefer it to a lie."

"Then take an honest look inside yourself, Nick, and face the beast you don't want to know exists. You know your mother. Better than anyone. What do you think happened?"

Nick grew silent as his thoughts went to a place

he very seldom allowed them to go. It was so dark and so painful there, that he'd always told himself it couldn't be. That surely, he was wrong to even suspect it.

But the words were there and they weren't his. It was like they came from some kind of ancient prophecy or ordinance that had been handed down throughout the ages. "I was conceived in violence to do violence, wasn't I?"

"The Malachai always is."

Nick cursed under his breath. Well, at least now he knew what not to do to father his future heir and murderer.

But if that was true . . . "Then how can she stand to go near him?"

"He's your father. To her, blood means more than anything else. Blood makes family. And I'm sure if you asked her, she'd tell you that he gave her the greatest gift of her life . . . you."

Yeah, some friggin' gift he was.

Sick to his stomach over the truth, he wanted to puke. His mom deserved so much better than to have been saddled with something like him. From beginning to end, he'd ruined her life.

"I shouldn't have yelled at her."

"You were hurt, Nick."

And she wasn't? His hurt feelings were insignificant when compared to what he'd put her through. What he had yet to put her through.

She's going to die because of me. . . .

He blinked against the pain that was concentrated at the center of his chest. "That's no excuse." He cringed at the horrific reality of his conception. "How can she even stand to look at me?"

"You are her son, Nick. Her flesh and her blood. I told you, in her eyes, that means everything." Kody raised her hands and formed a shadowy box between them.

Because of his scrying powers, he knew she was opening a window to show him events. But where he used his for the future, she was showing him the past.

He saw his mother screaming in the throes of labor. Just a baby herself, she was in the living room of Menyara's run-down apartment, where they had lived until Nick was five and the landlord had tossed the guy next door out for nonpayment.

"Make it stop!" she screamed at Menyara.

"Push, Cherise. Push. You can do this, child. He's almost here."

She let out a cry so shrill, it echoed in the room, and made Nick cringe at the thought of the pain he'd given her.

Menyara laughed as his mother collapsed on the pullout couch. The baby made a weird gurgling sound, then screamed out at the indignity of being brought into a hostile world.

After wiping him down, Menyara wrapped him in a blanket and handed him to his mother. "He's beautiful, child . . . just like his mother. And as *perfect* as he can be."

Tears flowed down his mother's cheeks as she stared at him. "Hello, baby. So you're the one who's been making me eat broccoli and cheese with chocolate syrup." She clutched him to her chest and held him as if he were the most precious thing in the world.

Menyara brushed a lock of hair off his mother's cheek. "You want me go and call that adoption lady, *cher?* She say all you had to do was sign them papers and they'd be happy to find him a good home. They be plenty of parents willing to take him."

Nick sucked his breath in sharply between his teeth. His mother had never told him that she'd ever considered letting him go.

"It makes him sound like pet to be adopted, doesn't it?" His mother looked up at Menyara. "But it would be the best thing for him, wouldn't it?"

Her eyes filled with nothing but love and loyalty, Menyara shrugged. "Perhaps. Perhaps not. For you, it would definitely be best, *ma petite.* Your parents said you could come home if you gave the baby up after he was born."

His mom glanced around the room that was decorated with Egyptian artifacts and artwork while tears glistened in her eyes that were identical in color and shape to Nick's. "I'm too young to be a parent. I can't even drive yet. Can't legally work or do anything except be a burden to you, and you've already been so kind to me. Above and beyond. I don't know what I would have done had you not taken me in, Mennie. Thank you so much for being so kind and decent."

And his mother hated being a burden to anyone.

"It has been an absolute joy having you here, Cherise." She smiled kindly as she cupped his mother's cheek. "And I don't mean because you do me laundry and clean me house, girl. Yours is a beautiful soul, and I will support whatever decision you make for you, and for your son." She dropped her hand to Nick's head that was covered with dark hair. "The adoption lady say that they were always in need of little boys. There be a long list of parents waiting to take him in and love him like he was their own."

"But he would never know *me*," his mother sobbed. "I could be in a restaurant one day and he could be sitting beside me and I'd never even know he was there. Every time I saw a little boy his age, I'd wonder . . . is he mine?"

Menyara sat down beside her. "Don't cry, Cherise. Births are always happy times. You have brought life into this world. Look at him, child. He's perfect. Beautiful."

She nodded against Menyara's shoulder. "He deserves only the best in life."

"All of us do, child."

Licking her chapped lips, his mother brushed her hand through his hair. "What do you think they'll name him?"

"I have no idea, sweetie. But, I'm sure it'll be a good name." Menyara reached for him. "Let me—"

"No!" his mother snapped. She buried her face against his chest as he wiggled angrily in protest. "I can't do it, Mennie. I can't. He's *my* baby. *My* flesh and *my* blood. He doesn't belong to somebody else. I'm the one who's been talking to him and I'm the one he's been kicking. How can I let someone else have him now?"

Menyara drew her brows together into a fierce frown. "Are you sure about this, Cherise? Life is hard on everyone. But you keep that baby, and it will stomp on you in ways you can't even imagine."

She lifted her head bravely. "It's going to stomp on me anyway. And I want to be there when it hurts him. I want to be the one who holds him and tells him it's going to be okay. I won't be able to give him much. But I can give him a mother who loves him with all of her heart. One who didn't abandon him the moment he was born so that her own life would be better. He deserves more than that."

Menyara bit her lip before she spoke again. "You are condemning both of you to a life of poverty."

"Maybe, but that could happen even if I give him up. My parents threw me out already over something I couldn't help. What's to keep them from doing it again? I can't trust them. I know that now. When I needed them most, they turned their backs on me." She curled her lip in anger. "You made your bed lie in it." The way she spat out those words told Nick she was repeating what her parents had said to her. "But I didn't choose this." She cringed as if the memory was more than she could take.

"Are you sure about this, Cherise? That baby will always be a terrible reminder of the horrors you've been through. Will you not think of it, every time you lay eyes on him?"

She shook her head. "He's a reminder to me of how strong I am. That I can survive anything the world throws at me. I won't be a victim again and I won't be defeated." She sniffed back her tears. "Look at him, Mennie. That little baby head. Those baby eyes. How can you not love something so adorable?"

Menyara brushed the hair back from his mother's face again. "He is precious. So what are you going to call him, then?"

His mother's hand went to the saint medallion she wore around her neck. It was the same one she'd given to him at his confirmation. "Nicholas, after the patron saint of children. My Nicky will be my victory over sorrow. My little champion. And every time I look at him, I will see just how strong I am. Not for me, but for him."

"And what other name will you give him?"

She smiled proudly. "Ambrosius."

Menyara screwed up her beautiful face "Ambrosius? Child, why would you ever give him a name like that?" She shivered.

But his mother wasn't swayed. "It was one of my grandfather's favorite stories that he used to tell to me whenever I spent my summers with them. And those were some of the best days of my life. I want to share that with my baby. Ambrosius Aurelianus was an ancient Saxon warrior that my grandfather said they called the king of all kings. He was supposedly a sorcerer of great power who protected his people and united a war torn Britain. A real man that time has shrouded in mystery—that's how my grandpa described him. Some say he was the older brother of King Arthur or Arthur himself or even Merlin. And the name means 'immortal.' Two strong, proud names for my perfect son. I can think of nothing better to call him. Nicholas Ambrosius Gautier."

Menyara let out a low whistle. "Child, he's going to hate you when he has to learn to spell that in school."

"True, but at confirmation, he already has his saint's name. So it serves more than one purpose. I think he'll like it." She smiled down at him. "You are going to like it, Mr. Baby. I insist."

Nekoda closed the window and brought Nick back to the present. "It's amazing the things we never know about the people we share our lives with, isn't it?"

Yeah, it was. "I had no idea she'd planned to give me up." He wouldn't have blamed her if she had.

Kody swallowed. "Life is about making decisions, Nick. Large and small. Every day and with every breath we take."

And it was about family. Those you were born to, those born to you, and those you let into your heart. That was how Simi defined it. Ironic really when you thought about it. The best definition of family he'd ever heard, and the only one he agreed with had come out of the mouth of an orphaned demon.

And while Kody's powers had shown him things about his mother he'd never suspected and confirmed his worst fear about himself, he had a newfound respect for his mother. Through everything she'd gone through, she had never lost her courage or her fire. Neither her dignity nor her ability to find the one bright spot on the dirtiest mirror in the room.

Menyara was right, his mother was a beautiful soul. And if she, a mere human mortal, a child no less, could stand and fight for him, then he stood a chance to become something more than his father.

As Kody said, life was about choices. And his choice was not to be a tool for evil.

He would *not* become Ambrose.

I am Nicholas Ambrosius Gautier. And I was conceived in violence to fight *violence.*

Ambrose had fought against it, but he, Nick, would fight harder.

And he would save his mother, even if he had to kill himself to do it.

In raven form, Caleb landed on the sill of Adarian's cell. Unfortunately, or maybe fortunately, Adarian wasn't in there. Not that he was surprised. This time of day . . .

The beast could be anywhere.

Caleb launched himself up toward the sky and circled around the yard, searching for him. It wasn't until his second pass that he finally spotted his target, sitting on a table all by his fierce lonesome.

It was actually frightening how much Nick looked like his father. Give the boy a couple of years, and they'd be indistinguishable from each other.

Except for their personalities. Nick was most often amusing and, as much as Caleb hated admitting it, endearing, even fun at times. No matter how bad a situation was, Nick could find something amusing about it. On the other hand, Caleb had never once seen Adarian crack a single smile unless it was a cruel one. And the only thing the senior Malachai found humorous was torturing others.

Yeah, they were nothing alike.

Caleb swooped toward Adarian's white picnic table. Because of Adarian's murderous nature and cruel tendencies, he was kept isolated from the other inmates. Four guards, shotguns cradled at the ready, stood around Adarian's area that was separated from the general prison population by a fence topped with razor wire.

Luckily, he could fly right over it and not get cut.

Caleb landed on the table behind Adarian and cawed to let him know he'd arrived.

Adarian released a breath of supreme annoyance. "What are you doing here, Malphas?" he asked in a low tone after he'd covered his mouth with his hand so that the guards wouldn't hear or see him talking to a bird.

You've been found.

"By?"

No idea. Whoever they are, they tried to access Nick's room. They didn't get in. But if they found him . . .

Adarian cursed.

I think it would be best if you left here.

"I'm not going anywhere. They won't find Nick. Even if they do, they won't mistake that guttersnipe for me."

Caleb scoffed. *You willing to risk your son's life on that?*

"No, but I'm willing to risk yours."

Of course he was. Why not? If Caleb died, Adarian could always find another. *I will keep him safe.*

"Oh, I have no doubt you will. You've seen what happens to creatures who disappoint me."

He'd also seen what happened to people who helped him. Either way, Adarian screwed you.

"Now go and protect him."

Yes, my lord and tormentor.

Adarian turned to watch Malphas leave. So something had located him. It wasn't the first time. Five years ago, he'd come close to being captured by one of his enemies. Death had never been an option.

Not until Nick had hit puberty.

Now that brat could take his place as Malachai.

Kirast kiroza kirent. Conceived in violence to do violence and to die violently. That was the promise written in the first language, on the Malachai symbol.

No sooner had that thought gone through his head than he felt his Malachai mark heat up. It was a warning that something from Azmodea was here.

A spark of electricity danced up his spine. Who or whatever it was, was watching him. Not that he cared.

But his end was coming soon. No matter how hard he fought against it, he knew the truth. He could feel it deep inside his bones.

If he didn't kill Nick soon and absorb his powers, he would have to die. And that he wasn't about to do. Not now.

He could always breed another son. One more malleable than Nick. One he could control and then kill.

Bitterness rose in his throat as he considered the son he'd only seen a few times. Who would have ever dreamed his wilting waif of a mother would possess a core of strength that was so staggering? Cherise had always been full of surprises.

But then so had he.

One of his guards snapped his head toward Adarian in a manner that was as recognizable as it was ludicrous. Some spirit had possessed the man. Which told him all he needed to know about the pathetic creature watching him.

"Lower forms don't scare me," Adarian said to the demon. "Higher forms either. Go home and leave me before I pull your wings off and shove you in a specimen jar."

The possessed guard glared at him. "You're the one who's going to be shoved into a jar. And then we're going to tear your son apart. Right in front of you."

Adarian laughed at the fool. "Bring it."

The demon attacked.

Adarian caught him up against his chest and held him tight. He choked the demon as he spoke to him in their native tongue. "How do you know about my son?"

"Everyone knows. We've known about him for centuries."

Adarian frowned. Centuries? Nick was barely a decade old. What was the imbecile talking about?

"Malachai! Let him go or we'll shoot!"

Adarian glanced askance at the moron who was interrupting them. "How did you find out about him?" he asked the demon in his arms.

"It wasn't easy. Zeus took away his emotions. His lack of hatred shielded him from us for a long time. But that ban is weakening and we now know he exists and where to find him. That was sneaky of you, Malachai. Impregnate a goddess. But it won't work. You *will* die. If not by me, then by one of my brethren."

The guards opened fire. Adarian shielded himself with the demon he held. The human part of the guard's body screamed as bullets pummeled him and sank in deep. Once the guard was dead, the demon pulled out and vanished.

Disgusted, Adarian hissed at the sensation of bullets ripping through his flesh. They wouldn't kill him. No mortal weapon could ever kill a Malachai. They just hurt.

One of the guards grabbed him and threw him to the ground. "You're going to pay for that."

Yeah, right. They had no idea. Any more than they had a way to cause him harm.

But as they handcuffed him on the ground, his thoughts turned to something he'd never suspected before. He had another son out there. One who was grown, who had the blood of two gods flowing through him.

While that son might not have the Malachai powers, he was a god and if Nick were to die. . . .

Adarian could infuse his other son with enough of Nick's blood to combine all three.

Oh yeah, this was better than he'd ever dreamed.

Nick's life was growing shorter by his heartbeat.

And it was time he paid his son a long overdue visit.

CHAPTER 7

Alone in his room, since Kody and Caleb had decided he was relatively safe for the time being, Nick yawned and checked his watch. He needed to go by Liza's before she closed and pick up Rosa's gift, then stop by Timeless Treasures to grab the present he'd put on layaway for her. If he left now, he'd get back in time to walk his mom home. He pulled his phone out of his pocket and called.

"Sanctuary on Ursulines. Jasyn speaking. How can I help you?"

"Hi, Jasyn, it's Nick. Is my mom around?"

"Oh hey, kid. Hang on and I'll grab her for you."

Nick waited until his mother picked up the phone.

"What do you need, Nick?" There was definitely ice in her tone, and it made him feel awful to have put it there.

"Hi, Mom. I—um—I need to go pick up something for Kyrian at Ms. Liza's. It won't take long and then I'll be back to walk you home."

"You don't have to do that." Yeah, she was still upset at him and it more than showed.

"I know, Ma. But I like walking you home . . . and I'm really sorry, okay?" He held his breath, waiting for her to respond in kind.

She didn't.

Instead, he got more of her icy shoulder. "I'll see you in a little while." She hung up.

Now I feel like total rolled over crap. She was probably thinking she should have signed the papers and tossed him to the nearest couple.

Trying not to think about it, he locked the door and left.

It was just starting to get dark. And that went a long way in cheering him. He loved this time of day the most, before the tourists started their heavy drinking, and when the Royal Street business owners began closing up for the night. They were always so cheerful as they left their premises and made their deposits. It was also that last few moments of the day before the real predators, the ones bullets and guns wouldn't stop, came out to prey.

"Hey, Mrs. Clancy," he said as the owner of the Masquerade store locked her door to leave.

"Evening, Nick. You headed the wrong way to get to your mama. You going to Bubba's store? Tell me that boy ain't holding any more of his zombie survival classes."

Nick laughed. "I imagine he'll be behaving himself tonight since *his* mama's in town."

"Oh good. My worst fear is he'll start a fire in his store and it'll burn all the way down to here."

"Always a possibility with Bubba." He grinned. "Good night, Mrs. Clancy."

"'Night to you, too."

Tucking his hands into his pockets, Nick headed toward the Cathedral.

He wasn't far from Jackson Square when he heard someone call out his name. Since he was a regular in the Quarter and knew most of the people who worked and lived in it, he paused.

Nick was about to ignore it when he finally spied another kid his age just in front of him, down the street a little ways. It was Bristol from school.

"Yeah?" he asked.

"I was actually on my way to your house to see you. Can you come here for a sec?" he asked, motioning Nick into the alley that led to a closed clothing boutique. "I want to ask you something about school."

His gut tightened and told him it wasn't a good idea. But it was Bristol. He'd known him for years. What could be wrong with going to speak to an old friend for a minute?

Nick headed over. "What's up?"

The moment he was deep inside the alley, Bristol shoved a piece of paper in his face. "What is this crap of bull?"

It took a second for his eyes to focus on the printout

that listed him as a source, claiming Bristol was gay. It also said that he knew it for a fact as he was gay, too, and had partied with Bristol a few times.

Nick curled his lip. "I didn't say that, crap."

"Yeah, right. You told the same lie about Spence."

"I didn't say nothing to anyone. I don't do things like that."

"And I'm supposed to take the word of a piece of Cajun trash whose mom's a stripper and whose dad is in jail for multiple murders? Really?"

Nick's temper exploded and he ached to pulverize him. "I did not say that," he reiterated, enunciating each word with the malice he felt.

"You're a liar." Bristol shoved him.

Don't hit back. . . . His mom wouldn't be able to take two fights in one day. He'd never hear the end of that.

He thought about Wren walking away earlier in Sanctuary. Wren definitely possessed the power to rip out the throat of anyone who annoyed him.

You can walk away, too. No time to learn like the present. Taking a deep breath, Nick turned to leave.

The moment he did, Bristol punched him in the back so hard, it knocked the wind out of him. "You don't turn your back on me, punk. You're the one who's trash, not me."

Yeah, right. But Nick wasn't going to fight him. Not now. Not after the argument he'd had with his mom. "Look, Bristol—"

He punched him again. This time in the jaw.

Nick staggered back. He had to get out of here before he struck back. Turning around, he took two steps and then pain exploded through his skull. . . .

Kody? Is that you?"

Nekoda frowned at the panicked sound of Cherise Gautier's voice on her phone. "Yes, ma'am. Can I help you?"

"Is Nick with you?"

"No, ma'am. Why?"

Cherise hesitated before she spoke again. "He was supposed to walk me home after he picked up something for Kyrian at Liza's store. I got off work almost thirty minutes ago and he hasn't shown up yet. When I called Liza, she said she hasn't seen him, either. I know how upset he was earlier . . . you don't think he's done anything stupid, do you?"

No. The most likely scenario was something had gotten ahold of him and eaten him. "I don't, Mrs. Gautier. He was feeling much better when I left. Let me make a few calls and see if anyone's seen him."

"I already called Bubba and Mark. They said he left with you."

"I dropped him off at your house." She left it at that since his mother frowned on anyone being in their apartment when she wasn't home.

"I'll stay here in case he's just running late. Please let me know if you find out anything."

"I will." Kody hung up the phone and immediately called Caleb. "Hey, is Nick with you?"

"No. Why?"

"He's missing."

Caleb cursed. "I'll start searching."

"Me, too. See you later." She hung up and closed

her eyes. Using her powers, she tried to sense Nick's whereabouts.

For once, it didn't work. She had absolutely no idea where he was.

Fine, this was why she'd given him her class ring. He thought it was normal, but she could always use it to locate him.

Sure enough, she picked up on it immediately. Letting out a relieved sigh, she allowed it to pull her to his side. She materialized in a dark alley that appeared to be in the middle of the Quarter somewhere. She glanced around, but didn't see anything. Why would it have brought her here if there was no Nick?

She was just about to leave when she heard a low, soft groan in the shadows. "Nick?"

It sounded like it could have been her name, slurred. Maybe. She couldn't tell for certain.

Her heart pounding in fear, she ran to where it had originated. At first, she only saw garbage on the street. But after searching some of it, she found a body on the ground, partially covered by refuse.

Please don't be Nick. . . .

Panic swelled inside her as she uncovered the

wounded human. A small pool of blood had formed around his head and shoulder.

"Nick?" she breathed, kneeling down by his side so that she could turn him over and confirm his identity.

Yeah, it was him. She should have known by his tacky shirt. But his face was so battered and bloodied that she wouldn't have known it was him except for the clothes he wore.

Okay, how do I get him help? If she flashed him into the hospital, they'd know immediately that she wasn't human, and they'd notify the authorities to come lock her up.

Think Nekoda, think. What was it that humans did for help?

Ambulance. *That's right. That was it.* She reached for her phone and called 911. It took a few minutes before a woman answered it.

Kody's hand shook as she wished she had the powers to heal Nick so that he wouldn't have to suffer. If only . . . "Hey, I found my friend in an alley where he was viciously attacked, and he's bleeding really badly."

"Is he conscious?" the operator asked.

"No, ma'am."

"I need your address."

Kody ground her teeth as she used her powers to locate it. She gave it over to the woman, and stayed on the line as she waited for help to come.

She conjured a cloth to help wick away some of the blood on his face. "Hang on, Nick. I've got an ambulance coming for you. They'll be here any minute."

Only it seemed to take forever.

As soon as she heard the sirens approaching, Kody ran toward the street to flag down the ambulance so that they wouldn't miss her alley.

They pulled up on the corner and grabbed a box before following her to where Nick lay on the ground.

"What happened?" the male EMT asked.

"I don't know. I found him like this a few minutes ago. He was supposed to be with his mother at work, and when he didn't show up, she called me to help search for him, and here he is. I called you guys as soon as I dug him out of the garbage."

"And you are?"

"His girlfriend, Kody."

They knelt down on the ground and started inspecting Nick's condition.

"What's his name?" the woman asked.

"Nick."

"Nick?" the female EMT said gently. "Can you hear me, son?"

"I didn't fight," he mumbled.

The EMTs exchanged a frown.

"Nick?" the woman tried again. "My name is Patrice. Can you hear me?"

"Patrice," he said raggedly.

"Good boy."

The man ran to get the stretcher while Patrice stayed behind to insert an IV in his arm. "Can you tell me how old you are, Nick?"

"He's fifteen," Kody answered.

"Thank you." She wrapped a brace around Nick's neck while speaking to Kody. "Do you have his mother's number?"

"I do."

"Why don't you go call her while I take care of him, okay? Tell her that we'll be taking him to Charity

Hospital and we'll need her there to sign papers for him."

Kody made the call while they stabilized him, then put him on the stretcher.

She'd just hung up when they started past her with Nick. He reached out for her and took her hand.

"It's going to be okay, sweetie," she assured him.

"You want to come with us?" the man asked.

"If I can, yes."

They put Nick into the ambulance before the woman went to the front to drive and the man stayed in the back with them. Kody sat by the door while the EMT continued to tend and monitor Nick's vital signs.

"Do you know what happened?" he asked her.

"Not a clue. He was supposed to run an errand and didn't show up. His mother called me and I went looking for him. It's a miracle I found him."

"He's lucky you found him, that's for sure."

Nick was trying to speak, but with the oxygen mask on, they couldn't understand him. The EMT pulled it back.

"What's that, Nick?" she asked.

"Tell . . ." He coughed, then groaned. "Tell her I didn't fight."

"I will." The EMT returned the mask to Nick's face. "Did you hear that?"

"I did, but I'm not the 'her' he's referring to. He means his mother. They had a verbal altercation earlier, and he promised her he would never fight again." She cringed as she surveyed the damage done to him. It was absolutely brutal.

The EMT leaned over Nick to pluck a vial out of his case. "No offense, kid, you should have fought back. I don't think they could have hurt you any worse if you had. And at least you would have gotten some kind of personal satisfaction out of it."

Kody couldn't agree more. And she couldn't understand why he'd allowed himself to be hurt this badly. Not even for his mother. *Nick, I want to hurt you for this.* But that was part of what she loved about him. When he gave his word, he meant it.

Placing her hand on his leg, she closed her eyes and used her powers to discover what had happened. She saw Bristol hit Nick in the back of the head with

SHERRILYN KENYON

a board he'd picked up from the alley. Caught completely off guard and temporarily blinded by the viciousness of that first surprise blow, Nick had fallen to the ground. His eyes blazing with murderous fury, Bristol had given him no reprieve. He kept bashing Nick with the board, blow after blow, never allowing him time to recover. All Nick could do was curl up in a ball and try to protect himself. Dazed and disoriented by the rapid succession of blows, Nick hadn't had a chance to call for help before he'd passed out in the alley. Cringing in horror, she finally saw the sanity return to Bristol's eyes. Only then did Bristol panic as he realized how badly he'd hurt Nick. Terrified that Nick was dead or dying, he'd grabbed Nick's wallet and had thrown garbage over him to hide his body. Then, he'd run off, leaving Nick to bleed out on the cold sidewalk.

Never had she wanted to hurt anyone as much as she did Bristol right then. How could he be so cold? He'd known Nick for years. Had been in countless classes and had been his study partner for several subjects.

But then Bristol had felt justified in beating Nick, and that was the most dangerous human emotion imaginable. Whenever someone, no matter how warped their reasonings, thought they had a justified cause for taking action against someone, they were capable of unimaginable cruelty. Bristol had thought Nick had lied about him, and rather than believe Nick was the one telling him the truth, he'd beaten him senseless for no other reason than he felt it was what Nick deserved.

Sickened by it, she released Nick and tried to focus on his getting better.

It wasn't until they'd reached the hospital, and the admitting staff started asking her questions about him while he was whisked off to a room where she wasn't allowed to go that she remembered to call everyone else and let them know what had happened. Caleb appeared next to her in the shadowy alcove of the waiting room before she could speak more than a handful of words.

"Is he all right?" His sincere concern surprised her. The way Caleb acted and spoke to Nick, she'd assumed he could barely tolerate him. But that wasn't mere tolerance or adherence to duty in his tone and body language.

Caleb was genuinely concerned.

Wow. . . .

Kody slid her phone into her purse. "We know he can't die from a mere beating, but the human who attacked him made a mess of him. He looks terrible."

Caleb narrowed those beautiful dark brown eyes suspiciously. Because she knew him for what he really was, it was easy for her to see past his human beauty, but right then when he let his tough protector façade slip and she saw the vulnerable heart beneath his demon's aura, he was every bit as handsome as Nick.

"Are you sure it was a human who attacked him?" Caleb asked.

"Positive. I think it's why he was trying to walk away from the fight. Had it been one of us, I'm sure Nick would have torn into him."

Caleb made a sound of supreme irritation. "I would kill his mother for causing this latest bout of stupidity, but . . ."

"I know. At this moment, I'm not happy with her, either."

And speaking of his mother, Cherise finally arrived. She paused in the double doorway to scan for a familiar face. As soon as she saw the two of them in the back corner, she rushed toward them. Blonde, skinny, and petite, she was absolutely beautiful even with tears streaming down her cheeks. "Where did you find my baby, Kody?"

"In an alley off Royal. Not far from Liza's."

Menyara arrived just in time to hear her response. No taller than Cherise, and every bit as skinny, she had her dark sisterlocks tied back in a red scarf and was dressed in a red blouse and jeans. "Oh my poor Nicky," she breathed. There was something about the depth and cadence of her voice that always reminded Kody of Eartha Kitt.

Her tears flowing even harder, Cherise turned toward Menyara, "Who would do such a thing to my Boo? Why Mennie, why? It doesn't make any sense. My Boo such a good boy, and I was sharp with him when he called to tell me he was going to work and then coming to walk me home. I swear I'll never yell at him again. Just tell me he's going to be all right."

"I hope so, Cher. I do."

Kody started to explain what had happened during the fight, then thought better of it. Since she hadn't been there for the beating, she couldn't very well tell any human how she knew so many details about it since she hadn't arrived until about an hour after it'd taken place.

So she settled for the most obvious explanation to soothe his mother. "It looks like a mugging."

Cherise's legs buckled. Caleb moved like lightning to catch her and keep her from hitting the floor. He swung her up in his arms, then carried her to an empty chair so that he could set her down for Menyara's care.

Menyara sat beside her and took her hand. "It'll be all right, *ma petite*. He a strong boy. It'll take more than a beating to take him away from us. I promise you."

"I pray you're right, Mennie," she sobbed. "Nick's all I have in this world. If I ever lost him, you'd have to dig two graves. I can't live without my baby. I can't."

She broke off into gut wrenching sobs that brought tears to Kody's eyes.

Trying to catch her breath before she gave into her own fears where Nick was concerned, Kody looked up to see a shadow of fierce pain inside Caleb's eyes. Something about Cherise's reaction haunted the demon.

But what? If Caleb had ever possessed a mother, he never spoke of her. Was it possible that he might have been married in the past? Had a family?

Demons mated, too, and some species of them were even more monogamous than humans professed to be.

Caleb's daeva species was one of the ones most notorious for their loyalty to family ties.

I really don't know anything more about him than he knows about me. For the first time, her blinders were torn off and she realized that even though the three of them spent so much of their lives together . . . that as much as they interacted with each other- her, Nick and Caleb- were really nothing more than intimate strangers . . .

How sad for us that this is what we're relegated to.

But then how many people lived like that? How many people either were or felt like they were strangers in their own home? Or that no one in their family really knew or understood them?

In so many ways, we are all nothing more than orbiting satellites that occasionally collide with each other whenever our paths overlap. People formed social bonds to keep from feeling so isolated. But in the end, the only constant in any life was its own soul. And even that was transitory.

Souls could be, and were far too often, bought and sold like used shoes in a consignment shop.

And yet when two of those souls slammed into each other hard enough, they *could* form a single unit so strong that nothing and no one could tear it apart. Those unions were rare and she'd been around long enough to know that for a fact.

But she'd also seen those unbreakable bonds. Like the one Cherise shared with her son. There was no force in existence that could shatter their love and break it apart.

It was a love bond Nekoda had only felt with her brothers and one other person.

Don't go there.

The pain of their loss was still too great for her to bear. And her nerves were already shot from what had happened to Nick. While their love wasn't that strong yet, she could feel it growing every day and doubling with every new discovery she made where Nick was concerned.

He was so much more than what he knew. For the first time in centuries, she had hope.

And she owed that to a creature she should hate with every fiber of her being.

Life was so strange. Seldom did it make sense. As her brother would say, *'life isn't a puzzle to be solved. It's an adventure to be savored. Let every challenge be a new mountain to climb, not an obstacle to get in your way and stop you. Yeah, it'll be hard, but once you reach the summit of it, you'll be able to see the world for what it really is. And at the top, it never seems to have been as difficult a feat to climb there as you first made it out to be. Most of all, you'll know that you beat that mountain, and that you rule it. It does not rule you.'*

I miss you, my brother. Even after all these years.

Life had no guarantees, except one. *You will never succeed until you try one more time.*

Even though her people didn't believe Nick could be saved, she did. Tonight proved it.

Please be all right, Nicky.

Over the next hour as they waited for an update about Nick's condition, the room began to fill with people eager to check on him. Wren. Aimee. Dev and his brothers. Jasyn. Mama and Papa Peltier. Talon. Acheron. Kyrian. Rosa and her son Miguel. Brynna and her father. But the one that caught them all off guard was when Bubba and Mark came in with Bubba's mother.

Without a single hesitation, Dr. Burdette made her way straight to the counter to speak to the staff on duty. "Hey, sweetie," she said to the triage nurse stationed there. "I'm Dr. Bobbi Jean Burdette from Perry County, Tennessee. And I'm a pediatric surgeon out of Vanderbilt and St. Jude's. A friend of my son's was brought in about an hour ago and I wanted to see if there was anything I can do for him."

"His name?"

"Nicholas Gautier."

The nurse turned her attention to her computer monitor as she searched for information on Nick.

One of the ER doctors approached Bubba's mother slowly, as if he couldn't believe what he saw. "I'm sorry, ma'am. Did I overhear you say that you were Dr. Bobbi Jean Burdette?" The Dr. Bobbie Jean Burdette who performs surgery at both Vandy and St. Judes, and who is a former Executive Board member for the World Health Organization?"

She smiled what had to be the warmest smile Kody had ever seen. "Why, sugar, when you say it like that, I almost sound impressive. That is indeed me. Believe me, no one else in their right mind would take on that much work if they didn't have to. But that being said, honey, it is some of the most rewarding work you can ever imagine. Ain't nothing prettier than the smile on a mama's face when you hand her, her baby and tell her that baby's going to live when she thought she was going to have pick out funeral clothes for him. Mmm mmm mmm, thank the good Lord that He chose me to have a few abilities to help out some of those in need. I am truly grateful for my many blessings, and for being able to help as many people as I can, as best as I can."

He held his hand out to her. "It is such an honor to meet you, Doctor. You are a living legend. The things you've done for and with the WHO . . . Wow." He turned toward the triage nurse who was now paying serious attention to Bubba's mama. "Stacey? This woman, right here, has gone into some of the most war torn and worst natural disaster areas of the world to do volunteer work to save children's lives. She's been one of the first responders to set up clinics everywhere you can think of, including here in our own backyard." He smiled at Dr. Burdette. I just can't believe you're here. In front of me. In New Orleans."

"Aw now, honey, bless your heart for your kind words. But don't be blowing sunshine at me and making me out to be more than what I am. You just might blind me and I need my eyes to see clearly. In the end,

I ain't nothing more or less than anybody else here on this earth. You ever want to know my flaws, and believe me, they are many, sit down with my bridge partners and they'll spend hours enlightening you." She shook his hand, then clasped it between both of hers. "And it's a wonderful pleasure to meet you, too . . ." She glanced down at his name tag. "Dr. Ferguson. And I'd love to chat with you, I really would, but I'm trying to find out information about a patient who was admitted here a little while ago."

While he conferred with the triage nurse about Nick, Cherise approached her slowly. Kody could tell Cherise knew her, but was timid about speaking up.

"Dr. Burdette?" she finally said, touching her lightly on the sleeve.

Bobbi Jean turned around with an arched brow. Until recognition lit up her entire face. "Cherise! Oh my goodness, child, I haven't seen you in what? Ten, twelve years?"

"Fourteen."

Bobbi Jean gaped. "Has it really been that long? Goodness me, how time gets away from us." She held her hands out at Cherise and smiled like a proud mother. "And look at you, honey, all grown up and every bit as beautiful as you ever were, if not more so. Now tell me how that wonderful little baby boy of yours is doing?"

Tears welled in her eyes. "Nick Gautier is my baby."

Her face blanching, Bobbi Jean covered her mouth with her hand. "I am so sorry, honey. I should have recognized the name. But Nick Gautier isn't exactly uncommon, and here I thought your baby should be younger. It just never occurred to me that they'd be the same person. What a small world it is."

Menyara went to Cherise and allowed her to cry on her shoulder.

Bobbi Jean pulled a tissue from the box on the counter and handed it to Cherise. "Now don't you worry none, baby. I'm here and I'm going to make sure your little Nicky has the best care possible. You hear me?"

Sniffing back her tears, Cherise nodded. "Thank you so much. You've always been so good to us."

Bobbi Jean rubbed her arm and offered her a kind smile. "It's all right, sugar. We didn't pull that baby of yours through all that misery just to lose him now. That I promise you. If I have to barter with the devil himself, we'll keep that boy here, alive, and perfectly healthy." Bobbi Jean turned back to the doctor. "May I please see Nick?"

"Absolutely."

Kody's frown deepened as she met Caleb's icy gaze. There was something about all of this that troubled her. "Surely, it can't be a coincidence that Bubba's mother just happened to have saved Nick's life when he was an infant. What do you think?"

Caleb shrugged. "The universe is random. Seldom does it make sense. I mean, explain to me the statistical anomaly that out of twenty people in a room, two of them will invariably share an exact birthday. And yet time and time again, they do."

"Yeah, but I don't believe in random. There's a reason for everything."

Caleb snorted. "That's because you are a blind optimist and I see things for what they really are."

Sure he did. But her gut told her otherwise. "You say that with conviction, but I don't believe you."

"Why not?"

"I've seen you in action, Caleb. Everything you do denies your words with neon clarity. You say you don't feel or care about anyone or anything. You don't believe in anyone or anything. Yet you've put yourself under the guillotine for Nick for no reason whatsoever, more times than I can count."

He scoffed. "I have a reason and it's a good one, too. If Nick dies on my watch, I die, and no offense, Caleb don't wanna die. Especially not for Nick Gautier."

"You don't fear death, Malphas. Everyone knows that."

Kody jumped at the sudden sound of Acheron's deep, rumbling voice behind her. She hadn't even realized he'd drawn near.

Besides being eerily sexy, the man moved like a wraith. Standing at a full six foot eight, with lean, hard muscles, he should never be able to sneak up on someone, and yet he was completely silent when he walked. More than that, he moved languidly, sensually. And yet when he fought, he could strike faster and deadlier than a nest of cobras.

Even though he was over eleven thousand years old, he appeared to be in his late teens. In fact, he'd been twenty-one when he'd died and become a Dark-Hunter. No one knew why. But he'd been the first one Artemis had created and he was now the unofficial leader of them all.

Always dressed in Goth attire, he wore a pair of tight black jeans, a white long-sleeve henley shirt pushed up to his elbows, with a ragged Sex Pistols T-shirt over it. His red biker boots each had a black skull and crossbones on the silver tip and a white vampire bat on the heel. His long purple hair fell to the middle of his back, and his humongously large, graceful hands were covered with a pair of thin, fingerless gloves. Even indoors, he wore dark sunglasses so that it was impossible to tell exactly what he looked like. Still, his features were so perfectly formed that it was obvious without those sunglasses on, he'd be even more devastating than he already was.

More than that was his aura of lethal power and pure intensity. It was so fierce that it sent a shiver down the spine of anyone who stood too close to him.

There was no doubt that this was a man skilled in battle and in other arts that were usually reserved for private time.

Caleb raked a disinterested stare over Ash's body. "What do you know about me, Acheron?" He actually pronounced his name with the full Greek accent so that it came out as "Ack-uhr-ron" instead of the "Asheron" most non-Greek people used when referring to him.

Acheron adjusted the black backpack over his shoulder—one that bore a white anarchy symbol on it. "We're brethren, you and I. Both damned by our own actions. Both . . . unique. I know you a lot better than you think."

Caleb rolled his eyes. "Don't try to play sage with me, Atlantean. I'm a lot older than you are."

"I know. But that doesn't stop me from seeing you. Though I have yet to understand why you're watching over Nick. What do you care what happens where he's concerned?"

"Why do *you* watch over him, Atlantean?" Caleb countered defensively. "What interest do you have?"

Ash's answer was simple and honest. "We're friends."

And it was one Caleb seized and turned on him. "I, too, am his friend."

An evil grin spread across Ash's face. "Your kind doesn't have friends."

"Neither does yours."

Acheron inclined his head to him respectfully. "Touché." Then Kody fell underneath his bold, intense scrutiny. "And the same holds for you. I have no idea why you'd be guarding him."

Kody smiled. "Aren't you the one who always says that sometimes things have to go wrong in order to go right?"

"I also say that just because you can, doesn't mean you should."

Those words haunted her. Did Acheron know about her ultimate orders where Nick was concerned? A tremor went down her spine at the thought.

No one, man, beast or other, could know why she was really here. Nick wouldn't take it well. And neither would her higher ups.

For that matter, neither would she.

They stopped their conversation as Dev Peltier approached their small group. He opened up the bag he was carrying, which held soft drinks and bottled water. "I figured we could all use something to drink. Aimee has snacks in her bag."

"Thank you," they all three said.

Acheron wandered off to talk to Kyrian.

Kody opened her water and resumed her conversation with Caleb. It was odd to her that he was technically more beautiful than Nick. Where Nick had reached that strange phase of turning from boy to man and his body wasn't quite proportional yet, Caleb was perfectly formed—no doubt enhanced by his demonic powers. His black wavy hair was fashionably cut and his body perfectly formed. Right now, he was leaning forward with his elbows on his bent knees. The ties from his hoodie fell down, brushing against his Coke can. The white of the hoodie was a stark contrast to his dark olive skin.

Yeah, he was made of the stuff that would have

both teenage girls, their mothers, squealing, and clawing at each other for his attention.

She might have had stomach flutters for him herself had she not known what he really was. Instead, it was Nick with his boyish charm and the promise of his hotness to come that lured her against her will even when she knew she should stay as far away from him as possible.

Which returned her to his earlier trip that they had yet to discuss. "You never did tell me what you learned from Adarian."

Caleb snorted as he set his Coke can down on the floor and stared at her from beneath his bangs. Something about his current position reminded her of a panther in the wild, eyeing the prey it wanted to bring down. "He's going to come after Nick."

That news jolted her. "What? Why?"

Caleb straightened up, then leaned back in his chair so that he could stretch his long legs out in front of him. "Not really sure. And he didn't admit it to me. But I felt it, and it was unmistakable."

"Is he the one behind this attack, then?"

Caleb shook his head. "This was human. I can smell a demon attack from a mile away, and this does not have that stench."

Maybe, but there was always a first time for being wrong. "Haven't you ever been fooled?"

He gave her a droll stare before he crossed his arms over his head, against the wall. "No. I'm not a loler." That was the term his kind used for low-level demons. "Even though I'm technically a mid-level class, I was one of the strongest generals in the Primus Bellum. With more kills than anyone except Jared. And I'm not saying he was the better fighter. We never battled against each other, but I would lay skills against his any time. Any place."

That news shocked her silent. While she'd known Caleb was old, she'd had no idea he was *that* old. Wow. . . . "Are you serious?"

He didn't react to her questions physically. Instead, his dark eyes alone taunted her. "Before you judge me, 'cause I can feel the hatred surging inside you against me, let me explain my political ties in that war. I personally carried the banner for Verlyn, and I was the one who led the whole of his armies against the Obsidian Triad."

That news was even more shocking. "You're not evil, then." It was a statement of fact.

He sneered at her comment. "You're as bad as the humans. C'mon, Kody, *you* should know that we don't all serve the dark powers."

"Yeah, but you do now. . . ."

Pain flashed in his eyes so fast that she wasn't sure she hadn't imagined it. "We all make mistakes, Kody. Sometimes I think the only point of our miserable lives is simply to learn how to live with the consequences of the bad decisions we've made."

By his tone, she could tell his were severe. "I'm sorry, Caleb."

"For what?"

"Whatever it is that brings that light of hurt into your eyes. The worst wounds, the deadliest of them, aren't the ones people see on the outside. They're the ones that make us bleed internally."

Caleb didn't respond in any way. But as he pulled his watch out of his pocket to check the time, a strange sensation went through her. She saw him then, on an ancient battlefield in full demon armor.

She tried her best to home in on the image, but it was gone almost as fast as it appeared. Still, it left her with one thing that was undeniable, and it explained a lot about his idiosyncrasies.

"You're not just a demon. You're a demigod."

Caleb went perfectly still, then he relaxed. "I don't know what you're talking about."

"Yeah, you do," she said, her voice rising at the end with bitter amusement. "That's what Acheron meant when he said you were similar creatures."

Caleb scoffed. "I'm *nothing* like him. He's cut from a very different bolt."

Maybe, but that brought her back to their original topic. "What you said about Adarian doesn't make sense. I thought he wanted Nick protected."

"That's what he told me originally."

"Then why do you doubt him now?"

Caleb shrugged. "There's no reason to. And yet . . . He's coming for him. Soon. I can't tell you the exact minute. Or even the day it'll happen, but I can feel it building like a simmering pot getting ready to boil over."

While she didn't welcome that news, it didn't really disturb her. "We'll stop him when he does." They had to.

"No, Kody," he said drily. "We won't. You and I don't have the ability to defeat him. And I know this for a fact. The one and only time in my entire military career that I was knocked flat on my rump and viciously defeated was by the first of the Malachais. One who didn't possess a third of the power of the current elder Malachai. When Adarian comes, Nick will die. There's nothing you and I can do to stop him."

She didn't believe that for a minute. "Nick can't die. We cannot allow that to happen under *any* circumstance. I know you see what I do. The next Malachai—"

"Will free Noir from his hole, and rain a complete slaughter down on all of us. But there is something even worse than that outcome."

In that instant, she could swear she had an ulcer—even though it was an impossibility for her species. *I don't want to hear this.* But she had no choice. If something was out there worse than their next enemy, she had to know about it.

Forewarned was forearmed.

"What?"

"Adarian doesn't have to *kill* Nick. He can *absorb* him."

Her throat went dry at the horror of *that* thought. Whenever a creature like them absorbed the powers of another, they took all of their powers and strengths, and combined them with the ones they already had.

Should that happen . . .

The Malachai wouldn't kill them. Oh no. That would be too kind. They would all become the outlet for his voracious cruelty.

And the *only* one who could fight Adarian successfully and possibly defeat him was currently in a chemically induced coma. . . .

I might as well get a tattoo on my forehead. Abandon hope all ye who see this 'cause we're about to get royally screwed.

CHAPTER 8

Nick couldn't see anything. He felt like he'd been swallowed whole by darkness. It was so thick and stifling that it made it hard to breathe.

Where am I?

The last thing he remembered was Kody holding on to his leg in the ambulance while she talked to the attending EMT. Everything else was a total blur.

Am I dead?

Where would a dead Catholic Malachai spend eternity, anyway? That was a scary and sobering thought. And a question he didn't *ever* want to have an answer for.

All right, if I'm not dead, the next baboon who hits me with a board is going to get it shoved someplace real uncomfortable on his body. In fact, Nick would turn his attacker into a human or demon Popsicle with it.

Yeah, that'd learn them.

Smelling something rancid in the thick opaque air, he grimaced and held the back of his hand to his nose to try and block it. Gah, what was *that*? Smelled worse than burned powdered eggs, and he'd mistakenly thought nothing could outdo those. Well, nothing other than the one and only time he'd made the mistake of walking into the men's restroom as Stone was walking out of it.

Oh yeah, *that* was definitely worse than this. He didn't know what werewolves ate on a regular basis, but whatever it was, it rotted them from the inside out. No wonder Stone had perpetual PMS.

"Hello, there!"

He jumped at the unexpected voice coming from something that was within touching distance. "Excuse me?"

"I said, 'hello.' Do you not know that word? Do you not speak English?"

Not sure what to make of the strange voice, Nick stepped back from it. "I'm not sure how to respond to that. But I do speak English . . . most days and I understand you and the word 'hello'."

"Ah," the disembodied voice said as if relieved, then he added, "I am speaking English, right?"

Nick scowled. "Um . . . yeah. Pretty sure."

"Good. Sometimes it's hard to tell. Languages come and they go. Sometimes I know them, sometimes—"

"Who are you?" Nick asked, interrupting him. "Where are we?"

"Which is it?" the stranger asked in an exasperated tone. "Who or where? Might as well throw a what in there too, just to hit all the bases. Oh, and I forgot how and why. That is all of them. At least I think it is."

The voice paused, then counted them off. "Who, what, when, where, how, and why. Yes, that's all of them," he said proudly, then his tone turned to one of fretful anxiety. "Though the answer to some of them,

I don't know. Like how did you get here when you don't know where here is? That's kind of hard to do, isn't it? I mean if you went someplace, shouldn't you know how you got there and then by default, you should know where the where is because you got yourself there. Right?"

Nick felt like he'd blindly stumbled into a Who's On First skit. Whoever this guy was, he wasn't firing on all burners. Dude was seriously listing to port and about to capsize.

"Nor do I know why you're here," he continued without even stopping to take a breath. "That baffles me, too, if you don't know where you are. Why would you go someplace when you don't know where it is? And people call me names. At least I know where I am and who I'm talking to, and I never go anyplace without knowing beforehand where it is I've gone. Or at least where I was trying to get to. Except for this one time . . . we won't go there. Not because I don't know where it leads. I do. It leads to a bad memory I've no wish to revisit. Kind of like smelly relatives and nasty bosses. I don't want to revisit them either, unless it's to give them nightmares. In that case, game on."

Nick gaped the whole way through his tirade. Yeah . . . This was the strangest person he'd ever met, and when you took into consideration that the captain of his football team was a werewolf, his boss an immortal vampire slayer who had a ninja-like, knife-wielding housekeeper, his tutor was Death, his best friend a demon, and his girlfriend something else entirely, and then there was the Simi . . .

Yeah, boy. Nick knew every variation of weird even when it didn't slap him in the face. Most days, he was drowning in it.

But this guy . . .

He took weird to a level all his own.

When he finally paused for a breath, Nick quickly interjected, "How about starting with the first and then answering the latter?"

"Why didn't you say so? I declare . . . some people are so strange. My name is Asmodeus. And you're home. Did you not know that?"

Nick scoffed. "Dude, this is not my home. For one

thing, my house isn't this dark, even when my mama gets cheap and refuses to use lights in it. Bourbon Street ain't *ever* this dark."

Asmodeus made a sound of disgust. "Can't you see in the dark?"

Was the guy totally off his gourd? No one could see in something *this* dark. "Dang it, Jim, I'm not a bat. I'm a boy."

"Okay . . ." he stretched the word out. "My name's not Jim. I just told you, it's Asmodeus. And why can't you see in the dark?"

Obviously not a *Star Trek* fan. But why would he even begin to think that Nick could see in pitch-black nothing? "Not really."

"Hmmm. Odd. Okay." He took Nick's hand.

Nick pulled back. "Dude, don't touch me."

"Why not?"

Why not? Really? He had to explain stranger-danger and personal space? Where did this guy live that he didn't understand grabbing another dude's body parts without an invitation was a first class ticket to a major butt-whipping event.

"Look, I don't know you, and we're not dating. So keep your hands off me."

Again with the annoyed noise. "Then how can I lead you if I can't touch you when you can't see?"

"How 'bout you don't lead me anywhere?" Nick was beginning to like the darkness. Unlike Asmodeus, it was quiet and rather peaceful. And it definitely didn't give him a headache.

"But you said you couldn't see."

Nick was aghast at the way this guy's mind worked. "That doesn't mean you can touch me."

"I'm so confused."

That made two of them. Obviously, this place had a whole different code of conduct than what he was used to.

All of a sudden, someone grabbed Nick from behind and hauled him backward.

"What are you doing here?" the man snarled in his ear.

Anger set fire to Nick's blood and sent it thrumming through his veins like molten lava. His mother was the only one who used a tone that angry with him.

And occasionally Kyrian.

Menyara and Rosa from time to time. And he really should add Talon, though the Celt did better than most.

His teachers and principal, of course. He definitely couldn't leave them out..

Yeah, okay, so he ticked a lot of people off. But . . .

"Dude, I don't know you. I dang sure don't have to answer you."

"Dude," the voice said in a mocking tone with pauses between the words as the man did a bad Valley girl imitation. "I'm like so gonna kick your annoying ass."

Nick stiffened as he assumed his Cock of the Walk stance that said he was ready to battle. "I'd like to see you try."

The man shot through the darkness so fast that Nick didn't hear or feel him moving until he had Nick by the throat. "Word to the wise, punk. Don't dare someone until you know who and what you're dealing with, and what they're capable of. You'll live a lot longer, and stay in one piece, if you memorize that. Trust me."

"Trust you?" Nick choked out through his constricted throat. "I don't even know what species you are."

"Precisely my point." He let go of Nick and stepped back.

One second they were in the dark, in the next, they were inside a room that looked like something out of the Middle Ages. There was a fireplace so big that Nick could easily walk into it and have a spread out brunch for three people. Two comfortable-looking chairs with giant wings were set in front of it, over a lion-skin rug he was pretty sure had blood and bite marks still on it. In the far corner was a black desk that had ornate skeletal carvings on the wood.

And the man . . .

Not what Nick had expected at all. He looked like a banker or stock broker or something . . . Normal. Dressed in an elegant navy pinstriped, double-breasted suit, his shirt was crisp and white with a bloodred tie that flashed with something Nick would swear was living skulls inside the fabric. His dark blond hair was slicked back from his handsome face.

But it was his eyes that were terrifying. Cold. Merci-less. Mean. It was like looking at Death, and since Death tutored him, he ought to know it when he saw it. A frigid green, his eyes were so clear that they gave the illusion of glowing.

Asmodeus was a little more typical. Spiked white hair framed an impish face. His gray eyes showed exactly how mischievous he could be. And he glanced around the room as if he'd never seen it before.

"Who are *you*?" Nick asked the man in the suit.

A wry smile curved his lips. "I've been called many things by many people. But those who want to live usually refer to me as Thorn. And they do so in a rev-erent tone."

Not a soothing name by any means. Ranked up there with the Dark-Hunter named Venom, and Venom was definitely not someone you wanted to mess with, either. "What are you?"

Thorn quirked an offbeat, wry grin. "That's easy . . . and yet so complicated that I have no wish to venture there with *you*. Suffice it to say, I'm a carbon-based life form. And I'm one of the deadliest things that call the shadows home. And you, Malachai, are in a place you shouldn't be."

"And that is?"

"Azmodea."

Nick felt ill with that knowledge. How the heck did he get *here*? Like Asmodeus had said, how could someone go someplace and have no clue how they got there?

Asmodeus grinned. "Unfortunately, it's not named after me. Rather, I'm named after it. That part kind of blows. Got me bullied a lot as a small demon. Really hasn't helped my adulthood all that much either. And when it comes to females, I'd really like to find my father and repay him for this hideous name he stuck me with."

Thorn held his hand up in a dismissive gesture. "Demon, go home or shut up. If you continue to annoy me, you'll be a stain on my floor. Understood?"

Asmodeus nodded.

Nick was still trying to make sense of everything. "I don't understand. How did I get here?"

Thorn placed his hand on Nick's shoulder again.

In the next heartbeat, his eyes flashed silver, then red, and settled on a hazel brown. "Nick, your body is lying unconscious on a hospital bed. I cannot stress to you enough that you can't let yourself do that. Ever. Under any circumstances."

"What do you mean? I can't sleep?" That would stink. He had visions of *Nightmare on Elm Street* dancing in his head. Now where was a sugarplum when you needed one?

Releasing him, Thorn laughed. "That could be entertaining. A Malachai with hallucinations brought on by sleep deprivation. But no. Sleep is different. You're still in the world of man when you slumber. Half in, half out. Any little disturbance will wake you, and snatch you back to the conscious realm. However, when you're medically unconscious, you're beyond the realm of man and are fully on this side of the Nether Realm. Without being anchored in the human realm, your geist, or essence, rather, will automatically bring you here to serve your master. It's also why you can't ever take drugs or drink alcohol, my friend. The minute you lose control of yourself and alter your mental state, you open yourself up for others to manipulate and harm you."

"You could even be possessed," Asmodeus said with a hopeful note in his voice.

Thorn cast an evil glare at him and he literally retreated two steps.

"Well, he could," Asmodeus murmured.

Nick gave Thorn a droll stare. "Have no fear about the drinking and drugs, waking up in my own urine and vomit, or freaking out from a psychotic episode doesn't appeal to me in the least. Have no plans to do either, and I still don't know *what* you are."

Thorn's features hardened. "Forget Ambrose, *I'm* the person *you* don't want to become. If you want some free advice, and I know everyone does," he said sarcastically, "stop caring about anyone but yourself. So long as you care more for someone else than you do yourself, you're screwed. You'll never stand tall and you'll always have a weakness that will stop you dead in your tracks and bring you to your knees." He leaned forward until their noses almost touched. "Always put yourself first, kid. With all the regrets I have, and believe me, I have many, that's my biggest one. The dumbest mistakes of your life will all come from the choices you make, trying to protect what you love."

"Wow. Thank you, Mr. Sunshine," Nick said with feigned enthusiasm. That was the complete opposite advice of his mother, who believed you couldn't live happily unless you cared about someone. To her, that was the point of life. Making connections. Valuing someone else above yourself. *Without that, Nicky, we're just meat sacks waiting to be free of the misery of our lives. You'll never know true happiness until you find that small handful of people you'd die to protect.*

Nick clapped Thorn on the back. "I'm so glad you came out with your sunny disposition and thoughts to cheer me up, 'cause I just didn't feel crappy enough today. Thank you, Mr. Sun Meister, Meister Sun."

Thorn rolled his eyes. "Don't listen to me. Fine. Whatever. I didn't listen either, and you see what lush and lovely housing it got me." He gestured toward the sinister hole they were in. "Talk about sunshine . . . we don't get, well, any here. And it never fails to

amaze me how you can explain everything to someone, right down to the smallest detail. You show them
exactly what not to do in order to be happy or success-
ful, and still they don't do it. They don't listen. They
come up with more excuses than a felon in prison.
Fascinating . . . Disgusting, but fascinating. You can
lead a demon to water, but you can't force it to bathe."

Sighing, Thorn glanced around the room, then
back to Nick. "And right now, we have to get you out
of here before someone else, who is not a good friend
of yours or mine, senses you." He cut a pointed stare
to Asmodeus. "And no one is going to tell anyone or
anything on the other side of that magic wall that you
were here, either. Not unless they want to see the
truly ugly side of my temper."

Asmodeus gulped audibly.

Nick was about to speak when something slammed
against the door. Hard. And from the deep sound of
it, it was large.

And most likely, ugly.

"And look, lucky us, they're here." Thorn said something else in a growl that might have been a curse, but

the language he used was so strange that Nick couldn't be sure.

In the flash of a nanosecond, Thorn was covered in scaly armor that had spikes protruding from his shoulders and elbows. He glanced at Nick. "You've no real powers, do you?"

"Oh *contraire, mon frère.* I'm able to annoy all adults in ten syllables or less. Sometimes, I don't even have to speak at all. I just walk into the room and it rankles them."

"I can see that," Thorn said drily.

Nick tensed as armor appeared on his body, too. "What's this?"

"In the event they get past me and Asmodeus, who is going to fight with me or find himself disemboweled at my feet, let's hope that keeps them from dragging you off to somewhere you don't want to go."

Before Nick could ask him to elaborate, the door burst open.

Thorn let fly a ball of fire into the chest of a tall, black blob. Asmodeus moved to stand in front of Nick and behind Thorn.

Asmodeus flashed a grin at Nick over his shoulder.

"Let's hope they don't make it through the big guy, huh?"

"Where's Adarian?" the blob hissed.

With both of his hands on fire, literally, Thorn stood at the ready, but he didn't launch his fire at the beast. "You missed him."

"I smell him. He's here."

Thorn's hands flared brighter. "Do you see him anywhere? Now get out before I decide to answer this attack with one of my own."

"I smell him," it insisted. It sniffed the air like a bloodhound. Then it froze and turned its black eyes to Nick. "It's you!" As he started to rush forward, he burst into flames.

Shrieking, it hit the ground and became a dark stain at Thorn's feet.

By the look on Thorn's face and the way he immediately went into warrior death match stance with both hands throbbing fire, it was obvious he wasn't the one who'd caused the demon's spontaneous combustion.

Out of the burning remains of the demon rose a glistening, translucent shadow. It grew larger and turned denser until it formed the shape of a man. Muscular and fierce, he had dark brown dreadlocks. His locks were shorter than Wren's, and much more attractive—probably because, unlike Wren, he wasn't completely antisocial. He actually styled his locks. And his goatee was every bit as perfect. He had sharp, angular features, most of which were covered by a pair of opaque black aviator sunglasses. Dressed all in black, he was even more frightening than the demon he'd killed.

But the oddest part about his appearance was what flashed through Nick's mind when he looked at the newcomer. He saw him on a black horse in greenish-silver armor that flickered like a living creature. The man held a blood-soaked banner as he gleefully spread out his arm and sent misery to everyone, everywhere he rode.

What the. . . .

"Bane," Thorn said in greeting, relaxing only a tiny degree. And as he did so, the fire on his hands turned down to a low, simmering flame. "To what do I owe the honor?"

Bane wiped his biker boots on the smoldering remains of the demon he'd killed. "I smelled a Fringe Guard and wondered what he was doing here, since this is not their domain." He turned his head in Nick's direction and quirked a sinister smile. "Now, I understand completely. So this is the baby Malachai Grim's been teaching. Interesting . . ."

Nick looked to Thorn to see if this was friend or foe. From Thorn's reaction-

He could tell absolutely nothing.

Until the fire on his hands finally went out. He gestured from Bane to Nick. "Nick, meet Bane."

Interesting name. "Bane?" Nick asked. "What? Did your parents not like you?"

Bane let out an evil laugh. "Not really. But that's all right. It meant that I didn't have to worry about mourning them after I killed them."

There technically wasn't anything threatening in that, and yet . . .

Bane was not someone you wanted to meet late at night. Especially not when you were alone.

And unarmed.

Take that back, Nick wouldn't want to meet him in a full suit of Kevlar wrapped in C-4 with a grenade launcher over his shoulder. Even with all that protection on your body, Bane would still be terrifying.

Asmodeus vanished from in front of him, only to reappear by Nick's side so that he could whisper in his ear. "Bane is a good friend of Grim's."

Nick hesitated as his earlier vision of Bane and this latest tidbit came together and forced a realization on him that he didn't want to have.

No. It wasn't possible.

Was it?

Nick cleared his throat. "For the record, you're not . . ."

A slow, taunting smile curved the right side of Bane's mouth. "One of the Four Riders of the Apocalypse? Yes, Nick, I am."

Stunned to the core of his being, Nick could barely accept that. Strange, right? He could handle his boss being an ancient Greek general. Acheron being an eleven-thousand-year-old whatever, and all the rest of the paranormal crap he stewed in.

But this . . .

It seemed truly impossible. *After all you've been through, you're really going to doubt* this?

Yeah, he'd seen that episode of *X-Files* a few times too many, and while he wanted to deny Bane's words all day long and into the next millennia, he couldn't.

Scarily enough, it all made sense.

Nick raked a curious frown over Bane. From the tip of his biker boots to the top of his dreads. Aside from the obvious Faith No More wardrobe rip-off . . . "You look so . . . normal. Man, would my priest be disappointed." Father Jeffrey expected the Riders in flowing robes like they had been depicted in some of the Tarot decks Nick had seen the psychics using outside the Cathedral in Jackson Square.

Bane wasn't amused. "I now understand Grim's need to pull the heart out of you. And here I just thought it was Grim. Nope. You really are that annoying."

Nick arched a brow. "And this explains what Grim meant when he said anytime he got together with his friends, it didn't go so well for humanity. You guys are . . . bad for crops."

Bane took it in stride and returned with a counter. "The same could be said for *you* and *your* friends."

Maybe.

Well, then again, whenever Bubba and Mark got together, it did tend to go nuclear. As much as he hated admitting it, Pestilence had a point.

Thorn returned to wearing his posh navy suit. "So Bane, why are *you* here?"

"Same reason everyone will be converging on you soon, and it's not for your gory hospitality. The Malachai is back in Azmodea. People tend to notice."

Thorn welcomed that news as much as Nick did. "We've got to shield him."

Bane snorted. "Good luck with that."

Thorn crossed his arms over his chest. "No, not luck, Bane. *We're* going to shield him."

Bane shook his head in denial. "That's not *my* agenda."

"Is today, buddy," Thorn said with a wry grin, "unless you're tired of breathing. I do know a few people who'd be willing to replace you on the cosmic food chain."

Bane let out a long suffering sigh. "I don't understand you. Why are you fighting for the worms?"

Thorn shrugged. "Because some of us believe in doing the right thing even when we shouldn't. And you're going to do the right thing where Nick is concerned because I have your number, and I'm not afraid to dial it."

Bane's eyes glowed a wicked, fluorescent green. "I hate you, Thorn."

"Feeling's mutual, Bane. Now, man the perimeter and shield the Malachai."

Grumbling, Bane stepped over the still smoldering remains of the demon. "You owe me, Leucious."

"Pestilence, Pestilence, Pestilence . . . I've already paid you back. You're walking out my door. And in one piece, no less. Will my mercy ever have limitations?"

Flipping him off over his shoulder, Bane left them.

Thorn sobered the minute he was gone, and turned to face Nick. "You want to know what I am, Nick? I'm a creature like you. Conceived for only one purpose—to be a tool for evil."

Yeah, okay . . . No news to him there. Thorn didn't exactly hide that fact. Rather he embraced his role with both arms and a mighty hug. "Isn't that what you are?"

Thorn laughed. "I can see why you'd think that. But no. I am my own man. No one tells me who I am or how to behave. Who to kill and when. Or how. I define myself. Not my birthright or supposed written destiny. Definitely not my biological donors. I, alone, control me."

Strange as it was, Nick took comfort in those words. "So I don't have to become the Malachai?"

"No. That's not what I'm saying. You *are* the Malachai. Just as you're part human. Nothing will ever change that. But, you don't have to let that birthright consume or define you. It's hard to fight against your nature. Like an addiction, only this one is genetic and hardwired into your DNA. That impulse to harm rides you with spurs. Eats you alive. But you can't let it win. You have to remember that the evil part serves you as much as the good part does. There's a time for peace and a time for war, and sometimes you have to embrace them both. Most of all, you have to control them."

"Can you teach me?"

Thorn shook his head. "Only *you* can walk in your shoes, my friend. And I'm certainly not the voice in your head you want to listen to. I literally have destroyed everything I ever loved, either on purpose or by total accident. Believe me when I say that second chances are even more rare than finding true love. If you ever get one, don't squander it, kid."

Those words haunted him. "You know about Ambrose?"

Thorn's eyes glowed the same bright green that Bane's had done. "Have you ever heard the term 'Metaverse'?"

"Yeah, contrary to my mother's most highly held belief, I really do things other than play video games and text my friends. I know about alternate universes."

Thorn inclined his head to him. There was a note of respect in his eyes. "Then you know that simultaneously, every outcome of everyone's life is constantly in motion. One in each of the universes. Nicks *infinitas*. And yet, here we are in this life."

Yeah, but one thing he'd never been able to figure out . . . "How do we know that *this* is the right existence? How do I know one of the other universes isn't the one I should be living in?"

Thorn gave a low laugh. "How do we, indeed? That is *the* question. Who's to say if this is the right life or not? And while I have an answer, you don't need it, other than for me to mention that this is the only version of *you* and Ambrose that *you* know. In order to save *you*, Ambrose has bent the fabric that none of us are allowed to touch. He has breached this existence and is trying to gain access to the outcome that was achieved in an alternate universe and by another Nick, and make it happen here. The problem with that is—"

"You can't have the same outcome in two different dimensions."

"Exactly. Each one *must* play out as a different dance. In quantum mechanics, it's termed the uncertainty Principle, which says that the more you know about the position of one matter, the less you can control, determine, or know about the momentum of the other. When Ambrose came back and began interfering with the timeline of this universe, he created a buckle or bridge between the planes of existence. Things are now coming into this universe that weren't here before. Things he can neither control, nor see the potential problems it'll cause you both down the road. You see what I'm saying?"

"Yeah, by trying to help me, Ambrose screwed us over big time."

Thorn gave him a sarcastic salute. "That's a little harsh, but true. Now no one can predict what will happen to you. How this newest twist will unravel. But one thing you can bank on, *you* are the grand prize in a bloody contest. Whoever can bring you in to Noir will dominate this world and be rewarded greatly. Nick, my boy, to the preternatural creatures of this universe, you're infamous, and there's a bounty on your head that's staggering. Hell, you're lucky I'm not turning you in."

The way Thorn said that, it made Nick wonder if

one day Thorn might not change his mind and hand him over.

Kody stood up as Dr. Burdette came out with Nick's attending physician to speak to his mother.

Her eyes swimming in tears, Cherise went over to them. Kody followed with Caleb until they stood behind her and Menyara. The others stayed back, giving Cherise room.

"Will he live?" Cherise's voice shook.

Dr. Burdette pulled her into a tight hug. "Sugar? Didn't I tell you we weren't going to let that baby die? We have him stabilized and he's resting."

Cherise's blue eyes widened. "That sounds like there's a 'but' in there."

It was the male doctor who answered. "There is. He's in a coma and we're not sure why."

Frowning, Cherise reached out for the support of Menyara before turning her attention back to the doctor. "I don't understand. What do you mean?"

The doctor sighed. "He has no reason to be in a

coma. His injuries weren't *that* extreme. Don't get me wrong, they *are* bad, but not life-threatening. Not to mention there's a lot of brain activity going on that we can't explain. It's like he's not really in a coma . . . that on some level he's highly alert, but nothing we do can revive him. . . . I've never seen anything like this."

Kody exchanged a nervous glance with Caleb. "Are you thinking what I'm thinking?" she whispered.

"Yeah. Nick's somewhere he doesn't need to be."

"If it's where I'm thinking, I can't go."

Caleb growled low in his throat. "Yeah, that would wreck my sucky day even worse than what I'm about to go do." He winked at her before he headed out the door.

Dr. Burdette squeezed Cherise tight. "I can't imagine he won't come out of it in a day or two, honey. He will be fine, Cherise. You'll see."

Cherise drew a ragged breath. "I have told him so many times not to fight. Why couldn't he, for once, just listen to me and do what I say? Why didn't he give over his wallet and—"

"He didn't fight his attacker," Kody interjected, wanting to protect Nick any way she could.

Even from his own mother.

Cherise frowned at her. "What?"

"That was the only thing he'd say until he passed out. He wanted me to make sure you understood that he'd done what you asked and hadn't fought back when he was attacked."

"She's right," the doctor concurred. "All of his wounds were defensive, and not a single mark on him says he fought back in any way. From the looks of his injuries, I'd say he was on the ground in a fetal position, covering his head with his arms the entire time he was being beaten."

Cherise sobbed even harder. "So I'm the one who got him hurt like this. . . ." Tears rolled down her cheeks. "Oh God, what have I done?"

Kody rubbed her back. "He just wants to please you, Mrs. Gautier. He'd eat broken glass for breakfast if you asked him to."

But the self-loathing and torment in her blue eyes said that she wasn't going to forgive herself anytime soon. "Can I see him?" she asked his doctor.

"Sure." Dr. Burdette led her to the back while Kody

closed her eyes and tried to sense Caleb's location. He was completely gone from this plane of existence.

If he had descended into the Nether Realm to find Nick, it wouldn't be fun for him. Unlike her, he'd known the horrors of that place firsthand. What little she knew about it had come from others.

You're too close to the Malachai, Nekoda. You're losing your objectivity.

She knew that deep masculine voice inside her head. It came from Sraosha. His title was her guardian, but in truth, he was more like a warden who reported her every move to their superiors. *I've lost nothing.*

He grumbled, but didn't speak again. She knew what he and the others thought of her. That she should kill Nick and move on to the next Malachai.

But her brother had promised her that within the balance that had allowed one of the Sephirii to turn against his own and bring them down, the Malachai could do the same. A Malachai would be born with equal balanced parts inside him—just like Jared had been, and that that one special beast could be turned to their side and used against Noir and his sisters.

Nick was the only one, in all these centuries, who'd been born with that unique criteria. And there would never be another. He was their one and only hope.

If she and Caleb could turn him, they could stop Noir. Without his Malachai, he would be controllable.

Forever.

However, Sraosha and the others were correct. If they failed to kill Nick before he came into all of his powers, because of that mixed blood he would be the only Malachai who could destroy all of them. He would truly be invincible.

And they would all be dead or imprisoned.

We are not assassins, she reminded Sraosha in her head. *Especially not of children.*

He's not a child, Belam. You know that. He is the deadliest creature ever born. For now he's weak, but every day, he grows stronger. Deadlier. Meanwhile, you're growing weaker where he's concerned.

I'm not weak. She had never been weak. *Don't mistake my mercy for weakness. I assure you, if I know he is lost to us, I will cut his throat myself and deliver his heart to all of you.* Because if she didn't, he would destroy everyone she loved.

The only problem was, he was fast becoming one of the people she loved most.

You will do your duty. Sraosha pulled back from her.

Yes, she would do her duty, and she would keep her promise to her brother.

Even if it killed her.

And especially if it meant killing Nick.

CHAPTER 9

In his raven form, Caleb drew up short as he found Nick in the last place he'd expected.

Under Thorn's protection in the center of hell. Or more pointedly, in Thorn's office, learning how to sword fight . . .

The bright summer sun is shining in the darkest corner of Tartarus. That, and snow in August in New Orleans would be more likely than the sight below him as he used his powers to see inside the massive black mansion. Thorn hated everyone. No, not hated. That was too kind a word for the utter contempt and disdain he held for every living and undead creature in existence. His hatred was so intense it practically oozed out of his molecules.

Centuries ago, the two of them had been friendly. At least as friendly as anyone could be with something like Thorn who only trusted others to screw him over. Ironically, that was what had bonded them together—their mutual disdain and mistrust for everyone else in existence.

A true nihilist, Thorn believed in nothing. And nothing believed in him.

Well, not entirely true. Caleb believed in Thorn's willingness to kill any and every thing around him, especially if he found it or them annoying.

This can't be good. Thorn taking a liking to you had to be the same as trying to befriend a starving bear. Sooner or later, it was going to look over at you and think, *Lunch.*

Yet there he was, protecting and teaching Nick.

Talk about a mind freak. It went against all natural laws as Caleb knew them. Next thing, cobras would be sleeping with mongeese. Not mongooses, 'cause that just sounded stupid to him. LSU and Alabama fans would be having cookouts together, and one might actually put the other out if he or she caught fire.

Yeah, and the mighty war god Ares would go picking roses with a Girl Scout troop.

All of the above was much more likely than Thorn helping Nick.

And Caleb refused to believe there was some selfless reason motivating this. There had to be something in it for Thorn, or he wouldn't do it.

But what?

Tucking his wings in, Caleb swooped down to dive bomb them through an open window.

Please don't let Thorn be sadistic enough to have glass there. . . .

For the first time ever, Nick heard the voices in the ether speaking. Some were left from past spirits who'd gone on, while echoes of their life forces remained trapped. Most were from the living . . . the thoughts they let out into the universe, never realizing beings who were sensitive could pick them up and hear their innermost secrets. The rest were warnings from the living things people didn't know they could communicate with.

All you had to do was listen.

It was like hearing static on a radio. Just noise at first and then above the friction, total clarity. The more carefully you tuned in, the clearer it became. And once you had the right frequency, you heard every nuance.

Thorn cupped Nick's head in his massive paw of a hand. "That's the source of life you hear now. Feel your place in the universe and see how vast it is. How many beings call it home."

He was right, it was vast. But . . . "There's so many people in pain." It was overwhelming. While he'd known people suffered, to actually hear it . . .

Their combined pain opened his eyes. While he'd felt alone in his suffering, he realized that he was merely one of billions who felt exactly the same kind of impotent frustration that he did, that they were alone and that no one understood them, or their situation. That they had no control over the things that battered their souls, one after another, until they were reeling from shock.

Thorn narrowed those eerie green eyes on him. "Everyone's in pain, Nick. Some just hide it better than others. As William Goldman so eloquently put it, 'Life is pain, Highness. Anyone who says differently is selling something.'"

Nick nodded as he finally understood. "The whole point of life is learning to live with the consequences of the bad decisions we've made."

Thorn scowled at him as if trying to read his mind. "Where did that come from?"

"It's something Caleb says a lot."

His frown deepened until he appeared to have an epiphany. "You mean the demon, Malphas?"

As if on cue, a raven cawed, then flew between them, driving them apart.

Turning around to face the raven, Thorn unsheathed his sword for battle.

With a bright flash, the crow became Caleb in his full demon form. The black armor he wore appeared to bleed from every crevice. Rivulets of red ran all over the metal and dripped silently to the floor. With long orange hair, he had yellow eyes like a serpent. If that didn't clash enough, his skin was as red as the ooze on his armor. His black, leatherlike wings expanded and twitched as if daring Thorn to attack him.

"Dude," Nick said drily. "We've got to see a plastic surgeon about your unfortunate birth defect. And the orange hair . . . really? We need to talk L'Oreal. Black's a better neutral. You know? It wouldn't clash with your skin tone so much."

Flashing his fangs at Nick in irritation, Caleb stepped aside to give Thorn a clear path to him, and swept his arm out as if putting Nick on display. "If you want to kill him, Thorn, I won't protest."

Thorn laughed. "How many fools have fallen for that tactic?"

"Not enough, unfortunately. *He* still lives. And here I am. . . ." Caleb cocked his head to study Thorn intently. His gaze narrowed on the sword Thorn had yet to lower. "Are we fighting?"

"I don't know. You plan to attack me?"

"Only if you attack the boy."

"Well then . . ." Thorn sheathed his weapon and shook his head at Caleb. "I can't believe even Adarian would waste a good daeva's talent on babysitting."

"Daeva" was Caleb's demon classification. Though as a rule they were mid-level demons, Caleb's powers were infused by something that allowed him to function much higher than that. He also had powers most daeva didn't.

There had to be a reason for that, but Caleb wasn't into sharing. Not even when Nick begged.

Caleb slid a suspicious stare toward Nick. "We have got to get you out of here. Immediately."

"Good," Nick agreed, "'cause Toto wanna go home, Dorothy." He clicked his heels together. "There's no place like home, there's no place like home."

Grimacing, Caleb glanced up at the sky. "If someone drops a house on me, I'm going to be really upset at both of you."

Thorn snorted. "That would require a good witch. *Bon chance* finding that here, *mon ami.*"

"Good point. We are in the bowels of all evil, after all, and yes, Thorn, I do include you in that category. I've spent enough time around you to know how deep your wicked tendencies run."

Thorn laughed. "If you were a woman, Malphas, flattery like that would get you lucky."

Caleb tucked his wings down around his body so

that they formed another layer over his armor. "I am not even going to respond to that. Now, while your brain's functioning, any idea how to get snot-wit out of here?"

Nick gaped at the uncalled-for insult. Snot-wit? "Excuse me?"

"Really wish I could, Nick," Caleb said under his breath.

Thorn considered the answer before he spoke. "Other than making him regain his consciousness . . . no."

Caleb manifested a mace, then took a step toward Nick, who quickly backed up.

Thorn grabbed the mace out of his hand. "I said conscious, Malphas. Not dead."

"Oh c'mon, demonspawn. Just one little concussion . . . please. I've earned it. If for no other reason than he made me have to come here to get him."

Nick would be offended if he didn't know Caleb was joking. At least, he hoped Caleb was joking. "That was a joke, right?"

Caleb patted him on the cheek. "'Course it was, punkin'. Why would I want to kill little old you?"

Yeah, that sent a chill down his spine as reasons stockpiled in his mind.

But that was mild compared to the all-out panic that set in a second later when Bane appeared in Thorn's office.

"We got a problem." He passed a stern look from Thorn to Caleb.

"What?" Thorn asked.

"Noir has caught a scent of your little buddy and he's about to declare war on you to get him back. He thinks you've found him and are planning to use the Malachai against him."

"Of course he does. Paranoid idiot." Thorn threw his hand out and illuminated the opposite side of the room. Images flashed until they focused on one of the walls that surrounded his fortress. There were all manner of entities headed their way. Nick could only identify a small percentage of the demons, the rest . . .

"Are those bugs?"

Three heads turned to give him a look that questioned his intelligence.

"Yes," Bane said, his voice dripping with sarcasm.

"The baddest ass in all the universe is attacking us with big giant bugs. Help me, I'm being clobbered by a flea. Quick, Malphas, fetch the Raid."

Nick rolled his eyes. "What are they, then?"

Caleb sighed. "You know how Greeks have a three-headed dog that guards their Underworld?"

"Yeah."

"Those are what Noir uses to guard his. Basically, they're bloodhounds with exoskeletons so that certain classes of demons can't hurt them or escape them." He flashed an evil grin at Nick. "For the record, kid, you happen to be on that list."

Oh. And the bug-dogs could climb straight up a wall, as was proven when they reached Thorn's territory and, without hesitation, walked straight up it.

Caleb looked at Thorn. "How much fire can you conjure?"

"Not enough to take all of them out. It would drain me too fast and leave me at Noir's mercy."

Nick's heart raced. "We're dead, aren't we?"

"No, Nick," Caleb said in a deceptively calm voice, "we're worse than dead."

Nick widened his eyes. "What's worse than dead?"

Smiling, Bane clapped him on the shoulder. "Lucky you, you're about to find out."

K*ody!* Nekoda literally jumped where she stood in Nick's hospital room as Caleb screamed in her head.

What? she asked, projecting her thoughts to him so that the other people in the room wouldn't think she'd lost her mind.

Which she most likely had, but she didn't want to be confined to one of the mental floors for it.

Wake Nick up.

She glanced over to Menyara and Cherise, who were talking in a low tone to Dr. Burdette on the other side of Nick's bed. *I can't, Caleb. Not exactly alone here.*

Yeah, well, if you don't get him conscious, he's about to be enslaved to Noir.

Terror consumed her. That was all they needed. *Are you serious?*

Do I sound like I'm kidding?

No, he sounded panicked. Which made her blood race even more. Caleb didn't panic as a rule. He was always eerily calm no matter the threat. If he was rattled, it was bad.

But how could she get Cherise, Menyara, and Bubba's mama out of the room?

If she set it on fire . . .

That would be bad. And it'd most likely get her banned from the hospital.

C'mon, Kody, think. . . .

Caleb's voice was even more insistent. *Nick's about to die, Kody. We can't hold them. . . .* His sentence ended in a sound of anguish.

Glancing around, she tried to find something to use to distract the women so that she could wake Nick. But the hospital room was about as bare as anything could be. Drat!

If she went over there and started shaking him while he was hooked to all that equipment, they'd think she'd lost her mind. Her luck, they'd call security.

I have to do something.

Fast.

With no choice, she focused on Cherise and pushed her thoughts into Cherise's mind.

His mother shook her head, then scowled. "You know," she said to Menyara and Bobbi Jean, "I think I'm hungry all of a sudden. Why don't we grab a quick bite downstairs in the cafeteria while he's still sleeping?"

Both women looked at her like she'd lost her mind. Especially since she'd insisted the entire time that she be near Nick.

"You sure?" Menyara asked.

Cherise nodded. "We won't go far. We can rush back if something changes."

Menyara and Dr. Burdette exchanged frowns, since that had been their argument for hours as Cherise refused to leave in case Nick needed her.

Kody prodded them. "I'll stay with Nick and let you know if he wakes."

Cherise smiled. "Thank you, Kody."

Kody waited until they were gone before she rushed to the bed. "Nick?" She shook him gently. "C'mon, baby, wake up."

But he wasn't responding at all.

She shook him more vigorously. And still he didn't move.

Caleb? She tried to reach him again.

He didn't answer, either. Panic consumed her. What was going on?

Was she too late? Had Noir already captured them?

No, it couldn't happen. It didn't bear thinking on.

Her heart racing, she kept trying. She was the only hope they had.

I won't let you guys down. I promise.

Nick was quickly learning that on the paranormal food chain, he was kibble. And everyone else above him on that chain wanted a bite out of his hide.

That being said, Bane, Caleb, and Thorn were taking the brunt of the fight so that they could keep him from being dragged off by one of the others.

If only I'd brought my sword with me.

He knew better than to let that out of his sight. It

was one of the few things he'd been given that never let him down. The sword always worked the way it was supposed to. Pointy end went into his enemies and made them bleed.

Simplicity of design and dependability were beautiful things.

Oh, wait a second . . .

A weird thought occurred to him as he bashed one of the demons over the head with the book in his hands.

Could he summon his sword into this realm? It was infused with part of his DNA. Supposedly it was in tune with him, and he'd been working for months on the ability to summon his sword when he needed it. It was supposed to come to him on his command.

Nothing else worked the way it was supposed to, why should the sword obey him? Especially since he was in another dimension.

Still, it was worth a try. An effort wouldn't cost him anything.

Not trying was a guaranteed failure.

Closing his eyes, Nick did his best to imagine the

sword in his hand, its ornate hilt filling his palm. Just as he started feeling the heft of it in his hand, he was struck in the chest.

Nick staggered back as something else hit him and pain exploded through his entire body. He opened his eyes to see mortent demons right on top of him. Ah now, that was just rude. And he was tired of dealing with mortents. They smelled and they were just plain old obnoxious.

Other demons had Thorn on the ground. Caleb was bleeding profusely and Bane was pinned into a corner.

Man or mouse . . .

Time to be judged and he better not be lacking.

Nick opened himself up to the ether and let it whisper to him, at the same time he called for his sword. Light exploded all around them. Half the demons hissed, shrinking back from it.

Holding his hand up, Nick continued to whisper even as he was forced to avert his eyes from the light to keep from going blind.

The other half of the demons renewed their fight to reach him. And as they drew so close that he could feel their fetid breath on his skin, a clap of thunder rang out in his head. One second, they were nipping at his heels, in the next, he drove them back with a booming blast that sent all of them tumbling.

Nick started to laugh, until he realized that he couldn't turn whatever it was off. Worse, it was building up, faster and faster, trying to take control of him. He cried out as pain rushed through his veins. It felt like he was burning from the inside out.

Caleb shouted something at him, but he couldn't hear it.

I'm dying.

And there was nothing they could do to stop it.

CHAPTER 10

Nick felt his life force draining out of him. Then, just before the darkness took him under completely, he fell back into nothing. Desperate, he tried to grab on to something to stop his rapid descent. Anything.

Still, he fell.

Until he hit a sharp object that stabbed him so deeply, he was surprised it wasn't protruding through his chest. He waited for . . .

He didn't know. Disoriented and sick, he only wanted to wake up at home and have everything back to normal.

But that was easier said than done.

I have to face whatever it is.

Opening his eyes, he went rigid, unable to believe his sight. For once, it wasn't something from a horror movie. Instead, he stared into the face of heaven and it was smiling brightly at him. "Kody?"

She clutched his hand. "I thought I'd lost you."

"So did I." He tried to move, then groaned as absolute misery pierced him. "Did you beat me?"

"I didn't, but someone did."

Bristol.

How could he have forgotten? The worm had jumped him on his way to Liza's.

All of a sudden, Caleb appeared in human form on the opposite side of the bed. Thank goodness, he lived, but the peeved light in his eyes said he wanted to finish what Bristol had started.

Then, he glared at Kody. "Could you have cut that *any* closer?"

She gestured to Nick. "Talk to your friend here. He was the one who wouldn't wake up."

"Yeah," Caleb breathed, turning his vicious glare back to Nick. "What was that you did?"

He scowled. "What do you mean?"

"Do you recall the Nether Realm?"

Duh. Not exactly something you'd forget without massive amounts of electroshock therapy. "Of course I do, and I *never* want to go there again."

"That makes two of us."

Kody glanced back and forth between them. "So what happened?"

Caleb jerked his chin toward Nick. "Your boyfriend turned into a human torch and annihilated a number of demons before you yanked him out of there."

She appeared impressed by his description. "A torch? Really?"

Caleb nodded. "So what happened, Gautier? What'd you do?"

Shrugging, he tried to remember. "What always seems to happen when I'm under attack. I was trying to summon my sword and then something from deep inside me grabbed ahold of me. Next thing I know, you're yelling at me to not use those powers. I kill a bunch of stuff and then you yell at me again for not listening to you."

Caleb didn't appear nearly as amused by his

explanation as Kody did. "You need someone to yell at you."

Nick snorted. "Got plenty of volunteers for that job. Really don't need any more."

Caleb made a sound of supreme annoyance.

"Is he awake?"

Kody stepped back so that his mother could run to the bed and throw herself over him.

Nick grunted as his mother struck one of his sore ribs. "Ma, you're killing me."

She lifted her head to glare at him. "Good, I want to kill you. I swear, Nick, you're going to be the death of me."

A stab of pain lacerated his heart at her words. It was a bad reminder of why Ambrose was doing this.

To keep his mother alive from whatever he'd done that had gotten her killed.

Guilt gnawed at him. Not just over what he'd done in the past to hurt her, but over whatever future stupidity he was going to commit. He'd put her through enough. He didn't want to do anything else to make her cry. "I'm sorry, Mom."

"No, baby. I'm the one who's sorry. When I told

you not to fight, I didn't mean for you to not protect yourself. I never, ever meant for that."

Her words confused him even more. "But Mom, all my fights are me defending myself. I never throw the first punch."

She grimaced at him. "Why didn't you ever tell me that?"

His indignant anger begged him to lash out at her for *that* comment. But he held it back. "I've tried, repeatedly, and all you do is 'don't but Mom, me, Nick' and then you refuse to hear anything I say."

Sniffing, she swallowed hard. "I'm sorry about that, Boo. I'm going to try and do better. I promise. And you can fight anytime you want, okay? Just don't let them hurt you like this ever again. I'd much rather bail you out of jail than put you in a cemetery."

"Better to be judged by twelve than carried by six," Dr. Burdette said from behind her. "That's always been my motto. And it's the one I raised Michael on. I told him that I would never get on to him for defending himself, but if I found out he backed down from someone out of fear, his back porch was gonna be pink."

"Michael?" his mom asked.

Nick snickered. "Bubba."

Dr. Burdette made a painful moan. "Please, don't call him that. I cringe every time I hear it."

His mom frowned. "Why do you hate it so? I've known a lot of good Bubbas."

Dr. Burdette made an irritated sound in the back of her throat. "Lucky you, Cherise. My animosity goes all the way back to my first day of school. Bubba Clark, may he roast his tenderloins in the devil's hottest pit. There I was, all pristine in my white handmade dress my mama had worked so hard on. I felt like a fairy tale princess. Had my little pale yellow hat, and a matching patent leather purse. I thought I was the cat's meow and felt all pretty and girly. Next thing I know, I get shoved from behind and fall, scuffing my purse, my shoes, and putting dirt on my dress. Even worse, that little rat refused to apologize for it. Being the child I was, I laid into him with everything I had. And I might have been a little girl in a frilly pinafore dress, but I had three older brothers who taught me how to lay a man low, and sister, that day I did. I had him on the ground, crying like a baby after milk. Therein started a rivalry that goes on to this day. Bubba Clark has made me miserable any time he can, right down to pretending to be a policeman when I was on dates with Michael's father. Anytime we kissed, he'd shine his light in our windows—until the day Bruce beat the tar out of him for it. So I cringe whenever I hear the name, and the fact that Michael would use it . . . I'm going to start calling him Mickey again just to watch *him* make the faces. That'll learn him."

Nick laughed, then groaned as a stabbing stitch went through his middle.

"You all right, hon?" Dr. Burdette asked before placing her hand over his abdomen.

"Yeah. I got kicked pretty good a few times."

"Yes, you did. Do you know who did this?"

Instead of answering that question, Nick found a new fascination with the ceiling.

"Baby," his mom said, brushing his hair back from his forehead. "Answer Dr. Burdette's question so that we can file a police report."

While he wasn't happy with what Bristol had done, he didn't want him to go to jail over it, either. Bad things happened whenever kids from his school got locked up. Besides, he could handle this on his own. Had he not been so sore from his mother's reaming, this wouldn't have happened anyway. He and Bristol would have tossed words, maybe a few punches. In the end, they both would have walked home. So no, he didn't want to see Bristol in jail for this.

"I don't remember." Gah, how he hated lying, especially to his mom.

"Nick . . ."

He cringed at her tone, which said she knew he wasn't being honest. "I just can't, Mom."

She narrowed her gaze at him before she sighed. "Fine. I can't force it out of you. But I think you're making a mistake. You let someone get away with this and they'll keep hurting people until someone stops them."

And normally, that someone would be he.

Squeezing his hand, his mother stepped back. "By the way, I've been told that you're the most popular patient on the floor."

"How so?"

"There's a herd of folks outside, wanting to see you. And all of them worried about you. The nurses said that they get calls day and night asking about you and that if you think this—" She pointed to the all-out florist in his room. "—is a lot of flowers, you haven't seen anything. They had to store some of them in the staff offices."

Wow. It was a lot of flowers. "You sure they're not thinking I'm dead and sending them to the funeral home?"

She scoffed. "You're so bad."

Yeah well, he hated to see all of the flowers go to waste. Just what was against one wall would fill up their apartment. "Seriously though, would you make sure that the nurses take the ones they want?"

"I knew you'd feel that way. I have the cards collected so that we can send out thank-you notes to everyone." That was the thing about his mother, hard times might have caused her to live on the streets for awhile, but she was always polite.

And always a lady.

He realized she hadn't been exaggerating about the number of people asking about him once she started letting his visitors in. Dang, it *was* impressive. He'd never known before how many people cared about him. Funny, huh? Most of the time he felt like an outsider, sometimes even in his own home. But mostly at school and around other people. Looking at the visiting crowd coming in, maybe he wasn't as alone as he thought.

Even Kyl Poitiers and his dad came for a visit, as well as Casey Woods, and Amber Cassidy, who'd been one of Brynna's best friends since kindergarten. And then the half of the football team that wasn't in Stone's pocket. It really stunned him. Especially since they hadn't visited him in the hospital after he'd been shot. But then, he'd interacted with them a lot more over this last year. Strange how much could change in only a few months.

After they were all gone, Aimee, Dev, Alex, Kara, and Mama and Papa Bear Peltier all came in together and brought him a chocolate chip cookie basket. Yeah, not to be rude, but folks could keep the flowers. Choco-chip . . . *Now we're talking.*

Load me up till I burst. Then bury me behind the Chips Ahoy factory.

Dev tsked at him. "Next time you want to play ping-pong, I suggest you use a ball and not your head. Slim, you look awful."

"Thanks, Dev. That was just the look I was going for. Got up this morning, glanced in the mirror, and said, 'Nick, you're just too dang handsome. You need to find us someone to kick the crap out of you and bruise you all over. That'll make you feel all better.'"

Aimee laughed, then popped Dev in the stomach with her hand. "Holy cow, I think we may have found the one person in existence who can give you a run for your sarcasm. Go, Nick."

He didn't know why, but there was something about Aimee that drew him to her, and it wasn't just because the blonde waitress was exquisitely gorgeous. For that matter, he didn't think of her like *that* at all. She was more like a big sister. One who could be really raw with people. He'd seen her take the heads off anyone who was rude to her or any of the wait staff at Sanctuary. But when she wasn't riled, it felt good just to be in her presence.

"I have bad news for you," Papa Bear said in a serious tone.

Dread rushed through him. Standing at a cool seven foot three and weighing in probably around three hundred well-muscled pounds, Papa Bear Peltier was *not* someone you wanted to upset.

"Sir?" Nick asked, scared of the answer.

Papa Bear tsked. "Quinn unplugged the Galaga machine. Your nine-hundred-thousand score was erased."

Nick scrunched his face up. "Oh the humanity! I'll never score that high again." He groaned in miserable agony.

"Papa," Dev teased. "Tell him the truth." He grinned at Nick. "He *had* Quinn unplug it because he couldn't beat your score."

Papa Bear flashed an evil smile. "All right, I'll own that. But it'll teach you to get hurt and leave your successes unguarded, won't it?"

Nick shook his head, grateful that was what had upset the bear.

They all traded jokes with him for a while, then left.

After they were gone, Wren came in alone. He hesitated in the doorway. Something that probably sprang from the animal part of him. It was as if he respected other creatures' territory and didn't want to enter into it unless he planned to kill them. Not that he'd ever killed anyone to Nick's knowledge, but the day wasn't over yet.

"How you feel?" Wren asked.

"I'll live."

"Good." Wren pulled the bills out of his pocket that Nick had given him and held them out for him to take.

Nick frowned. "What are you doing?"

"I appreciate the thought, Gautier, but I don't need the money."

"Dude," he chided, "you're a busboy."

"Yeah?" He said that like he didn't get what Nick was saying.

Nick didn't want him to feel bad about what he did to earn a living, but Wren was probably not much older than he was and he didn't seem to have any ambition to make more money. He would assume then that Wren needed every cent he made for whatever it was Wren did when he wasn't working, which wasn't often, but still . . . "I know the Peltiers pay well, but . . ."

Wren's face twisted into a pained expression before

it settled into a wry grin. "Nick, I don't work at Sanctuary for money. I don't have to."

"What? You secretly loaded?" Nick laughed. "Or you won the lottery?"

With his head bowed low, Wren sheepishly rubbed his thumb down his cheek. "Um, Nick, my last name is Tigarian. As in Tigarian Industries, Electronics, and a dozen other corporations that fall under our heading. I'm the sole heir to *all* of it."

Nick gaped. Oh yeah if that was true, Wren was insane. "Why in the world would you work as a busboy if you have all that money?"

"Money doesn't buy everything."

"Then you ain't shopping in the right stores. Sorry, but having been poor most of my life, I stringently disagree. Because you swim in it, money may not work for you. For me, hellooo Versace, Armani, and all those other highfalutin' names I have to consult a dictionary to pronounce."

Wren snorted. "I've never been poor, so I can't argue."

"I'm sorry. My mind is so boggled right now. I

can't imagine working if I had access to your inheritance. I just don't get it."

Wren shrugged nonchalantly. "You could if you'd walked in my tracks. As my father used to say, everyone loves a self-made man. But they passionately resent his spoiled, rich son . . . even when the son was never spoiled. When you have a lot of money, you don't have a lot of friends. Only people wanting a loan, or scheming some way to take it from you, rather than work to get it themselves. Especially if you've inherited it. Then they feel justified plotting against you. After all, you didn't earn it, so you owe it to them."

He'd never thought about it that way. But Wren was right. He'd known his share of people who thought that very thing—kids at school who would tell other students they should pay for their lunch because their parents had more money. *You're rich, man. You can afford it.*

His mom had never been that way. And she'd hammered her beliefs into him.

You'll never be able to hold your head up with dignity so long as you hold your hand out for charity.

Wren held the money out again. "So please, take this back. While I deeply appreciate the gesture, I really can't keep it when I know you need it more than I do."

Nick took it and inclined his head respectfully at the gruff billionaire. What had life done to Wren that with all of his wealth, he'd rather live in a room at Peltier house, cleaning up after people, hauling around a monkey in his apron pocket, than travel the world and enjoy his money?

You really couldn't look at anyone and tell much about them. Where they'd come from or what demons rode their souls with spurs on.

And he remembered what Thorn had told him. *Everyone is in pain.* No matter where they come from or what you think of them. Sorrow spares no one, and scars respect no person. He also thought of Grim's lesson. People put up shields in an attempt to protect themselves from harm, but one trigger word could breach those defenses and leave them bleeding on the floor.

Nick knew for himself that words were far more

damaging than any weapon. The body healed and the scars faded, but the internal damage was eternal. It echoed anytime you let your defenses fall. Even with the money he had access to now, he still felt like a hobo, begging for handouts. Whenever he went to Brynna's house or Kyrian's, he kept waiting for them to call the police to put the trash out on the street where it belonged.

He had no way of knowing if that feeling would ever leave him. But he was learning not to gut himself over it like he used to. Every day, things got better. If anyone had told him a year ago that this would be his life in just a few short months... That his mother would have a job with people, or rather shapeshifters, who treated her like a lady, that he'd be hooked up with one of the prettiest girls in school, and that he'd have an apartment on Bourbon Street, he'd have laughed in their face.

Yet that had become his life. *All* of it.

Wren hesitated at the door. "You know, Nick, you're a real decent man, and there aren't many of them in this world. So do us a favor and don't get killed. There are too many jerks we need to off. We can't afford to lose someone who actually has manners."

"You sound like Caleb."

"Maybe we both have a little demon in us." And with that, Wren left.

After the next round of friends, which included Brynna, who appeared a lot better mentally than she had the last time he'd seen her, Nick was ready to sleep.

Until Bubba and Mark came in.

Mark sighed as he scanned the room. "Gah, dang, Bubba. Look at this place. Have you ever?"

"Nope. It's totally unprotected." He handed a satchel to Mark. "Let's get started."

Nick frowned. "What are you two up to?"

"Pay us no nevers." Bubba pulled the doctor's stool over to the window so that they could stand on it and start painting symbols with holy water on the wall above it.

"Hey, did you remember to get more salt?" Mark asked.

"Of course I did. What kind of demon/zombie kit would it be if it didn't have salt in it?"

"Just checking. What with your mom coming in

and it being this time of year and all, you haven't been as sharp as normal."

"Tell me about it. But I ain't totally dumb neither. I still have a modicum of intelligence. You wanna grab the thistle and take care of the door?"

Bubba might have his intelligence, but his sanity was still under debate.

But then, after what they'd gone through over the last year, Nick wasn't about to chance it. If their seal could keep some of the things out he'd met in the Nether Realm, they could wrap him in tinfoil, shave his head, and call him Sue.

Mark opened a bottle of something that smelled worse than his usual duck urine cologne.

Even Bubba groaned. "Mark, take a bath, son. You're stinking up the place."

"Ha, ha, ha," Mark mocked. "It's the sulfur stinking."

"Uh-huh, sure it is." Bubba snatched it from him and smelled it. Shaking his head and grimacing, he quickly put the cap back on. "Wha-aa-dude," he sputtered. "Dog, this stuff smells like you after three days at Comic Con. Are you trying to get us thrown out?"

Yeah, 'cause standing on the doctor's stool and painting holy water all over the walls would make them so happy. They might even offer them a job.

After they got out on probation.

Nick whimpered as he continued to laugh over their antics and it made his bruised sides ache. The two of them were priceless. He didn't know what was funnier. What they said or what they did.

Unfortunately, just as Mark set fire to the thistle, the nurse came in. She let out a war cry before running to call security.

Bubba and Mark started putting their things away. Given Bubba's height and muscled body, it always amazed Nick how fast he could move. Mark, on the other hand, was ripped, but lean and wiry. You expected speed out of him.

"We got you covered, brother," Bubba said. "That should keep out almost anything. Now, we're gonna haul before we get hauled out by security. My mama is just ornery enough to make me spend the night in lockup if I get caught again."

Nick laughed at the idea of a man the size of Bubba being so scared of someone as tiny as Dr. Burdette.

Until he remembered the fact that he was taller and thicker than his mother, too. And she scared the crap out of him. Yeah, okay, so he couldn't legitimately harass Bubba for Mamaphobia. Whoever had said that the hand that rocked the cradle ruled the world must have had a Southern, born and bred, mother.

Sobering, he inclined his head to them. "Thanks, guys. I'll see you later."

They ducked out the door like two spies avoiding camera relays.

Nick was still smiling when the nurse came back. "Where'd they go?"

When unsure of how to respond, the best tactic? Stupid. "Who are we talking about?"

She huffed at him. "You know? The men who were burning things in here. Where are they?"

"I didn't see anyone burn anything."

She glared and he could swear he saw the promise of a painful shot in his future. "We'll find them. With or without you."

He wished her luck. One thing about those two, they were slipperier than a greased gator on the hunt in the bayou.

Although, the worst thing she could do was catch them.

It'd be like trying to keep a cobra in a shoebox. Not a good idea.

Grinning, Nick leaned back and closed his eyes. He turned his thoughts to something even better than two lunatics outrunning the authorities.

Nekoda.

Instead of sending her off with Caleb to get some eats, he should have kept her here. He didn't know why, but just the sight of her soothed him. No matter his *beaux-beaux*, she always made it better.

At times, he thought he was in love with her. At others . . .

How did anyone know for sure? Were there bells or whistles, or . . .

What?

Life really needed to come with cartoon bubbles over everyone to explain what was really going on inside their head.

The saddest part, he didn't know anyone to ask about it. His mother had never been in love. Aside from him and his father, she refused to have any man near her. *I ain't bringing no man around while I got a baby at home. Anyone hits my Boo and I'll gut him.* For the longest time, he'd felt guilty about that.

But after what Kody told him, he knew the real reason why she didn't date or see men. And that broke his heart.

Menyara would only give the standard, *There are some things in the universe that defy explanation. But trust me, when it strikes, you will know.*

Kyrian didn't want to talk about his wife. Ever. Acheron scoffed at the idea of love as the ultimate stupidity. *You know what love is, Nick? It's a woman's way of controlling the relationship and controlling you. In the wrong hands, it's the worst, most painful weapon imaginable. So when you give your heart away, make sure it's a mutual exchange. 'Cause once you let them in, cutting them out again is like being gutted with a dull spoon.*

He didn't want to know what had happened to Acheron to make him so jaded, especially given the fact that Ash had died at age twenty-one. To have that kind of hatred eleven thousand years later. . . .

Yeah, someone had hurt Ash badly.

The Were-Hunter shapeshifters had their mates chosen for them by the Fates, so they didn't really date like humans, and they definitely didn't have a choice or say in who their spouses were.

The only people he knew who were married, he didn't feel comfortable enough to ask. Or they were divorced, which didn't bode well since they'd obviously made a mistake when they picked someone.

But Kody . . . she made him feel things no one else did. He could be having the absolute worst day and with one smile, she could make him forget all about it.

"Did you enjoy your time in Azmodea?"

Nick curled his lip at the familiar voice. Why would Ambrose bug him now? Couldn't he have five seconds to decompress before his insane older self came in to rough him up?

Yawning, Nick answered without looking. "It certainly wasn't Disney World—unless Mickey sold his soul to Satan. Not that I've ever been to Disney World. Heck, I haven't even been to Six Flags and it's just over the bridge."

The power from Ambrose made the hair on his arms stand on end.

Ambrose's aura practically sizzled with its lethal capabilities. "I can't believe you got out of there in one piece. I had to betray the closest thing I've ever had to a friend to escape it."

A bad feeling went through Nick. While the voice was definitely Ambrose's, the story wasn't.

No . . .

It couldn't be.

Opening his eyes, he saw a man who bore a frightening resemblance to Ambrose. Except this one had short, military-cut jet-black hair, and he stood about two inches taller. Even more telling, he was covered with prison tattoos.

Definitely not Ambrose.

This was his father.

Soc au lait!

CHAPTER 11

Nick tried to call for help, but he was completely paralyzed. He couldn't even blink. If he so much as thought about Kody or Caleb, a sharp pain pierced his brain.

Was he being stabbed with an ice pick?

His father gave him a crooked smile. "Oh the powers that awaited you . . . the things you were born to do . . . Too bad you won't live long enough to experience any of them."

Fighting with everything he had, Nick did his best to break free.

He couldn't. Never had he experienced anything like this. It was terrifying. Forget being Force-choked by Vader, this was even more terrifying and debilitating.

If I get free, old man, you're going to bleed.

Yeah, okay, so it most likely wouldn't be much of a fight, but he was going to put up as much of one as he could. There literally was nothing he could do.

Adarian's gaze was frigid as he moved to stand over Nick. He pressed his thumb against the inside corner of Nick's left eye. In his head, Nick screamed from the raw agony of it. But the sound wouldn't leave his throat.

He was the only one who heard it.

His father had him completely paralyzed.

"That's it," Adarian whispered before he sucked his breath in with pleasure. "Feed me with your pain. Let me bathe in it."

"What are you doing, *tchu!*"

Nick's eyes widened at a Cajun insult he'd never heard his mother use before. In fact, she went into a full *babiller* on his hide, using words that shocked him and some *he* didn't even know she knew the meaning of.

Her shrill voice ringing off the walls, she ran toward

them. She actually slammed all of her body weight against Adarian to shove him away from the bed. Given the fact that she was about a foot and a half shorter and probably weighed less than one of Adarian's muscled thighs, her ability to move him was impressive. "You get away from him! You hear me?" she snarled through gritted teeth.

"I just wanted to see him. He is my son, after all."

She backed Adarian into a corner like a Chihuahua cowing a Doberman. "You shouldn't be here and you know it. How are you here? I know you didn't make parole. No one's dumb enough to ever let you out again."

Adarian's gaze softened as he faced her anger without flinching. "I'd forgotten how beautiful you are." He reached to cup her cheek.

His mother slapped Adarian's hand away. "You are not going to touch me again. Ever!"

Nick kept trying to move or speak, but whatever Adarian had done to him, it was holding him solid.

Averting his gaze with a glaze in his eyes that told Nick he was listening to the ether, Adarian went ramrod stiff. When he looked back at his mother, his face was a mask of disbelief. "You're the one who turned me in to the cops after I robbed that bank, aren't you?"

"Yes, I did," she said proudly between her clenched teeth, straightening up to her full height, which barely reached the middle of his father's chest. "I didn't care what you did to me. I didn't. But when you hit my baby . . . nuh-uh. It was on like Donkey Kong. Nobody touches my boy. Not you. Not anyone. He's all I got in this world and I will slaughter you like a hog at Christmas if you even look askance at him again. You hear me?"

Adarian appeared as stunned by her attack as Nick was. "You turned me in." Disbelief haunted his voice.

"I. Did," she repeated.

The hurt in his eyes was tangible. And it was telling. Adarian loved her.

Dis-gus-ting . . .

No, worse than that. His father's love was a perversion. . . . *Because he's the Malachai.* They weren't born to know that emotion. They were born to hate and to slaughter. That was what Thorn had told him.

The only reason Nick had any concept of love was

because of his mother's blood, and the fact that she'd kept him and nurtured her 'baby'. Nick was the only Malachai ever born who'd been shown love and who understood it.

His father had no idea how to cope with it. For that matter, Adarian had probably never felt it for anyone else.

"How could you?" Adarian's tone was more like a child being tortured by its parent.

His mom shook her head at his continued confusion. "Are you . . ." Closing her eyes, she waved her hands around her face as if erasing a board. "Of course you're insane. I know that. Everybody knows that."

Biting his lip, Adarian held a light in his icy gaze that said he was one step away from hitting her.

Nick fought his hold even harder. He had to protect his tiny mother from the bear of a man who had fathered him.

"Is there a problem, Cherise?"

Since the only part of his body he could control was his eyes, Nick turned his gaze to the door, where Kyrian stood in a major power stance that let everyone know he was more than willing to get bloody if he had to. Dressed in black from head to toe, he was almost the same size as his father. And he was every bit as buff. Kyrian's black sunglasses covered his eyes while he stood with his arms crossed over his chest.

Adarian did the alpha strut as he closed the distance between them. "This doesn't concern you."

Kyrian didn't break his tough-guy stance at all. "The hand you had on that lady says it does."

Adarian laughed. "You don't know who or what you're dealing with."

"And neither do you." Kyrian's voice was as smooth and emotionless as if they were discussing the weather. It always amazed Nick that Kyrian could speak so easily without showing even the smallest hint of fang. "So if you want to dance with me, let's take it outside where we have more room."

Invading Kyrian's personal space, Adarian was close enough to kiss him. Still, Kyrian didn't blink or flinch—and that in and of itself was a call-out to his father.

Adarian raked Kyrian with a sneer. "You think you can take me?"

Kyrian cocked an amused grin. "You're not the scariest thing I've ever seen. And you're definitely not the most powerful."

Adarian laughed. "There, you would be wrong."

Just as Nick was sure Adarian would attack, Acheron moved to stand directly behind Kyrian.

His father's eyes widened as he took in Acheron's seven-foot height, four inches of which came from the thick-soled, flamed Goth biker boots he wore. More than that, Acheron not only exuded lethal authority, anyone with a drop of paranormal blood in them knew he wasn't what he seemed. His powers surged in a way no one else's did.

In the land of Bad Ass, Acheron reigned supreme.

Adarian took one step back as if rethinking his position. After a few seconds, he turned his head to speak over his shoulder. "You can't keep me from my son, Cherise. He's my blood."

She shook her head. "No, he's not. He's *my* boy." She put a long emphasis on the "my" part. "And I'm not sharing him with anybody. That includes you. I know you think I'm nothing. But I'm no longer the

child I used to be and I'm not afraid of you anymore."
She pointed to Nick. "That right there is the only family I have. And I love him with every part of me. You touch him ever again and one of us *will* die. I promise you that. You can take it to the bank and spend it."

A tic beat a fierce rhythm in Adarian's cheek. And the promise in his eyes was loud and clear.

He would be back.

Sucking air between his teeth in a frightful hiss, Adarian brushed roughly past Kyrian and Acheron.

As soon as he was gone, his mother's legs buckled and she headed to the floor. Moving with preternatural speed and power, Kyrian caught her against him.

It was only then that Nick could move again.

"Breathe easy, Cherise," Kyrian said, scooping her up in his arms so that he could carry her to the recliner by the window. Gently, he set her in it and took two steps back.

She fanned her flushed face with a shaking hand. "I don't know what got into me. He could have killed me. I'm surprised he didn't."

"You're a mother who loves her child—who was

protecting her son." Acheron quirked a twisted grin. "That makes you the most dangerous creature on the planet. I'd face down a team of SEAL-trained mass murderers any day over one pissed-off mom, of any species, protecting her young. Believe me." Tucking his hands into the pockets of his spiked motorcycle jacket, Acheron paused next to Nick. "What did he want?"

Nick let out a long breath. "I don't know. I really don't."

His mom launched herself from the chair to his bed so that she could check on him. "Did he hurt you, baby? Why didn't you call me?"

"I couldn't. He had a Vulcan death grip of some kind on me. I couldn't move or do anything."

His mom brushed the hair back from his brow. "Well, he's gone now and we're done with him. I don't ever want to see him again."

Kyrian nodded. "We'll make sure he stays away from both of you."

She turned and offered him a grateful smile. "I can't thank you enough, Mr. Hunter. I know it's not your place. God love you for your decency. You've been so good to us."

Her heartfelt praise made him bristle. Nick had noticed that Kyrian, in spite of having been a prince when he was a human in ancient Greece, didn't like to be thanked. "I believe in helping people out whenever I can. I know you and Nick don't really have anyone to watch over you, and while you're both very capable, we all need a cavalry once in a while."

His mom nodded. "I hate admitting it. But you're right. It's not in me to ask for help for nothing." She glanced from Kyrian to Acheron. "And with the two of you and Menyara, I never have to." Tears welled in her eyes.

"Mama?"

Blinking against her tears, she took Nick's hand. "I'm okay, baby. It's been a very emotional day. A lot has happened and the roller-coaster ride is making me a little sick to my stomach. But don't you worry about me, Boo. I'm all right."

Yeah, his mom had a core of steel unlike anyone he'd ever known.

Acheron dropped his backpack by the bed. "Why don't you go on to work, Kyrian. I'll take first shift of Nick watch duty."

He inclined his head to Acheron, then turned to Nick's mom. "If you need anything, call me."

"I will. Thank you."

"Anytime." Kyrian knuckle-bumped Nick. "Take care, Cajun, and if you don't stop getting hospitalized, I'm going to start docking your pay."

"Yeah, and I'll start scratching your car paint."

Kyrian laughed. "You know I value my cars over your life, right?"

"I don't believe it for a minute," Nick called out as he left.

But Kyrian didn't respond.

His mom patted his hand. "You know, this got me thinking, Boo. You do need to learn to drive. If you'd been in a car going to Liza's, none of this would have happened . . ."

Joy rushed through him. "You're going to teach me?"

She visibly cringed. "Yes," she said in the most pathetic tone ever.

Acheron laughed. "Would you like me to teach him?"

She cringed even more.

"It's okay, Mrs. Gautier. I don't care if he bangs up my car, and I'm really, really patient when teaching people. Especially those with hot heads. I've been training folks for years."

Man, that was an understatement. It was all Nick could do not to burst into laughter.

His mother scanned Ash with a doubting stare.

"You don't look old enough to have been doing anything for years."

If his mom only knew the truth.

"Please, Mom?" Nick begged. "No offense, but I think I'd rather have Ash do it, too. He won't be screaming or grounding me if I make a mistake."

She opened and closed her mouth as if she wanted to argue, but she knew the truth as well as he did. "Fine. But if I had a Porsche, there's no way I'd ever let a fifteen-year-old in it, never mind drive it."

Acheron scoffed. "He won't be learning in my Porsche. It's a standard. I think it'd be best to teach him in an automatic. Let him get used to the feel of the car and traffic rules before we complicate it with a gearshift. Last thing King ADD needs is one more distraction."

"Hey!" Nick protested. "I'm not that—hey, did you see that?" He pointed to the wall as a joke.

"Ha, ha," Ash said.

"So whose car will you use to train him in?" his mom asked.

"One of my others."

His mom quirked a brow at that. "Others? How many cars do you own?"

"Ummmm . . ." Ash stroked the side of his face with his fingers. "A lot."

"You don't know?" she asked, aghast.

"Not really. Most are kept in storage and I have them delivered when I want to drive them."

She pinned him with that suspicious look that meant she thought he was a drug dealer or a car thief. "What do you do again for a living?"

"Wrangle people."

Her eyes widened. "You work in the sex trade?"

"No!" Ash practically roared that word.

Nick sucked his breath in. There was one of Grim's trigger words. Wow. That was a violent reaction. He'd never seen Ash explode like that to anything.

His breathing labored, Ash clenched his teeth, then seemed to get ahold of himself. "Sorry. That's a subject I take very seriously. Children should be protected, not . . ." His nostrils flared. "Anyway, I train and consult personal security personnel."

Nick was impressed with Ash's spin on what Dark-Hunters did. Personal security personnel.

For the whole world.

"Why do you call it wrangling?"

Ash shrugged. "My people get moved around a lot. The logistics can get hinky at times. I have several coming into town for Halloween, in fact. And it's why I'm not always here. I travel a lot to different cities and countries where we have staffs."

His mother's jaw gaped. "That's so impressive. Especially for your age. How old are you exactly?"

Nick arched his brow, waiting to see what Ash would come back with.

"Older than I look, Mrs. Gautier. *Much* older than I look."

Yeah, he looked like he was in his late teens. No one would believe he was an ancient Atlantean who was over eleven thousand years old.

She smiled. "I understand. I don't like giving out my age either. Sorry to be so personal. But I feel even better having you here now that I know what it is you do. Have you ever had to deal with someone as . . . special as Nick's father?"

Acheron burst out laughing. Hard. "Uh, yeah. All the time. My people specialize in the truly unruly."

"Good." She stepped away from the bed. "If you two will excuse me, I'm going outside to make a call to Menyara. I'll be back in a few minutes."

"Take your time, Mrs. Gautier."

"Call me Cherise," she said with a smile. "I think we all know I was never married. But I appreciate the gesture. Thank you."

"Any time, Cherise."

After she left, Acheron sat in the recliner. "So what went down?"

"With my dad?"

"No, the mugging."

Nick sighed. "I don't know. There's some weird crap going around my school."

"Please tell me it's not zombies again."

Nick laughed. "No, Madaug's been banned from making games. If his brother Eric ever finds one again, he has a giant magnet he's going to set down on Madaug's prized computer."

"Ouch."

"Exactly. Not that Madaug needed the threat. He learned his lesson quite well."

Acheron nodded. "I imagine so. Anyway, back to school. What's going on?"

"Someone has set up a Web site and they're posting garbage about my classmates. Mostly made up, but enough truths to make it look authentic. Now students are going at each other's throats over it."

"*Echrichta.*"

"Bless you."

Ash laughed, this time giving Nick a flash of his elongated fangs. "In Atlantean the Echrichta were the children of Pali, the god of strife, and Diafonia, the goddess of discord. Their grandfather was Misos, the Atlantean god of war and death. Before wars broke out, the Atlantean gods would unleash the Echrichta to stir up emotions and get the people ready to attack each other."

That had to be the coolest accent in the world. There was nothing to compare it to, but in spite of the fact that Acheron was male, Nick loved to hear him speak his native language. "How do you say that? Ecka—encha—Encharada . . . Enchilada?"

"You have to catch and roll the uvula in the back of your throat on the r's. So it's heck-RAH-ta."

"Yeah, I'm gonna quit before I embarrass myself. So were they human in appearance? Ugly snot monsters? Or what?"

"They were extremely beautiful. At least on the ouside. Inside . . . Echrichta literally means 'she who stirs excrement.'"

Nick burst out laughing. "What? Are you serious?"

Acheron nodded. "I swear. In my day, in Atlantis, men were respected. Women were feared . . . and for good reason. Hell hath no fury."

Nick agreed with that. Women and girls carried a grudge like nobody's business. Sue Tilling was still mad at him for bumping into her on the playground in kindergarten. "I have to say they scare the crap out of me most days. Kody can render me speechless with the raising of one eyebrow."

"Exactly. Men can beat each other to a pulp and still walk away friends. With a woman, once an enemy, always an enemy. Women will sit like a spider, *for years,* waiting for the chance to strike. They never forget and seldom forgive."

Nick cringed. "You're scaring me, Ash."

"Sorry. But just remember this. No woman has ever killed a man while he was washing dishes."

Nick scowled at him. "What?"

"It's another Atlantean saying. If you keep the woman happy, she's less likely to cut your throat."

"Man, y'all were whacked. So what did these troublemaking, excrement-stirring goddesses do?"

"The kind of stuff you're talking about at Your School. They'd go in and tell someone's secrets and claim they'd heard them from someone else, usually a friend. Or they'd just make things up to break apart friendships and homes. It was what they lived for. They'd go to humans and whisper in their ears, playing off their fears. Sometimes it was overt and other times it would be as subtle as saying, 'Hey Nick, I saw Kody this afternoon when at the mall. Man, she's looking really happy these days. And her friend Tom she was with . . . wow. You could tell he was loaded. Expensive clothes. Rolex. He was so impressive and smart.'"

"How would that upset me?"

"Let's say that Kody had told you she couldn't be with you that same afternoon because she had to study."

"Yeah, okay, that would not make me happy."

Acheron nodded. "And you'd probably fight with her over it, especially if she hadn't done it. You'd think she was lying about it, and she'd think you didn't trust her."

Nick let out a low whistle. He could see where that would get ugly fast. "It's kind of like an evil silkspeech."

Ash stiffened for a second. "How do you know what silkspeech is?"

Nick let his Cajun accent out in all its glory. "I be hanging with me some Goths."

That placated him. "Silkspeech isn't just the tool of demons and gods. While it's potent in their hands, it's deadliest when in the hands of a human who's incapable of feeling happiness. Or worse, one who takes happiness by hurting others. Jealous people who trade in gossip and who feel the need to take someone down a notch so that they can feel superior."

"Oh, I know people like that."

"Sadly, Nick, we all do."

Yeah. And it was sad.

The nurse came in to glare at Nick. "Those men got away. But I will find out who they were. What were they doing in here anyway?"

"Protecting me."

"From what?" she asked, arms akimbo.

Acheron arched a curious brow.

Nick didn't want to tell her or Ash about the demon part, so . . . "There's an escaped felon trying to kill me." There. The truth with vague details. The Echrichta might excel at lies, but Nick excelled at creative truth. Something that was a talent in and of itself.

"I'll warn security about this." She checked his IV bag, then put a needle into it.

Acheron cocked his head. "What are you giving him?"

"Just a small sedative."

One that was already kicking in. Man, it was strong. The room blurred. He heard Acheron saying something, but he couldn't make it out at all.

Freaky weird. It was even making him hallucinate. Instead of seeing the nurse, he saw his father.

No, wait . . .

That was his powers kicking in. The nurse *was* his father.

Nick tried to speak, but couldn't. All he could hear was the sound of him coding as he passed out.

CHAPTER 12

C ome home, child, and be rewarded."

Nick heard that tender voice. It was feminine, but not his mother's. Warmth suffused him as he tried to find that unseen woman through the darkness that enveloped him.

"Fight her, Nick." That was Kody. "Think of me, baby, and come toward my voice."

Nick hesitated. It wasn't in him to blindly follow anyone. "How do I know it's you?"

"You know me, Nick."

Yeah, but he wasn't stupid. Any more than he was trusting. "If you're really Kody, tell me where we met."

"In school."

That was a vague and safe bet. "Where in school?"

"In class, silly."

He made the sound of a warning buzzer. "And for the million-dollar question . . . you're absolutely wrong. No Nick for you, jerkweed!"

Now he was being cursed by a man's gruff voice. In the back of his mind, he wondered if that might be Noir, but there was no way to know for sure. And he wasn't about to ask since the last thing he wanted was for the dark god to get any kind of boost to his powers.

"Nick?"

He jumped at the sound of "Kody's" voice right behind him.

A dull greenish light flared so that he could see her. Only . . .

His mind locked up over the way she was dressed. Her brown hair was pulled back from her face and held high on her head in an intricate braid, with the majority of her hair falling down her back. She had a leather halter with fringe hanging down the front and back. Her short leather skirt was also fringed and leather bands that held sheaths were wrapped around her arms and thighs. Along with another sword and sheath that she wore diagonally across her back.

Ringed with heavy black eyeliner, her green eyes were the color of deep emeralds.

She smiled at him before she chucked him lightly on the chin. "Close your mouth, baby, you're drooling."

He probably was. Any normal heterosexual fifteen-year-old would. "My baby is h-a-w-t!" Then he remembered the masquerade trick. "You are my baby, right?"

She handed him his sword and grimoire. "Yes, I am."

Only the real Kody would have known to bring those to him, and where he kept them. Grateful she knew him so well, she took his weapons, then heard the sound of something beating loud and fierce in the sky above them. "Where are we?"

"The Fringe Realm."

She said that like he should know exactly what she was talking about. But, he had no clue. "I don't understand. Where's the Fringe Realm?" *What's the Fringe Realm?*

"Think of it like a protective membrane that keeps the worlds within their respective boundaries."

Nick placed one hand over his ear as the sound became louder. "And what's causing that?"

Before she could answer, *that* attacked. They were like flying monkeys that had mated with dragons. Their bodies were more humanoid, yet their faces were dragon-shaped and their pale tan skin made of scales. Large fangs curled like tusks out of their mouths.

Kody flipped around his back to catch the first one that reached them with a sword stroke. The others descended on them rapidly.

Pulling his sword hilt out, he held it in his palm and imagined it the size of a Scottish claymore. It quickly shot to that size so that he could fight. His heart pounding, he stood at Kody's back as they fought against the beasts.

"Don't let them separate us," Kody warned.

"I'm not letting them do anything." They definitely had the home team advantage, and were making use of it. *I'm not going to be kibble today.*

At least that was the intention. But intending something and being able to do it . . .

Much easier said than done. Nick crouched low as one of the dramonks came at him. He rose up and stabbed it in the middle of its chest. Screaming, it twisted around and reached a huge claw toward him.

One second, he thought he was a goner, and in the next, Kody pulled him back and was between them.

Instead of it grabbing him, it got her. She cried out in agony and anger as it snatched her from the ground and launched toward the black sky, clutching her in its claws.

In that moment, a rage he'd never felt before came over him. His vision dimmed as words formed themselves in his mind. When he spoke them aloud, they came out as a guttural growl, in a language he knew without ever having been taught it.

She is mine. Let nothing touch her save the Ambrosius Malachai.

The words rolled out like a sonic boom that shook the air around and ground beneath him. He let the words continue to fill the ether until he merged with it.

The ether is yours to command. Breathe, Ambrosius, breathe. Let it empower you. It is your blood. Your lineage. Your Right.

Nick felt it seep inside him, thick and heady. Something entered his mouth. It tasted like blood, but instead of repulsing him, he craved it. Leaning his head back, he drank his fill. And with every swallow, he became stronger and stronger. . . .

Death is my friend. He walks to my right. War walks to my left. I am their commander and I am the one they serve.

And Kody was his chosen one.

No one took from him. Not without paying with their lives. Lowering his head, he threw his arms out, spanned his black wings, and launched himself toward her. One of Noir's larger pets came at him. He shot a blast of fire at it. With one shrill scream, it burst apart.

Nick ignored everything as he closed the distance between him and Kody.

Kody saw the shadow that darkened the creature clutching her. She looked up, expecting another enemy.

What she found was so much worse.

Nick had converted to the Malachai. His skin was black and red swirled together into a beautiful pattern that faded into his ebony wings. His eyes were a vibrant reddish yellow. And yet, he was still incredibly handsome.

In that instant, she saw the real reason why he had to be saved.

He was unique. His mother's blood and his father's. He was a creature unto himself.

A creature of hatred nurtured by love.

One who would fight his own to save her life. No other Malachai would ever do such.

Flying with incredible speed, he grabbed the gritale by its head and snapped its neck. It let go of her. Kody fell through the dark sky.

Until a hand caught hers. Her heart pounding, she stared into the face of ultimate death. Into the blazing eyes of a creature known for its merciless cruelty.

The Malachai has no heart. It can feel nothing but hatred. It thrives on it. It seeks to feel it even when it shouldn't. That is its mother's milk. Its only pleasure comes from consuming the blood of its enemies.

For the first time, she feared him.

Nick placed her on a ledge above the cavern they'd been in. And as he rose, jet-black armor covered him.

Dark gunmetal spikes glistened from the shoulders. His hands were now vicious claws. From his left shoulder, there were three pendulums that fell down the front of his body. One for the past, one for the present, and one for the future. The epaulettes came down to the juncture of his biceps, where they formed a sharp point. And in the middle rose a deep, bloodred stone. A stone that had been named the eye of the dragon. They charged him and kept his armor invincible.

He's even conjured the suit. . . .

Nick was too young to know how to do that. It normally took a Malachai years to master this much power.

And when the others came in to attack, Nick exploded them with his fire blasts.

When the last creature had disintegrated, Nick turned toward her. In the dim light, she saw his eyes flash red. His features perfectly formed, he didn't look fifteen. She saw the man he would soon be.

No, she saw the Malachai. Eyes that flashed from red to yellow to blue and back again. Until they finally settled on their human blue.

Ironically, that was more eerie than when they'd been yellow or red.

It made him look human. Vulnerable.

Things the Malachai could never be.

He stalked toward her with a hatred blazing in those eyes that left her trembling. She braced herself to fight, but just as she would have lifted her sword, it went flying from her hands—torn out of her grasp by an unseen force.

"Nick?"

He tilted his head as if he didn't understand her. Flashing his fangs, he seized her by the throat and shoved her back against the rock wall. Kody grabbed his wrist, trying to force him to let go. Shrieking, she used every piece of strength she had.

It wasn't enough.

Help me. . . .

Nick smelled the blood of the woman he held. It was stronger than human. Heady. Sweet. He wanted to sink his fangs in and taste it. To hear her beg for his mercy.

We don't hurt people. That voice . . . it was vaguely familiar.

Like the woman he held.

Kill her!

He tightened his grip.

"Nick," she choked out. "Nick . . . please."

Nick. He looked at his hand. The skin was a swirling pattern of red and black. No. Not his hand. A stranger's hand . . .

Confused, he frowned at the woman he seemed to know. Memories surged. Or were they dreams?

He wasn't sure.

Until she reached up and laid one tender hand on his cheek. That one, soft touch, light as a feather's kiss, shattered the anger and hatred he felt.

His eyelids were suddenly heavy. But as he lowered them, he remembered her touch. Her taste.

"Kody," he breathed her name like a prayer even though his demon's voice rattled like thunder over the river. He allowed her to pull his hand away from her throat. Bracing himself for her attack, he felt his hatred surging again.

Until she kissed the hand he'd had around her throat.

Kody knew she had to move slowly. In this form, Nick was little more than an angry toddler in the body of the most lethal being ever born. At this stage, the Malachai controlled him and not the other way around.

He trembled as he cupped her cheek with his clawed hand.

"You remember me?" she asked.

Nodding, he dipped his head toward hers. Even in his demon's form, Kody welcomed his kiss. She should hate him, and yet, even like this, she saw the real him, and it wasn't a monster. Her Nick could love, and most of all, he held her heart.

Nick breathed her in as she kissed him, and his senses reeled. He was a creature of hate and brutality.

She was a creature of light and tenderness. It was in his blood to destroy her kind.

Only he didn't want to. Especially not when she wrapped her arms around his shoulders and held him close against her. And then she started singing to him in a low tone, her breath tickling his ear. A soft *berceuse* like his mother used to sing to him when he'd been a child. He let the sound of her voice and the softness of her hand in his hair wash over him. It bathed him in something even warmer than his hatred.

He was fully content to stay here.

Until a sharp, stabbing pain bisected his chest.

Kody pulled away with a gasp. As soon as she did, she saw the spear that was shoved into his back so deeply, it protruded from his chest.

Nick staggered. The agony was unlike any pain he'd ever known. It drove him to his knees.

"Baby?" The horror in her green eyes told him that she wasn't a part of this attack.

For some reason, that strengthened him. Turning, he saw the one who'd stabbed him.

His father.

Growling, he lowered his head so that he could hone in his demon's sight on the one who'd wounded him.

Adarian put his thumb on the center of Nick's forehead as he'd done before. Only this time, Nick didn't feel the piercing pain. "Sorry, son. But I need—"

His father didn't get to finish that sentence. Nick had broken off the blade protruding from his chest and used it to stab Adarian.

"Never underestimate a backwoods Cajun in a fight, old man." He shoved Adarian back.

Gaping, Adarian caught himself. He looked down at the gaping wound Nick had left in his abdomen, then back at him. His own blood covered his hands.

Nick licked his lips as the smell hit him. Whenever one Malachai consumed another, he took his powers. His strengths, but none of his weaknesses. If he were to mix Adarian's with his . . .

He laughed. No one would ever be able to command him then. He wouldn't have to fear Noir or anyone else.

With that thought foremost in his mind, he took a step forward.

Adarian turned and vanished.

Nick started after him. But just as he spread his wings to take flight, he felt that precious hand on his arm.

"Let him go."

Still, he didn't listen.

Not until her lips grazed his. That shattered his bloodlust and started a new fire inside him.

Kody smiled at him, then grimaced as if something pained her. It was only then he realized that his father's spear had gone straight through him, into Kody.

No . . .

Not her.

"Nekoda?"

Her legs buckled.

Nick scooped her up in his arms. Her blood was smeared across his armor and her beautiful skin. Her features paled.

She lifted her hand to touch his lips. "Your blood is poison to my kind."

His stomach shrank. "I'll get you help."

"You can't. I can't go to a human doctor." She closed her eyes.

"Stay with me," he growled fiercely.

A small tear fell down her cheek. One that ripped him apart. She was always so tough and larger than life that he forgot just how tiny she was. She barely weighed anything in his arms.

"You're a creature of death, Nick. You can't command me to live. That power doesn't belong to you."

Unimaginable grief tore through him as he thought about living without her. The hole it would leave inside him. It was bleak and painful . . .

He couldn't breathe.

And it was then he knew the truth.

He loved her. She was the strength that got him through his hardest days. The sound of her voice . . . the touch of her hand. Those were what he craved most. Not her blood.

Her life.

I love her. Now he understood what people had tried to tell him. *This* was what love felt like. But it wasn't pleasant. It stabbed him with more ferocity than his father had done. Gah, it sucked to realize that someone else meant more to you than you did. No wonder Acheron disdained it so.

The Atlantean was right. You gave a part of yourself to another. A part you couldn't reclaim. And it was gone before you even knew it.

He had no idea when or how he'd given her his heart. But he couldn't deny the desolation inside him with the thought of losing her forever.

I have to find help.

Bring her to me, Malachai, and I'll save her for you.

This time, he knew whose voice taunted him. "Noir?"

Yes. Come to me, Ambrosius. And I'll take care of you both.

Nick started to obey, then caught himself. Street-wise and tough, he wasn't anyone's fool. "I'll take care of you both" sounded like a threat to him.

Kody gasped, drawing his attention back to her and the seconds of her life that were running out of her and down his arms.

What should he do? She would die any minute now.

Her life or an eternity of slavery for him?

Kody's words haunted him now. *Sometimes our choices are only between lesser evils. But they are our choices alone to make.*

Was this fate or free will?

He didn't know. And honestly, right now, he didn't care. A decision had to be made, right or wrong.

Life or death?

Slavery or freedom?

CHAPTER 13

Kody came awake in the softest bed she'd ever been in. Panic tore her apart as she remembered what had happened. She'd gone after Nick to protect him and had been stabbed by his father.

The last thing she remembered was Nick in his demon's form. The form that kept him from feeling anything for anyone. Yet the fierce Ambrosius Malachai had been crying as he held her and begged her not to die.

Noir . . .

He'd offered Nick a bargain for her life.

"Oh Nick," she whispered. *Please tell me you didn't.*

Glancing around the room, she frowned. She lay on an old-fashioned Rice bed. The hand-carved testers rose almost the whole way to the ornate ceiling that formed a dome over her. The lower part of the tray was painted sky blue with clouds. In the high arch overhead, someone had painted it to look like an ancient temple. Her heavy down cover was a deep, rich navy laced with gold and burgundy threads.

She sat up, then immediately wished she hadn't as a wave of nausea and pain hit her. It was only then she saw that she was wearing a white flannel nightgown. Warm and toasty, granted, but . . .

This was starting to freak her out. Who had removed her clothes? What had happened to her?

Where was she? She knew she wasn't dead. Somehow she'd returned to the human realm. But how?

Looking inside her gown, she saw the jagged scar where she'd been stabbed. *All right, their fight in the Fringe Realm hadn't been a dream. . . .*

And now she was starting to get angry. Who had dared to touch her while she'd been unconscious?

What had happened to Nick? And most important, where was Nick now?

"So you're back among the living."

She lifted her head out of her gown to find Caleb standing in the doorway. He had his dark hair brushed back from his face, which only emphasized how handsome a man he was.

If he just didn't have that little demon infestation problem . . .

"I'm at your house?" she asked.

"You don't have to sound so offended. I do have people clean it, you know?"

"Sorry." She sighed wearily. "You have no idea how confusing it is to wake up in a strange place with no idea how you got there."

Caleb laughed. "Sure I do. Happens to me frequently."

She rolled her eyes at his frightening lifestyle. "Yes, but I woke up in this bed alone."

He sucked his breath in sharply. "Low blow, Kode."

Maybe, but . . . "Are you going to tell me how I got here and who undressed me?"

He held his hands up in surrender. "That be your boy,

not me. You want to bitch-slap somebody, I'll fetch Nick. He's the one who brought you here."

That concerned her even more. "Did he say anything to you about what happened?"

"Only that you two were attacked, and you went down. He needed someplace safe to put you until you could heal. We both decided taking you to his place would be a huge mistake. His mom would ground him until retirement if he did that, not to mention, she'd want to know how you got stabbed, and why you both weren't in the hospital.

True. On all accounts.

And none of this was allaying her fears. She should be dead. How had he saved her?

Not one of the possibilities appealed to her. They all ended with Nick doing himself harm.

"Where is he now?"

Caleb checked his watch. "As of an hour ago, Sanctuary. He and his mom should be heading over to school in a few, for parent-teacher conferences." He dropped his arm and narrowed his gaze at her. "You're making me nervous with the intensity of your interrogation. What do you know that I don't?"

"Noir offered him a bargain. We need to know if he took it."

Caleb went white as a sheet before he started cursing under his breath. "He seemed like normal Nick to me when I saw him. But now you have me worried, too. That boy finds more trouble . . ."

She wouldn't argue that. Much like Bubba and Mark, you couldn't leave Nick alone for five minutes that he wasn't getting into something he shouldn't. Or that something wasn't trying to eat him. Either way, watching his back was a full-time job.

She let out a long breath. "How long have I been out?"

"Almost four days."

She cringed in reaction. Four days? Really? "Are you serious?"

"Why would I joke about that?"

"I don't know. You're a daeva. Some of you can be really twisted."

"I'll remind you of that the next time you need someone to save your sorry butt."

She ignored his threat. He'd come when she called. He was terribly dependable that way. "So what all have I missed?"

"Main thing. School was canceled today, and no," he added quickly, "I didn't set anything on fire to cause it. It's that stupid Web site that we're still trying to locate. The owner has people going at each other like animals. There were eight fights before yesterday's homeroom alone. So Head has called meetings between faculty, students, and parents in an effort to allay parental fears and to find the party responsible . . . which makes me really glad I'm not Goth or Emo."

Weird segue that she definitely didn't take with him. "Why?"

He made a sound of disgust. "Who do you think they're targeting? Head is convinced it has to be 'one of those weirdo, depressed kids,' 'cause you know, they're all cutters and social rejects."

Of course they were. "He doesn't have a clue about his students, does he?"

"Nope. Even if you bought him one, I doubt he'd understand it. But given his attitude, I'd love to introduce him to Acheron and watch his head explode."

She gave a short laugh. Yeah, Ash would definitely throw his preconceived stereotype out the window.

"Give me a couple of minutes to get dressed. Then we need to go find Nick."

Nick sighed in frustration as they sat outside the office, waiting for the secretary to make a copy of his transcript for his mother's records. He was thinking the woman must have taken the long way to the copy machine, including a scenic route through Europe.

He had way too much to do to be stuck here. . . .

But at least Kyrian was coming to pick him up. After he'd been attacked, neither Kyrian nor his mom would let him near a door to the outside after dark.

Impatient to leave, he stood up and started pacing the small walk area in the center of the waiting room. He wanted to rant over the secretary being part snail, but he knew his mom wouldn't tolerate it.

Everyone deserves your respect, Nick. Especially those who are doing work for you and making your life easier. God bless them for it.

Yeah, she didn't have a sense of humor when anyone showed impatience with a worker.

"Oh hey, that's Nick! Nick!"

He turned to see Jill in the hallway with her brother and two older people who seemed vaguely familiar to him. Since they looked too old to be Jill and Joey's parents, he assumed they must be the tuition donors.

Jill came rushing over to hug him.

Awkward. Why did some girls do that? He didn't like to be touched much anyway. Unless it was Kody.

This . . . this was intrusive.

Help me.

She squeezed his arm as she made him walk toward the door. "Nick, you have to meet our sponsors." She smiled at them. "This is the Nick I was telling you about who has the same last name you do."

"Ah." The man held his hand out to Nick. He seemed decent enough. His graying hair appeared to have been brown in his youth. Dressed in a nice brown sweater and khakis, he oozed an aura of Garden District or Kenner old money. As did his accent and diction. "It's a pleasure to meet another Gautier. I know Jill thinks the world of you. It's Nick this and Nick that, all the time."

Giggling, Jill turned as red as her blouse.

"Most people do think the world of my Nicky . . . Dad. He's a good kid. Honor student. Here on a *full* scholarship. Was one of the best football players they had until he was benched with an injury. And he's already working, saving up money for college. Not to mention, he does a lot of charity work. Every morning, he gets up early and goes down to Ms. Liza's doll store so that he can wash off her sidewalks and balcony before she gets to work and he gues to school. He doesn't even charge her for it."

Nick wasn't sure what stunned him most. His mother's bragging on him or the fact that he was standing in front of his real grandparents.

No wonder they'd seemed familiar. Some part of him must have remembered them from the one time he'd seen them passing by in the mall.

And now that he knew, he definitely saw how much his mother favored hers.

Rising to her feet, his mother moved to stand beside him. "Nick, meet your grandparents. You've always been curious about them. Here they are."

Jill's jaw dropped while Joey went bug-eyed. "I thought you said you didn't have any children, Mr. Gautier?"

His grandparents drew up like two swollen cantaloupes. It was obvious they weren't happy with Jill remembering that.

Mr. Gautier looked down his nose at Nick. "I've heard he cheated to get into school here."

His mom cast a scornful glare at her father. "That's jealousy talking. But they did make him take the test twice, because they were so stunned by his superior performance. And he had the same score both times on two entirely different tests. One hundred percent. He missed nothing and even got the bonuses. Apparently in all the one hundred and thirty years the school's been operating, my Nicky is the only one to make a perfect score. He's been courted by some of the best Ivy League schools in the country ever since."

Wow, his mom never bragged about anything. She disdained it. *Be humble in thought and humble in action. Most of all be humble in tongue.* She'd harped on that as much as she did "honor thy mother" and the Golden Rule, et cetera.

It was Mrs. Gautier's turn to be snotty. "You still working in that henhouse, selling yourself for money?"

His mother curled her lip. "I *never* did that."

"Not what I was told."

"Then someone lied, and no, I don't work there. I'm a day manager for a restaurant. Have been for over a year now."

"You expect me to believe that?" Her father raked Nick with a sneer. "Anymore than I believe what you're saying about *him*. Good grief, look at him. How many fights has he been in?"

His mother opened her mouth to respond, but before she could, Kyrian came into the office to pick him up for work.

Dressed in a black Armani suit with a black shirt and black-and-white tie, he looked every bit the rich businessman and prince he'd once been. His blond hair was perfectly styled and if Nick didn't miss his guess, those were two-thousand-dollar-a-pair loafers on his feet.

And for once, he wasn't wearing his sunglasses inside.

He stopped gallantly in front of them. "Cherise, *ma petite,* am I early?"

She smiled up at him. "No . . . Kyrian." She no doubt had to force herself to say his name since she always insisted they call him Mr. Hunter. "Perfect timing."

He returned her smile. "Nick, I had to put the Bentley and Aston Martin in the shop for oil changes. I'm afraid I was stuck with only two-seaters to drive tonight so I'm in the Lamborghini. But since I don't want you walking home after that vicious mugging, so Ash said he'd be here in a few minutes to pick you up in his Jag. Is that all right?"

Nick was even more stunned.

Kyrian *never* threw his cars out like that. In that moment, he could kiss his boss for his mind-reading abilities.

"Sure." Nick smiled. "He's already promised me I get to drive it."

"Oh hey, Kyrian. Cherise . . . Nick, how you feeling, son?" Madaug's father, Dr. St. James, came into the office and put a kind hand on Nick's shoulder. "Madaug told me what happened. You poor thing. And on your way to help Ms. Liza close her store. She's so heart-broken."

"Yes, sir, and I feel terrible about that. I keep telling her it wasn't her fault, but she won't listen."

"Yeah, Liza's bad that way." Dr. St. James jumped then reached into his pocket. "Work as always. And I better answer this. Y'all take care. I'll see you later."

"Good night," Nick called after him.

His grandfather scowled. "How do you know Dr. St. James's son?"

Nick shrugged. "We became friends while I was tutoring him." Kind of true. But if he told them that they had bonded due to a mind-control game that had turned players into zombies that Madaug had unleashed on the school, it might not go over well.

"Tutor? Madaug?" his grandfather asked incredulously, as if he couldn't believe Nick could read, never mind help someone else. "But Madaug's a genius."

"In computers and science. He reeks in English and social studies."

Yeah, they didn't want anything to do with him and his mom. It was obvious by the revulsion on their faces, and disdain in their eyes.

"C'mon, Jill and Joey, we need to leave."

His mother didn't say a word until they were gone, then she turned around and hugged Kyrian. "Thank you so much for that, Mr. Hunter! You are the best."

Kyrian shrugged her hold away. "No problem. I live to please."

"And that you definitely did tonight. Thank you so much." She ruffled Nick's hair. "And you be careful and I'll see you later."

"Yes, ma'am."

As soon as the secretary handed her the papers, they all went outside, where Kyrian had his car parked on the street in front of the school.

Nick slowed down as he saw a parked police car and the officers walking around with a picture they were showing to his classmates. Police at his school was never a good thing.

When they got to Stone, he pointed to Nick. "He's right there!"

Nick went cold. What the heck was going on?

The police made a beeline right to him. The biggest of the two narrowed his eyes. "Are you Nicholas Gautier?"

"Yeah."

"Then you're coming with us."

Nick laughed nervously. "I don't think so."

"Yeah, well, we do."

"No," his mother said sharply. "My son isn't going anywhere."

"Yes, ma'am, he is. We have a warrant for his arrest."

"For what?" he and his mother asked simultaneously.

"Rape and theft."

CHAPTER 14

The look on his mother's face would haunt him forever as the cop grabbed him and shoved him against the hood of his squad car, right in front of the school for everyone to see. Nick grimaced as the cops rudely frisked him, then cuffed his hands behind his back. Once he was secured, the biggest officer grabbed him by the hair and wrenched him off the car.

"Mama, I didn't do it. I didn't. I swear to God!"

"That's what they all say." The cop looked over at his partner. "Wouldn't it be nice if, just once, they confessed and made our job easier?"

Tears glistened in his mother's eyes. He could

tell she wanted to believe him, but the doubt there . . .

How could she even think he'd do something like that? Even for a nanosecond. She'd been with him for fifteen years. How could she not know him better?

He did his best not to look at any of his classmates or the smirking faculty members who had no doubt he was guilty. That thought sickened him.

The only one who wasn't judging him guilty was Kyrian. "Don't worry, Nick. I'll have you out of there as soon as you're booked."

Booked. That word slammed into him so hard that for a minute, he thought he'd vomit.

"Good luck with that," the smaller officer scoffed. "With what we have on him, he's not going anywhere until trial."

What could they have on him? He hadn't done anything. Heck, he'd only been out of the hospital since yesterday.

As they were placing him in the backseat, Caleb came running up to his mom. He frowned at her as she told him what was happening.

Caleb winced, then kicked the front bumper of the squad car.

"Hey!" the smaller cop snapped. "What do you think you're doing?"

"What?" Caleb challenged. "I can't touch your car?" He kicked it again.

"Boy, do you want to go to jail?" the taller officer asked.

"For what?" Caleb braced his foot against the front fender. "It's a free country."

"Not when you're vandalizing state property it's not."

Caleb arched a defiant brow at him. "State property? My tax dollars bought this car then. Doesn't that make it *my* property?"

"Oh, that's it, you little punk." The cop went for Caleb.

Caleb scoffed. "C'mon, really? What are you charging me with?"

"Vandalism."

Caleb rolled his eyes, then shouted out to their classmates. "Come, see the violence inherent in the system! Help! I'm being repressed!"

"Get your ass in the car!" the cop snarled, his Yat accent coming out full force.

They put Caleb in on the other side.

Nick gaped at him. "What are you doing?"

Caleb glanced askance at the cops as they called in his arrest. "Where you go, I go, Gautier. And there's no way you're going into a jail without backup. You're about to find out why Adarian lives in a prison."

Nick wasn't sure what to think of that, other than the fact his father was a mass murderer. "What do you mean?"

The cops opened the doors and got in.

There are some things that defy explanation—kind of like . . . you know, you. Not to mention your loco mindset when you did whatever it was that you did when you saved Kody, or why the color of the dryer lint always matches the color of your missing sock. He projected his answer to Nick's mind. *A Malachai in jail is definitely one of those inexplicable things.*

Caleb turned his attention back to the police. "So what tort am I being held for again?"

They didn't respond to Caleb. Instead the larger cop sighed irritably. "I hate the smart-mouthed kids the most."

Caleb leaned forward in his seat. "So who's the meanest person you've ever arrested?"

"What are you doing?" Nick gasped.

Caleb cracked an evil grin. "You have things you can't resist doing. This is one that is a moral imperative to me." *Must rankle bullies.*

You're going to get jack-slapped.

Caleb frowned at him. *Jack-slapped?*

Slapped so hard you forget everything you know, i.e., you don't know Jack . . . jack-slapped.

Caleb rolled his eyes.

Nick didn't say anything else as he sat there, trying to figure out why they would think he'd raped someone when it was the most repugnant crime he could think of. Who had accused him?

And why?

When they got to the jail, they were gruffly hauled out of the car and into the building.

As soon as they stepped through the doorway,

Nick saw a familiar face, but he wasn't sure what to make of it.

Virgil Ward, attorney at law. And in Virgil's case, blood-sucking attorney took on a whole new meaning, since he was also a vampire. His dark hair was short, but slightly shaggy. With it brushed back from his face, he didn't appear much older than Nick or Caleb . . . to Nick, anyway. But Virgil managed to project a much older persona to everyone else. Those around him saw Virgil as someone in his midthirties. Dressed in a tailor-made, expensive black pinstriped suit and a pair of black Ferragamo shoes, he wore a dark purple shirt and a dark gray, purple, and black tie that had miniature skeleton bunny heads and crossed bones all over it.

"Gentlemen," he said, inclining his head to the officers escorting them. "These are my clients. I trust you'll take good care of them."

The larger officer growled in frustration. "I should have known. . . . I suppose you want them put into the special holding section."

"It would be prudent."

The other officer growled again. "They're not going to start eating each other or one of us, are they?"

Virgil laughed. "They're not zombies, men. But one of them does have special dietary concerns you might want to note."

The larger officer grumbled.

Virgil winked at Nick, then projected his thoughts to him. *Don't worry, kid. I know it's your first time here. But we're set up to deal with our* special needs *detainees.*

Special needs? *Dude, I don't ride the short bus.*

Good for you. 'Cause some days, I definitely do.

That was not comforting when coming out of the mouth of your attorney.

As they walked past a group of deadly-looking gangbangers, one of the bigger members lunged at Nick with a snarl as if he was going to attack him. The moment the man did, it sent an electrical charge through Nick. One that put all of his senses on high alert and made his heart race with gleeful expectation. Suddenly Nick saw and heard everything with a shocking clarity. And instead of cowering, he lunged at the gang member, wanting to taste his blood.

The man's eyes widened, before he backed down.

Against his conscious will, Nick tried to break out of the policeman's hold so that he could go back to the gangbanger.

Caleb cut him off. "Look at me, Nick."

For several heartbeats, he couldn't understand what Caleb had said.

"Nick!" he shouted.

That finally broke through the cloudy haze. "W-w-what?"

"Remember what I said about your father?"

Yeah . . . Nick felt it, too. Being around this many people who were corrupted by hatred and rage and violence, it was like being a wind-up toy that someone had snapped the spring in. His powers were fully charged and he felt more alive than he ever had. It was a heady concoction.

He looked at Caleb. "Do you get the same . . ." He wasn't sure what to call it.

"Thrill? Not to the extent you do. That fun little nugget is unique to your species alone."

And he was right. He totally got it now why his

father stayed in prison. It was like breathing in fresh air and sunshine. Bad analogy since only an idiot would breathe in the foul body odor, urine, and vomit stench that permeated the building, but that was the closest example he could think of.

The cops took them to a special booking room that was reserved for Virgil's clients. They were rudely searched, fingerprinted, and then photographed. Honestly, Nick wanted to cry as it brought back his one and only other arrest when he'd been a kid. And while they'd hauled him to the station in their car, they hadn't "booked" him. It was so humiliating. He glanced over to Caleb as guilt stabbed him. *He* was the only reason Caleb was here.

God love Caleb for his loyalty.

Nick cringed as he looked down at the bright orange jumpsuit they'd forced him to change into. Heck, they'd even confiscated his shoelaces. "I'm sorry, Cale. I didn't mean to get you into this."

He shrugged. "Trust me, this is neither the worst nor the most humiliating thing I've ever gone through. And while we're here, you should pray that this is the worst thing that ever happens to you."

Point well taken. Still, it stung. While he hadn't always been the best person and had done some questionable things, he'd never really thought he'd ever be arrested for real, with real felony charges that carried a hefty prison sentence if he was found guilty. That was the kind of thing that happened to people like his father and the scum his father ran with.

And now it had happened to him.

They were escorted to a room that had a single holding cell. Luckily, it was empty. The cops put them inside it, then had them hold their arms through the bars so that they could uncuff them. Once the cops were gone, Virgil came in to talk to them.

"Rape and theft, huh?"

"I didn't do it."

Virgil didn't respond to his statement. "They claim they have you on surveillance."

Nick shook his head. "It's a lie. I didn't do anything."

Caleb leaned against the bars. "When did the alleged crimes occur?"

Virgil pulled out his PDA and opened a file. "The theft was late last night just before midnight at a jewelry store, where you took cash and a single necklace. And the rape occurred around 3 A.M. Where were you at those times?"

"Home. In bed."

Virgil made a note. "You have any witnesses?"

"No. I was in bed alone."

"Poor you. In more ways than one. Without someone to corroborate your whereabouts . . . and with them having photographic evidence . . ." Virgil grimaced. "Look me in the eyes, kid."

Nick did.

After a minute, Virgil blinked, then made another note. "Okay, you're telling the truth. By the way, Nick, you have the most screwed-up life. You're either boring as all get out, or you're about to die. There's no middle ground with you. You might want to work on that."

No kidding.

"So what do you think they'll do to him?" Caleb asked.

"I wish I had a better answer for you, but . . . It all depends on who our judge is. We can have his mom say he was home. However, the prosecutor is going to say that kids slip out of their homes all the time without their parents knowing it. Nick has a bad record for violence at school."

"Defending myself!"

"They won't bring up the why," Virgil said coldly, "only the fact that you've been in trouble, many times, for fighting at school. And that you were recently hospitalized for fighting."

"I wasn't fighting!"

Virgil arched a brow at him. "Given your record, do you think any judge or jury will buy the fact that you laid on the ground while someone hit you and you didn't fight back?"

Nick winced. Another valid point. But . . . it was the truth.

"You should have filed a mugging report," Virgil said under his breath.

Nick growled at him. "I didn't want to get the kid into trouble."

"No good deed goes unpunished. And for that, you might spend the rest of your life in prison. Go you."

Nick refused to believe that. It couldn't happen that way. It couldn't. "I thought the law was all about getting to the truth?"

Virgil burst out laughing. "Stop watching *Law and Order*, kid. Courts don't care about the truth. The only thing that matters is what you can prove. It's not 'innocent until proven guilty.' It's 'I have an open case log thicker than the New Orleans and surrounding parishes phone books and I need to close some of them.' So until you prove to me that I arrested the wrong person, you're going to jail, buddy, and I'm closing at least one case this week."

Nicks stomach heaved. That was not what he'd been raised believing. But if anyone knew how the legal system worked, it would be Virgil.

"I just want to go home."

Vigil smiled sympathetically. "I know, Nick." He checked his watch. "Let me go see if I can rush this along and get you a bail hearing tonight. In the event I can't, or that you need something during daylight hours, let me give you my business partner's card. His name is William Laurens and he's one of the best litigators there is, second to me, of course." After pulling out the card, he handed it to Nick.

Nick frowned as he read the card. "This says Bill Laurens, paralegal."

"Ah crap, wrong card. Sorry. Have no idea why that's still in my pocket. Bill's my partner's oldest son and he interned with us as a paralegal while he was in law school. He's now one of our junior partners." He handed Nick the correct card. "You could call Bill, but I'd rather you deal directly with either me or William."

"All right." Nick tucked the card into his pocket. "By the way, who called you?"

"Kyrian Hunter called William and William called me. Be grateful. Without notice, you'd have been taken through general procedures, which goes a whole lot slower, and they would have put you in a holding cell with some exceptionally fun people."

"Believe me, I am grateful. Even if I am in here with an undesirable." Nick glanced askance at Caleb.

Caleb made a noise of pain. "Next time, Gautier, you go alone."

Virgil checked his watch again. "All right. You two sit tight for a few and let me go see if I can work some magic for you." His gaze went to Caleb. "Kicking a police car? Really?"

Caleb shrugged. "Car offended me. It was sitting right where I wanted to stand. What would you do?"

"Made sure there was no surveillance, then sucked the cops blood dry, and blown the car up."

Caleb laughed. "Hos-tile. I love it. You and me could be friends." He glanced over to Nick. "As for why, I had to do something for them to lock me up with snot-nose, and I didn't want it to be anything too serious since I would like to leave, sooner rather than later. I've got enough things hunting me. I really don't need anything else."

"I feel that pain myself, brother." Virgil slid his PDA into his pocket. "I'll see you two in a bit." He started to leave, then stopped. "I know you, don't I?" he asked Nick.

"About a year ago, you helped us out. We were with Bubba and Mark at the time."

His eyes brightened with recall, then they widened with substantial interest. He pointed at Nick, but looked at Caleb. "He's *your* Nick."

Caleb saluted him. "You're a little slow on the up-take tonight, Virg. You down a few pints?"

"Freshly fed and . . . we *really* have to get him out of here." He practically ran out of the room.

Nick turned a probing stare to Caleb. "What aren't you telling me?"

"The longer you stay in a place with concentrated malice, and let's face it, this is a cesspit of malice, the more it'll seep into you. Think of it like a tributary feeding a stream that turns into a river. The more you're around it, the more it feeds the demon side of you. The more you're likely to convert into the true Malachai."

He would be like the monster who'd almost assaulted Kody. "Is that why my father attacked my mother?"

"What do you mean?"

Nick didn't answer. Instead, he fell silent as memories went through him and he tried to make sense of it all. "I think my father loves my mother."

Caleb scoffed. "That's a delusion. Malachais are incapable of love."

Nick scowled. "I'm not."

"You haven't been fully converted yet. You're still an embryo."

Not as much of an embryo as Caleb thought. But Nick wasn't going to argue that right now.

Or let anyone know about the bargain he'd made.

"I disagree. You didn't see his face when she was yelling at him. He was hurt by it. And he couldn't have been that hurt if he didn't care about her." That was the first thing he'd learned in grade school. When someone insulted and yelled at you and you didn't have feelings for them, it angered you. Made you want to hurt them. But when you loved someone and they attacked, it raised your level of hurt more than it raised your temper.

Caleb fell silent as he considered that. "You know, that actually explains a lot about you. And a lot about Adarian."

"What do you mean?"

Caleb moved to sit on the cot underneath the bar-covered window. "Normally, a Malachai is born to parents who hate it. Both mother and father. The father because he knows if the child lives, he will die—most Malachai, including Adarian, murder their children as soon as they find out about them."

"You mean I had siblings?"

"Yeah, and he killed every one of them. Except you . . . which never made sense to me. You, he wanted protected. And the mothers hate because of the way their children were conceived, the babies. Again, your mother is different in that she embraced you. So if what you're saying is true, you are a Malachai conceived in love and nurtured. That, my friend, has *never* happened."

"Which means I can love, right?"

Caleb's gaze lost focus as he thought it over. "It means something. Not sure what. But . . ."

It gave Nick hope. Maybe he could avert his future and find a way to save them all.

Wishing he had an answer, Nick moved to the other cot, closer to the door.

"So, how did you save Kody, by the way?"

Nick cringed at the question, then hedged at the answer. "I took her to help."

"And that would be . . . ?"

"Someone who helped her."

Caleb growled low in his throat. "I don't want to play this game with you."

But it wasn't a game. It was serious business. Nick had made a pact that he knew he shouldn't have. One Ambrose had thrown down a tantrum over when he'd learned about it.

"What have you done?" Ambrose had snarled in his face.

"What I had to."

Ambrose had held his hands out like he was choking Nick. "A dog can't serve two masters."

"I'm not a dog."

Ambrose curled his lip. "You're so stupid. I knew I should have killed you."

Nick had snorted. "Wow, that hurts me in my tender place. Nice to hear me say I wished myself dead. Love you, too."

Ambrose shook his head. "You don't understand. I made your mistake . . . later in life, but I did the same exact thing. I bound myself to my enemy and it did not work out well."

"But we're changing the future. Right? For all you know, I might have already fixed things."

Ambrose had paused in the circle he was pacing around Nick's room. "That's where it gets tricky. There are things that will happen regardless of the actions we take."

"Such as?"

"You meeting Kyrian and working for him. No matter what I've tried, that always happens. I can't stop it. I can only change the events that lead up to it and the time in our life when it happens. That one moment of meeting him, however, is written in stone. But . . ." Ambrose squinted as he ruminated. When he spoke again, his voice was a full octave lower. "You might have found the answer for us."

"What do you mean?"

"Why did you save Kody?"

Nick pressed his lips together as he debated telling him. But in the end, it wouldn't matter. One way or another, Ambrose would learn the truth. "I love her."

Ambrose sneered. "Love? You don't even know the meaning of that word."

"Oh yes, I do. Don't you dare tell me I don't."

Ambrose shook his head. "You're too young to understand it."

"No, I'm not. I know what I feel and I know it's real. I would die for her."

"Then you're even dumber than . . ." Ambrose paused as his eyes danced around. He closed the distance between them and smiled a smile that made Nick's blood run cold. "We are destined to become a Dark-Hunter. That, too, I haven't been able to avert. Until now, the catalyst has always been the death of our mother. But . . ."

Nick wasn't sure he liked the sound of that word. "But what?"

"If you love another woman, a woman I've never known existed before, then maybe she's the one who dies instead."

Agony exploded inside him. "No! You're wrong."

"Think about it." Ambrose jerked him into a tight hug. "You're right, kid. You may have found the answer I've sought all these years. That has to be it. You love Kody enough to die for her. It only stands to reason that she'd be the one you lose to launch you into a DH."

That was not what he wanted to hear. While Ambrose might enjoy the thought, it made Nick ill.

"I won't let her die. I won't."

Anger turned Ambrose's eyes a deep shade of red. "Listen to me, moron. Who would you rather bury? Your mother or your girlfriend? 'Cause I'm telling you right now, one of them is going to die horribly."

"I won't allow it."

"You have no choice." Ambrose had spat those words out coldly.

Now, Nick was feeling the truth of Ambrose's prediction. By trying to keep Kody alive, he'd already screwed up. Badly.

And as he stared at the glass over the window, he saw images appear.

In one, he saw his mother in a chair inside a house he'd never been in before. Her lifeless eyes were wide open as he called out for her to wake up.

In the other, he saw an older version of Kody. Dressed in a white wedding gown, she lay in his arms, covered in blood. *Her* blood.

It's your imagination. It had to be.

Yet inside, he knew the truth. Those were the two

possible futures for him. Just like Ambrose had said. One of them would have to die.

He might not have saved Kody at all—only delayed her death. Ambrose had talked about rearranging time frames. He could change when things happened, but not the things that were destined to happen.

Instead of saving Kody, he might only have bought her a little more time. *That's better than nothing.*

Or was it? Had he let her die, his life wouldn't be so complicated. He'd have never made a bargain that might very well be the death of him.

The more he thought about it, the more he hated the Fates or Ambrose or whoever was causing this to be his future. It wasn't fair to see what was coming and to have no way to avert it. That was the cruelest blow of all. And the more his anger built, the more his body temperature elevated.

"Nick?" There was a note of panic in Caleb's voice. "What's going on in your head?"

Sitting on his cot in their cell, Nick lost his ability to understand Caleb. Instead, all he could see, hear, or feel was his own anguish. It wrapped around him until it suffocated him. No matter what he did, it only made things worse.

It killed the people he loved.

The darkness swallowed him again, but this time it was inside and not outside his body. And it hurt so deep in his essence that he felt like his very soul was being flogged and flayed.

He was standing out on a ledge, looking down at a landscape that terrified him.

This was his life and he'd already ruined it. Fifteen and it was over. The damage done, and so deep that it couldn't be unraveled.

"Nick!"

He ignored Caleb as his pain tripled. And in that one moment when it hurt the most, he had total clarity.

There was only one way to stop the pain. It was extreme, but . . .

If it worked, it would stop everything.

Don't do this. It would destroy his mother.

She dies anyway. Or Kody would.

And he heard Kody's precious voice in his head.

We all make our own decisions.

It was time he made his. If the darkness wanted him, it could take him.

With one condition.

The answer had been here the whole time. This . . . this crap would end tonight. He would make sure of it.

"Nick!" Caleb shook him, trying to make him understand his voice. But he wasn't getting through whatever had sunk its fangs into him.

Worse, Caleb saw the physical manifestation of the Malachai powers. Nick's skin flashed from its human tawny shade to the swirling demon skin. His eyes from blue to orange to red . . .

If Caleb didn't stop this, if he didn't find a way to reach Nick before the demon swallowed him, all of them would die.

CHAPTER 15

D o you really want to die?"

That question hung in Nick's mind, taunting him. In his dream, he looked out into a field and there he saw his future. For the next two years, he'd be a laughingstock in school. Everyone had seen him arrested.

Everyone.

Even his grandparents.

The horror of his mother's expression . . . The doubt in her eyes.

And what waited for him? More loss. Either his mother or Kody. And others Ambrose refused to name. Why should he continue living when the cost of it would be their lives?

If he were dead, there would be no reason for any of them to die. That would stop it completely. It would. They would be free. His father would no longer be after him to kill him.

The pain that had lived inside him since the hour of his birth would end. *I'm so sick of it all.* And he was. At fifteen, he felt like a battered old man. Life was so hard. Some days it seemed like the only purpose of it was to see just how hard it could kick him. How low it could make him sink. It had needlessly slapped him senseless most days. And for what?

Why did it have to be like this? Why did people have to be so mean for no reason whatsoever? Why did they have to attack? Bring someone down?

End it.

You can control that much of your life.

Suddenly, Grim was beside him. He was dressed in a flowing black robe, his face barely visible from inside his cowl. In his hand, he held a black knife that looked like a military KA-BAR. Silently, he held it out to Nick.

One cut.

One moment of one last pain.

Everything would be over. He would hurt no more.

As Nick reached for the knife, he felt another presence beside him.

"Don't do it, Nick. This isn't you." Kody. The sound of that sweet, soft voice reached out and touched him in places he didn't fully understand. She covered his hand with hers and then laced her fingers with his. They were so soft as they slid against his skin.

"Close your eyes," she breathed in his ear.

Without question, he obeyed. His head swam as images blurred through his mind in rapid succession. He didn't know what he was looking at. Not until Kody kissed him.

She pulled back and laid her hand to his hot cheek. Then she spoke to him in a language he'd never heard before. Yet, he understood her words perfectly.

"There's an enemy inside all of us, Nick, that wants to do us harm. It hates us passionately, and it wears us down with echoing insults we can't escape. No matter what we try or what we do. It's a never-ending play-back that torments us when we're alone. And especially at night when we're trying to sleep and there's no one else beside us."

The love in her eyes scorched him as she stroked his cheek with her thumb. "But somehow our sanity returns, and drives that madness away. And we are *not* what that voice says we are. We're stronger than that, and our dark, ugly interloper knows it. I think that's why it hates us so much. Because it knows that we alone can defeat it. We can send it back to the darkest part of our nature where it belongs. Bury it so deep that we drown out those voices that hurt and torture us. It does not have to control us, and we don't have to listen."

She smiled up at him. "No one is immune to the dark interloper. We all feel that those wounds won't heal. That they go too deep and let so much blood that it floods our souls with utter agony. That we have screwed up beyond repair. But it's not true. What we have, Nick, is one life. And every day of it is the richest blessing. The bad times teach us lessons about ourselves and others. But most of all, they show us just how strong we are. For we survive what destroys a lesser being, and every day that we live is victory over that interloper. You and I are like creatures. We are not sheep to be slaughtered. We are fighters, and in the midst of our darkest battles, we don't lie down and get stepped on. We shake our fists at the sky and shout, 'Bring me your worst. Because I intend to give you my best and I will win no matter what it takes. You may knock me down, I can't stop that. But I will get back up, and when I do, your blood will be the blood spilled.'"

He wanted to believe that. He did. "I'm so tired, Kody," he breathed. "It just keeps coming with no let-up. Everything I do is wrong. Everything I touch turns to crap, and I'm sick to death of being blamed for things I haven't done."

"That's the interloper talking, not you. I know my Nick. My Nick is strong."

He licked his lips as his pain intensified. "If I live, you or my mother will die. What's the point?"

"What's the point?" she asked incredulously. "The point is to savor and treasure every moment, every breath. They are precious because they are limited.

Nothing in abundance is ever held dear. It's cast off without any thought whatsoever. But happiness, victory, and life are sacred because they are fleeting and stingily measured."

"And the pain is never-ending." Talk about abundance. It was shoveled at him so fast, he was buried in it.

"Not true and you know it. Pain is even more fleeting than the other emotions. Yes, it stays for awhile sometimes, but it always goes eventually. Always. Do you remember what you told Brynna when you stopped her from killing herself?"

"That I wore tacky shirts?"

Smiling, she shook her head at him. "The rest of it?"

"Vaguely."

"You said, I know you're hurting. Believe me, I know how it feels to get your emotional teeth kicked down your throat so far that it makes you choke on the last shred of your dignity. That sick feeling in your gut that tells you, you can't take it anymore. That life sucks hard and it won't ever get better. That you're walking on the tightrope, trying to hang on with your toes 'cause you ain't got no safety net, and you're barely one sneeze away from being a stain on the floor. But you're not alone. You're not. You've got a lot of people who care about you. People who love you and who would be devastated if something ever happened to you.'"

"People who will die if I live," Nick reminded her.

"And do you really think we wouldn't be every bit as devastated if we lost *you*?"

No, he hadn't thought about that at all.

"There's always another side to everything, Nick. Two perspectives on all things. No two memories of any event are ever the same. They're all sifted through our emotional channels, which run deep, and they color every input into our brain. How many times have you argued with someone over a past event where they claim one thing happened, but you don't remember it that way?"

All the time. "But—"

She placed her hand over his lips to keep him from speaking. "Do you know what suicide is?"

"Yeah, death."

She shook her head. "It's the ultimate act of selfishness. Yes, death is painful for those who live on. Losing someone burns so deep that it never stops. Time doesn't heal it, it just dulls it for a little while. Believe me, I know. Unlike you, I *have* lost those I love. And I grieve every day of my life that I can't get ahold of them. That I can't hear their voices or see their faces. I would give anything I have, my soul, my life, if I could just hug them one more time and tell them that I love them. And how much I miss them. But again, it's because our time together is so fleeting and limited that it teaches us to savor every smile they give us. And having lived through their deaths, I can tell you this. I love them too much to make them suffer the way I have over their loss. I would rather say good-bye to them first than have them alive for years, aching for me the way I grieve for them. What do you think your mother would do if something happened to you?"

"She'd follow me to the grave." How many times had she told him that? *If anything ever happened to you, they'd have to dig two graves. I couldn't live if I lost you.*

"I *have* buried everyone I love, Nick. Please, don't be so cruel as to make me bury you, too." Tears glistened in her eyes. "I can't do it again, Nick. I can't. And I would rather give my life for you than have you give yours for me."

He covered her hand with his and savored the warmth of her touch and the words that branded themselves in his heart.

Nekoda tightened her grip on him. "If you doubt anything I say, ask Dr. Burdette why she's in New Orleans. Why she comes here every year at this time."

He frowned at her words. "Why?"

"Day after tomorrow is the anniversary of the death of Bubba's wife and son. And yesterday was the anniversary of the death of his best friend. Dr. Burdette's here because she's terrified that even all these years later, Bubba will kill himself to get away from the pain of losing the three of them."

"When did they die?"

"His wife and son, twelve years ago when his son was only two."

Nick's heart ached as he realized that Bubba's son

would have gone to school with him. They were almost the same age.

Kody nodded as she read his thoughts. "It's why
Bubba all but adopted you when you met. His son
had dark hair and blue eyes."

Just like him.

"And it's why he and Mark are such good friends."

Nick scowled at that. "I don't understand."

"Mark's older brother was Bubba's best friend. In
college they went out like millions of others their age.
They'd won a championship bowl game and had
wanted to celebrate. Bubba had too much to drink so
Mark's brother drove Bubba's truck that night. On
their way back to the dorm, for reasons no one knows,
their pickup left the road and overturned. Bubba was
thrown from the passenger side, but Mark's brother
was pinned underneath the truck. Had Bubba not been
drunk and passed out, he could have gotten help before
his friend died. Instead, Mark's brother bled to death
before another car spotted them and notified the authorities. Bubba has never forgiven himself."

That one bit explained so much about Bubba's idiosyncrasies. The poor man. And yet, Nick had known Bubba all this time, and he'd never had a clue about any of that. "Is that why he didn't go pro?"

"In part. He also didn't want to raise his son in that kind of lifestyle. Because he'd already lost his best friend, he didn't want to waste even a second of his time with his wife and child. He wanted a job that would have him home with them every night."

And still he'd lost them. It was so not right.

"But you see how our tragedies interconnect and shape us? Bubba wouldn't have had all the time he did have with his wife and son had he not lost his best friend."

Nick saw it, even though he didn't like it. "And he wouldn't teach self-defense courses if his wife hadn't died."

Kody nodded. "People aren't just ants rushing around over a crust of bread. Every life, no matter how isolated, touches hundreds of others. It's up to us to decide if those micro connections are positive or negative. But whichever we decide, it does impact the ones we deal with. One word can give someone the strength

SHERRILYN KENYON

they needed at that moment or it can shred them down to nothing. A single smile can turn a bad moment good. And one wrong outburst or word could be the tiny push that causes someone to slip over the edge into destruction."

She was definitely right about that. One touch of her hand could soothe him in a way nothing else did. Still, the voices were in his head and they were loud and clear, telling him how worthless he was. How ugly. How everyone would be better off without him.

"Do you really hear the self-loathing soundtrack in your head, too?" he asked her.

"Nick, I promise you, we all do. You know your friend Acheron?"

"Yeah."

"Have you ever seen him without dark sunglasses on?"

Now that she mentioned it . . . "No, I haven't."

"Ash is so embarrassed by his own eyes that he won't show them. At all. Not even to those he's closest to. If they ever do see them, he keeps his gaze on the floor. And have you seen the size of my butt? If it gets any bigger, it's going to be assigned its own zip code. And don't get me started on how thin and flat my hair is. Or the fact that I can't spell anything. I feel so stupid sometimes, and yet here I am able to summon powers from most dimensions. None of that matters to my inner beast that insults me every day of my life."

He narrowed his gaze suspiciously. "I think you're making all of that up. 'Cause, girl, I don't see a flaw anywhere on your body. Of course, I haven't seen your butt except when it's been covered with clothing. Maybe if you show me some of what you're talking about in the flesh . . ."

She wrinkled her nose at him. "You're awful."

He was, but in the worst moment of his life she'd made him smile. At least until his thoughts left her and returned to what had them here in this fringe area. What had possessed him in his cell. "How do you learn to function past the voices? They're always in my head on a continuous loop."

"Drown them out with music or logic. Yeah, I might not be that smart. Or beautiful. But that's not all there is to me. I matter to people. Not all people, but to the ones who matter to me, and they're the only ones in this world who count. To the darkest pit with the rest of them."

He leaned down and pressed his forehead against hers so that he could stare into her eyes. "I love you, Kody. And I hear everything you've said. But I don't think I'm strong enough to live without you."

"How do you think I feel about you?"

If that was true, she was right. How could he leave her to the agony of grief if he killed himself?

She tilted her head until she captured his lips and kissed him until his senses reeled. Her touch calmed and soothed him until he felt like himself again.

But with that sensation, he felt her leaving.

"Kody!" he called, reaching out for her. But she was already gone.

Suddenly, he slammed back into his body. Opening his eyes, he found himself in the holding cell with Caleb next to him.

Caleb let out a relieved sigh. "Thank the universe she got through to you."

Nick frowned. "What are you talking about?"

Caleb laughed bitterly. "You just experienced what I told you I couldn't explain. Whenever a Malachai gets into environments like this one, its base urge is to become violent. In the past, when that happened, it caused a Malachai to attack others. But you, my friend, turn in it inward instead of outward."

"Meaning what?"

"You become *self*-destructive."

Nick didn't understand the fearful concern in Caleb's eyes. "Is that not better?"

"Depends."

Nick was getting frustrated with Caleb's vague answers. "On?"

"If you want mankind enslaved by you or your father."

Great. Just what he wanted to hear. "You know, I'm beginning to think the only choice anyone has in life is between either a bad outcome or a worse one."

"You're right. It does seem to be the case, most times."

Nick grew quiet as three policemen came in.

"We're taking both of you to your bail hearing."

Caleb actually looked pleased. "Go, Virgil."

Nick was feeling pretty good about it, until he noticed something about the policemen. It was only a flash, but he recognized it as his powers warning him.

"Caleb, get back."

"Why?"

Using the trick Thorn had shown him, Nick summoned a firebolt. His hand glowed as a tennis ball–sized stone manifested in his palm. "They're lollers."

As Caleb moved back, one of them tossed out a bloodred chain that wrapped around Caleb's throat and held him in place.

Nick let fly his bolt into that demon's chest. He exploded into fire as the other two rushed Nick.

Caleb caught one before he could reach Nick, and broke his neck. The one attacking Nick threw a wide, telegraphed punch. Nick ducked and came up with a fist into the demon's jaw. The blow shattered his shell, causing him to disintegrate. Something that showered them with an odor so foul, Nick gagged on it.

"What kind are they?" Nick asked.

"The kind that shouldn't be here."

"How so?"

Caleb gave him a hard stare. "They're blood demons." He said that like Nick ought to know what *that* was.

Yeah. Clueless as normal. "Isn't that what Virgil is?"

"Damn, Nick, quit being bibliophobic."

Nick grimaced. "When did we quit speaking the same language?"

"Means you're afraid of books. I've never seen anyone stand toe-to-toe with a daeve and not have a shred of fear in him, yet if I hand you a book, unless it's manga, you act like it's going to bite you."

"It's not the biting that scares me, it's the boring. Besides, I like books with pictures. Manga can get pretty racy in Shonen and my mother doesn't confiscate it and ground me for reading it. Unlike other male materials that launch her into a three-week rant about how women don't look like that and how it's disrespectful to her to have it in her house."

Caleb growled at him. "You are so mature at times that you lure me into forgetting the fact that you're an embryo." He growled fiercely before he continued. "Vampires were human at one time. While humans call them demons, demons are a separate life form. I have never been human, thank the Source for that, and neither have blood demons. So named because they are created from the blood of a higher demon to serve him."

Now that sounded more interesting than scary. Definitely could come in handy one day. "Will I have that power?"

"If I don't kill you before you mature, yes."

Nick intended to stay off Caleb's menu. "Awesome. So what? Are they clones?"

"No. Not even. They're sent in to take something from the target and return it to their master so that he can gain control of that individual."

Nick went cold. "You think my father sent them?"

"No. Adarian has your blood. Besides, it's not his style. He's never subtle. Someone else sent them."

But who? "Who knows about me, or you, for that matter?"

"I don't know, Nick. But we've got to get you out of here before you break down again. Not to mention, we're both sitting ducks in this place." Caleb froze as if a thought had occurred to him. "I know you're not going to tell me because you knew it was wrong and that I should kill you for it, but do you think who or whatever you made your deal with could have sent them after you?"

Nick considered it for a few. "No."

"Any chance you'll tell me why you think that?"

"They already have something of mine. They wouldn't need to send out demons to claim any part of me."

Caleb ground his teeth until his jaw protruded. It was more than obvious he was super unhappy about Nick's bargain.

And Caleb didn't even know what it was . . . Yet.

"What did you give them?"

"Not my soul," Nick said, knowing that would be Caleb's primary concern. "Don't worry."

"I need to know. Should we get attacked—"

"We won't."

Caleb cursed. "What have you gotten us into?"

Before he could answer, Virgil returned with a single deputy. "You both owe me for this. I just laid down a critical favor to get you a bond hearing this fast."

"We won't forget," Caleb assured him.

But after they changed clothes and were hauled before the meanest-looking man Nick had ever seen, he wasn't so sure he wanted to be indebted. Virgil must have given up something big to get this guy to cooperate. He didn't know what, and he didn't *want* to know what.

The female prosecutor gestured angrily toward Nick. "It was a violent rape, Your Honor, and the defendant has a long history of violence. Look at the bruises on his face. Obviously, he was recently in another altercation with someone else. Not to mention his father—"

"I object, Your Honor." Virgil drowned out whatever she'd been about to say. "Relevance."

Glaring at him, she shoved her glasses up, higher on her nose. "Relevance is a family history of violence."

"His father is not the defendant here," Virgil fired back. "And unless you can produce a genetic expert showing that one has bearing on the other, it's irrelevant."

She bristled. "Psychologists say—"

"Do you have a psychologist who can testify?" Virgil asked.

"Not yet."

"Then I stand by what I said. I object."

The judge finally spoke. "Defense is right, counselor. The defendant's father isn't the one accused. Go on."

She sighed heavily. "Fine. I believe him to be a substantial flight risk and think that he should be remanded into custody until his trial."

The judge looked at Virgil. "Defense, what have you to say?"

"He's a child, Your Honor. Look at him. Clean cut, honor student."

"So was Ted Bundy," the prosecutor interjected.

The judge glared at her. "That's enough of that, Counsel." He returned his attention to Virgil. "Continue."

"He has two jobs and people who rely on him. He is not a flight risk. And I can produce seven upstanding members of this community who are here to give testimony as to his character."

"And I have a video of him—"

The judge banged his gavel. "Counsel, enough." He looked back at Virgil. "Where are your witnesses?"

They stood up. Nick turned to see Liza, Mama Lo Peltier, Kyrian, Mr. Poitiers and Mr. Addams, Dr. Burdette, and Madaug's father, Dr. St. James. His mother, Acheron, Rosa, Kody, and Menyara were also with Kyrian, and Bubba and Mark sat next to Dr. Burdette. Nick's insides shrank at the sight of them. While he was grateful they were willing to stand up for him, he was humiliated that they all knew about this.

Then again, who didn't know? Not like he'd been arrested in private.

He cringed at the thought of facing his classmates and school admin after this. No matter what, he'd forever be labeled as a criminal.

So this is how Brynna felt . . .

Virgil cleared his throat. "And Your Honor, they were the first seven I called. If you give me an hour, I can get you a dozen more. All of whom are willing to testify to Mr. Gautier's good character and upstanding morals."

The judge considered it. "Bail is set at a million

dollars and I want him under house arrest until his trial. He can go to school and work, but nowhere else. And he is not to be left alone."

"Uh, Your Honor," Virgil said, before clearing his throat, "his job for Mr. Hunter requires him to run errands all over the city."

"Then he is to be electronically monitored at all times and will be required to call in every hour on the hour outside of school."

"Yes, Your Honor. Thank you."

Caleb's hearing was much easier. The judge let him go with a promise that he wouldn't touch anymore police cars.

His stomach knotting, Nick headed for his mother. She wouldn't even look at him.

Kyrian clapped Nick on the back. "I've already given the bail money to Virgil to post your bond."

Nick nodded gratefully at Kyrian. "Thank you. For everything."

"No problem."

Acheron placed a comforting hand on his shoulder. "Don't worry, Nick. We'll find out the truth."

But it wouldn't change the hurt in his mother's eyes.

In fact, she refused to speak to him as she drove him home. He searched his mind for something to say, but nothing came.

He reached over to touch her hand. She pulled away before he could make contact. Anger and hurt pierced him straight through his heart. How could she doubt him?

Once they were home, he went to his room.

"Nick? I want you to leave your door open."

He started to say "But Mom," but he knew how that would play out. She'd shut him down like she always did. So he left his door ajar and went to sit on his bed. It was only then that he realized his mom had ransacked his room. "Mom? Where's my—"

"You're on restriction." There was a note of hysteria in her voice. "Sit in there and think about . . . things."

Bad idea, since the only thing on his mind right now was that he hated her for doing this to him when he was innocent.

And as he sat there, *thinking*, his fury mounted even higher until he couldn't stand it anymore. He sprang to his feet and went to the living room where she sat watching TV.

"What do you want?" Still, she wouldn't look at him.

Infuriated, he wiped his hand across his top lip. "I'm a virgin, Mom. I've never done anything more than kiss a girl, and Nekoda's the only one I've done that with. I know you don't believe me, but you can ask her. She's not a liar." And neither am I. But she'd never once believed him about anything.

Tears fell down her face. "I'm so sorry, Nicky. I know you're innocent. I do. But it's so hard for me to be in that courtroom with everyone judging me and you." She started sobbing.

Nick went to her and pulled her into his arms while she cried against his shoulder.

"You don't know what it's like to be the most popular girl in school and then . . . they were so mean to me. Once people knew I was pregnant, I went to my best friend's . . . We'd been friends since second grade, and her mother wouldn't let me in the house. She told me Ashley wasn't allowed to associate with trash."

Guilt slashed at him. He'd never meant to hurt her. "I'm sorry, Mama."

"Don't be, baby. You were worth it. You were. I've never once, ever, regretted having you with me. But it's been so hard. I'm always questioning myself if I'm doing the right thing by you. When you were an infant, I used to sit and hold you and cry while I apologized for bringing you into a world that was so cruel and bone mean. For keeping you in poverty and not being able to give you a better life."

"Don't cry, Mama. Please. I don't care that we had Christmases where the only gifts I got were clean socks and bubblegum. I don't. The only thing that matters to me is that you don't regret me. Please, don't look at me like I'm dirt."

She pulled back to cup his face in her hands. "I would *never* do that to you."

"But you have. A lot. I've seen it."

She shook her head. "No, Nick, that wasn't what you saw."

"Then why couldn't you look at me in the courtroom? Why did you pull your hand back in the car?"

"Because I feel like I failed you and that you were blaming me for being arrested. If I hadn't raised you the way I did, people wouldn't be so quick to judge you like they do. I know that's my fault. I offered to give testimony for you, and your lawyer told me it wouldn't be a good idea. Do you know how that made me feel? He might as well have made me wear a shirt that said 'trash' on it."

"Mama, no. Virgil isn't like that. He was only trying to keep you from getting chewed up by the prosecutor."

"Well, that's not how it felt."

Nick blinked his own tears away. "If you don't hate me, why am I on restriction and why wouldn't you let me close my door?"

"You have a B in chemistry. Remember? I told you at the school that you were on restriction for that."

Oh yeah, he'd totally forgotten. "And the door?"

"It gets really hot in this room when I have the TV on and you close it. What did you think?"

"I thought you thought I was a creep."

She glared at him. "Dang it all, Nick. I know you're not a creep. I've seen the way you are around Kody and other girls, too. You're bashful as you can be, and every time Kody touches your hand, you light up like a Christmas tree. Most of the time, you're scared to even touch her. It's like you're terrified of her."

He cringed. "It's that obvious?"

"Yes."

Would the humiliations never stop?

She wiped at her tears. "I can't believe you misunderstood me so."

"Same here," he said. "Have I ever said or done anything that makes you think I hold anything against you?"

"No, not really. But I hold it against me."

He scowled at her. "Then keep it on you. Don't let it run over here to me."

She placed her hand on his cheek. "I love you, baby. And I'm sorry you have to go through this."

Not as much as he was.

Then, to his shock, she handed him the remote. "I think you've been punished enough for one day. Sit here and watch TV with me."

Grateful beyond belief that he'd been wrong about her actions, Nick flipped channels until she snatched the remote back.

"You drive me crazy the way you watch TV. Pick something and stay with it."

"I have teenage ADD powered by male testosterone, Mom. What do you expect?"

She growled at him as she returned to her girl show. Nick tried not to grimace.

But that ended a few minutes later when a call came in. Since they were watching TV, his mom didn't get up to take it. Instead, she let it go to the answering machine.

"This is Principal Head from St. Richard's. I'm calling to let you know that Nicholas is being expelled from school immediately. If you will mail any textbooks he might have back to us, we would appreciate it. Likewise, we will box up his personal items and have them shipped to your residence on file. Thank you."

His mother's face turned bright red. "How dare he!"

Nick didn't respond. He was too busy feeling a crotch-kick for that. But then, what had he expected? Head thought he was a rapist and a thief. He was just protecting his students from a monster. . . .

Well, at least I don't have to face Head or anyone else

in school again. "Can I call Kody and Caleb to let them know?"

She hesitated before she nodded. "But this isn't over. I'm going to talk to your lawyer tomorrow to see if there's anything we can do."

"Uh, he's not really a day person. He works night court for a reason, so if you want to talk to him, call him before dawn."

She hesitated, then nodded. "Interesting. I'll do that right now. Don't worry, baby. We'll get you back in school."

Don't do me any favors. The thought of going back to school right now didn't appeal to him at all.

My life is falling apart.

He felt like crap, until he looked at his mother as she spoke on the phone, and tried to imagine the horror of what she'd been through by the time she was his age.

Yeah, getting thrown out of school sucked. Getting thrown out of your home was so much worse. Even now, her parents insulted her.

"Hey, Ma?"

She returned after leaving a message for Virgil to sit next to him. "What, Boo?"

"I am so proud of you. Thank you for not giving me away."

She scowled at him. "Oh baby, why do you obsess over that so much? It's like part of you keeps waiting for me to throw you out."

Because part of him *was* waiting for that. It was his worst fear. "I know what it cost you to keep me. I do. And as I get older, it's a lot clearer. By the time you were my age, I was walking."

She smiled. "Oh, I remember how beautiful you were. You didn't have any hair. You were such a bald little booger, I thought I was going to have to save up to buy you a toupee." She ruffled his hair playfully.

He laughed.

She leaned against him. "Don't worry, Boo. Everything will work out. It always does. Somehow, even if it's at the very last second, God always comes through for us."

And her faith never wavered. His was a little more bipolar. But his mother had constant and unflappable belief. He envied her that. And it was amazing given everything she'd been through.

Closing his eyes, Nick listened to the TV as he tried to relax.

And as he tuned the physical world out, he began to hear the ether voices.

Be careful. Be careful. Be careful. Be careful. It sounded like a reptilian voice that echoed around him.

Be careful of what?

My friend's enemy is my enemy.

Yeah, okay, so what did that mean? But there was no answer for his question.

Weird. Typical, but weird.

As he started drifting to sleep, he had an unmistakable feeling. Something was searching. Clawing. Slithering.

And it was here.

CHAPTER 16

Nick couldn't shake the feeling that he was being stalked. But other than his gut, nothing corroborated it. Neither Kody nor Caleb sensed it, which meant they thought he was out of his gourd.

Not the first time anyone ever accused him of being loco. Still . . .

"Would you focus, Nick?"

He blinked at the sound of Ash's voice. "Sorry. I just have a creepy, edgy feeling."

"Believe it or not, it could be the electromagnetic waves put off by your anklet."

Great. That was all he needed. Probably give him

leg or foot cancer one day, too. Just for good mea-
sure.

"Nick . . ."

All of a sudden the car slammed on its brakes.
"Hey!" he snapped at Ash. "I was going to stop, you
know."

"When? After you ran the light?"

"Maybe."

Ash shook his head. When the light turned
green, Nick eased onto the gas and took the right
that would lead him to Kyrian's house. For the last
two weeks while his mother fought the principal
and Nick waited for trial, Ash, in an effort to cheer
him up, was allowing him to drive to and from work.
Especially since it was the only time Nick could leave
the house.

At this point, Nick was going stir crazy. He couldn't
imagine being stuck in jail given how miserable his
life had been while confined to his apartment.

He pulled into Kyrian's driveway and waited for
the gates to open. The only upside to everything that
had happened was that his mother, since finding out

he was a virgin, was relaxing her strict rules for dating. She was even allowing Kody to come over and keep him company while she was at work.

"Ash?" he asked as he pulled up to the front of Kyrian's house. "Have you seen the video the cops have of me?"

"Yeah."

Virgil had shown it to Nick two days ago. "It looks just like me."

"I know."

Nick turned the car off. "I don't know if it's doctored or what. But you can't imagine how terrifying it is to think that there's someone out there who looks just like you. That if he does something, you're going to get blamed for it."

"Yeah, I have no idea." His voice dripped with sarcasm.

"What was that?" Nick asked as Ash got out of the car.

Ash didn't answer until Nick had come around to his side and handed him his keys. "Can you keep a secret?"

"Me and Tupperware, baby. We seal tight. Ain't nothing going to get out. Why?"

Ash tucked his hands into the pockets of his motorcycle jacket that had a skull and crossbones painted in red across the back. "When I was human, I had a twin brother."

Nick gaped. "No way. Are you serious?"

Ash gave a subtle nod.

"That must have been an awesome sight. The two of you, at your height, together? Wow."

"It wasn't the joy you're thinking. I only mention it to let you know that I know exactly how it feels. And I hated it."

"Yeah, but you loved your brother, right?"

Ash didn't respond as he walked up the stairs that led to the front door. Which told Nick everything. Whoever his brother had been, they must not have gotten along. Sad, really. He'd always wondered what it would be like to have a sibling. His mother was the closest thing to that he'd ever know.

Nick took the steps two at a time. He'd just stepped onto the porch when Rosa opened the door for them.

Even though she was in her forties, she was still incredibly beautiful. Her dark hair fell to her shoulders and she was dressed in a pink top and jeans.

"Hola, Rosa," Nick said, offering her a smile.

She returned his smile with one that was as warm as a mother's. *"Hola, m'ijos. ¿Cómo está?"*

"Bien, gracias. Y tú?"

"Muy bien." She closed the door behind him. "Nick, your Spanish is getting so good. Soon we no longer speak English together." Her smile widened at Acheron. "And how are you, Aqueron?"

"Bien. Is Kyrian up in his office?"

"He is."

Ash headed for the ornate curving staircase.

"So, Nick, *¿quieres tú comer?"*

He hesitated. "Wait, you threw in a new word." Then his memory kicked. "Food. No, eat! Do I want to eat. Absolutely. What we got today?"

She laughed at him. "I hope you marry a woman who cooks well. Otherwise, *m'ijo,* I think you will have a short marriage."

"That's what my mom says." As they neared the

kitchen, he caught a whiff of what was cooking. "Oh no you din't! Is that—"

"Si, pollo cacciatore, your favorite."

"Only when you make it." His mouth was already watering for a taste. No one cooked better than Rosa.

"I will make your plate while you take the trash."

"Yes, ma'am." But he did pause by the pan to inhale a good whiff of it. Man, he could live on that for days. . . .

Forcing himself away from it, he pulled the trash liner out and headed out the back door to where the cans were located.

As he was putting the lid back on the can, he heard something click. At first he didn't pay any attention to it. Not until a chill went down his spine, and in his mind, he saw himself being attacked.

Shaking his head, he'd just convinced himself he was being paranoid when all of a sudden someone tackled him to the ground.

"You little punk!" The man slammed a baseball bat down across his arm.

Nick cursed as he felt bones shatter under the

blow. He moved to roll over and escape. But the man hit him with three more furious strikes, then started kicking him. Nick tried to crawl toward the house, but blow after blow alternated with kick after kick.

I'm going to die. . . .

He knew it. He couldn't even defend himself.

All of a sudden, someone grabbed the man and hauled him off Nick.

Kyrian knelt by his side. "Nick? Can you hear me?"

"That little bastard raped my daughter! I hope he's dead!"

"Rosa! Call an ambulance! Pronto!" Kyrian pulled his jacket off and draped it over Nick's body. "Stay with me, Nick. Please don't make me have to tell your mother you're dead. She'll kill me."

Nick couldn't respond. He was so cold that his teeth were chattering. Behind him, he could hear Acheron on his phone, reporting the attack to the police.

Crying and praying, Rosa knelt down next to Kyrian and pressed her rosary into Nick's hand.

"How can you protect scum like that? What's wrong with you people?"

"He didn't do it," Acheron growled in the man's face. "You just assaulted an innocent boy."

"You think I don't know that little punk? I've seen him around the school. He's been in classes with my daughter for years. And I hope they lock him up for the rest of his life."

Nick was finally able to move his head enough so that he could see who it was.

Mr. Quattlebaum. Dina's father. His head swam from pain, but he tried to focus. He needed to think through this. Dina was one of Brynna's tight friends. He barely knew her. Quiet and shy, she seldom spoke to anyone. He couldn't even remember the last time he'd seen her.

Sirens rang out, drawing closer. *Don't pass out. . . .* Nick kept that thought foremost in his mind. He didn't want to go back to the Nether Realm. Not right now.

Kyrian left him to open the gate for the ambulance and police.

Nick tried to return Rosa's rosary. It'd been her First Communion present from her father, who had died of a heart attack not long after he'd given it to her. She counted it among her most precious possessions.

"No, *m'ijo*. You keep it for now so that God will watch over you. You can return it later."

As the EMTs started working on him, Nick heard the sound of laughter. Low and coming from the ether. At first, he thought he was crazy.

Until the police handcuffed Dina's father. The moment they hauled him toward the front of the house, Nick saw a demon shimmer out of Mr. Quattlebaum's body.

It was a demon he knew.

Where had he seen it? He had to remember, but the pain made it impossible. As he struggled to stay conscious, the ether voices screamed louder.

He saw his classmates as they read the lies and awful truths that had been posted about each other online. For weeks now, Brynna and the other girls had been harassed and accused of all kinds of vice. Fights had broken out constantly, even after the school meetings.

Trexian . . .

That was the demon he'd seen.

The EMT put an oxygen mask over his face. Nick tried to call out to Caleb or Kody with his thoughts to let them know what he suspected and what had happened. But before he could, the EMTs knocked him out.

Grim sighed as he watched Nick being placed inside an ambulance. Disgusted, he set his crystal ball aside to meet Bane's dark gaze.

"He's slipped out of your clutches again, huh?" Bane asked drily.

"Of course he did. I've never seen anything like it. He's worse than a cat."

Bane glanced to the crystal ball. "He's not out of danger yet. Could still get a nasty infection in the hospital. Maybe some kind of flesh-eating virus?"

"Don't tease me, Bane. I wish." *He* couldn't kill Nick. Stupid bargain.

All he could do was continue to hammer Nick's self-esteem and wear him down until he killed himself. But Nick was stronger than he looked. It was why they couldn't allow him to mature. Adarian was hard enough to deal with.

Ambrosius . . .

He would be the most dangerous Malachai ever born.

And Bane was right. Sooner or later, Grim would find the right person to influence. And then Nick would be nothing more than a bad memory.

A slow smile spread across his face as a new plan formed. And he knew just the entity to finish Nick off.

"I know that look. What are you going to do?" Bane asked.

"I'm going to give us the heart of a Malachai."

CHAPTER 17

✖

Nick opened his eyes, expecting to find himself in the Nether Realm again.

Instead, he was inside a temple with a golden roof that had forest scenes of deer and other animals on it. Sunlight poured in through the white columns.

Am I dead?

"No, you're not dead." The heavily accented voice was thick with an accent he knew extremely well. Greek.

Nick turned his head to see a vision in a long white dress that left her right shoulder bare. Her vivid red hair fell all the way down her back in thick, fat curls. Her skin was flawless as a goddess's should be.

"Artemis? What am I doing here?"

"We made a bargain, did we not?"

"We did."

"Well then, I can't have you being fought over by Thorn and Noir, can I?"

He supposed not. "Why am I so sluggish?"

"It's the drugs they're giving you. They affect you even in this realm."

Who knew? Nick tried to sit up, but it was useless.

"Just relax. Rest until you awaken in the human realm."

Nick nodded and closed his eyes. He saw himself again, summoning Artemis to heal Kody. At the time, he hadn't been sure it would work. But in addition to being goddess of the hunt, Artemis was also a healer, and a protector of children and women. At least that was what Kyrian had told him.

As a precaution should one of the Daimons or something else try to eat him while Kyrian couldn't help, he'd given Nick his ring that held Artemis's symbol. And then Kyrian had told Nick how to use the ring to summon the goddess.

In the beginning of their relationship, Nick had thought Kyrian crazy. But over the last year, he'd learned crazy wasn't what it used to be. And instead of selling Kyrian's ring, he'd kept it just in case.

Nick had been willing to give Artemis his soul. Instead, she had only taken some of his blood. But she'd sworn him to absolute secrecy. He couldn't tell anyone that he'd seen her.

"Why did you agree to help Kody?" he asked.

Artemis shrugged. "She's a warrior. A huntress of her own. I have a soft knot for such women."

Nick started to correct her mixed-up idiom, then caught himself. It was never wise to correct a god. "I still don't understand."

"It's not for you to understand. Now rest. Soon you will have a battle to fight and you will need all of your strength."

He tried to ask her what battle, but he was too weak to even do that. Against his will, he went back to sleep.

When Nick finally came to, he found himself in the ER again. At this point, they should just keep a room reserved for him—or a frequent patient card or something. What the heck? Name the hall after him since he was now on a first-name basis with half the staff.

Kyrian and his mother were there, along with Acheron and Kody.

His mother glared at him. "You are trying to put me in an early grave, aren't you?"

"Really not."

"You're lucky, Nick" Kyrian said. "You have a broken arm, but the rest of it is superficial."

"Thank the gods you have a hard head," Acheron added. "I honestly didn't think you'd make it given what I saw. That man was definitely after your life."

Even so, Nick felt bad for the man. While he didn't appreciate the beating, he well understood the man's motivation. "What about Mr. Quattlebaum?"

Kyrian sighed. "He was arrested for battery."

"He's lucky I didn't get ahold of him," his mother growled.

"Yeah," Kyrian agreed. "Come to find out, he's been stalking you for the last few days, waiting until he could get you alone and attack."

So Nick hadn't been imagining that. Someone was

watching him. Here Nick had been looking for something paranormal when it'd been a human . . .

Nick froze as his memory drifted to what he'd seen just before he'd passed out. Quattlebaum hadn't been alone. He turned his head to meet Kody's gaze. *There's a Trexian on the loose,* he projected his thoughts to her.

She widened her eyes. *Are you sure?*

He nodded. *I think it might be behind all of this.*

Trexians were very similar to Ash's Atlantean goddesses. They thrived on causing turmoil.

It all made sense.

And the only one who could find a Trexian was one of its victims. The earlier the victim, the easier to track it. And Nick had a pretty good idea who the first victim had been.

Hah, Caleb! I do *read.* And all that he remembered from the last time he'd consulted his grimore.

He turned his attention back to Kody. *I need you to get Brynna for me.*

One of Kody's brows shot northward as a little green monster flared in her eyes. "Excuse me?"

Everyone turned to look at her expectantly.

Kody's face flushed bright red. "Sorry. I didn't mean to say that out loud."

As soon as they stopped looking at her, she glared at him. *Brynna?*

I'm going to lay a bet that she was the original target, and even though I was one of his targets, because I'm not fully human, I'm not sure if my confronting the demon will work.

Okay, that makes sense. You're out of the doghouse. For now.

Good, 'cause he didn't like the scenery there. It was a cold, arctic place. While he could get into the doghouse with ninja speed, getting out of it wasn't usually this easy. *Let's hear it for near-death experiences.*

And once Kody left, he spent the next half hour arguing with his mother on why he didn't need to stay the night for observation. It was Acheron who finally convinced her.

"We'll keep an eye on him, Cherise, I'm sure he'll be much more comfortable at home."

Once she agreed with Ash, it seemed to take him forever to get out of the hospital and headed back home.

His mom ranted the whole way. Wow . . . too bad nagging wasn't an Olympic sport. His mom would easily take the gold. "I can't believe you were attacked again. He better be glad the police have him. If I ever lay eyes on him . . ."

"Mom, breathe. He only did what you're threatening to. He thinks I raped his daughter. We're both lucky he doesn't have your temper or a gun, otherwise, I'd be dead."

She reached over and squeezed the hand on his broken arm.

Nick yelped. "Now? Now you want to hold my hand? I swear, Ma, you're twisted."

She rolled her eyes at him, then parallel parked in a space in front of their apartment.

Nick got out and waited for her. "Are you going back to work?" *Please, please go back to work. . . .*

"I hadn't planned on it."

Of course not. That would make his life too easy. C'mon, *please, go to work. I'll be fine.*

"But you know, Nicky, you're looking fine to me. I think I'll go on."

Was that his powers? Could it be one of them was actually working?

She handed him her keys. "You can let yourself in, right?"

"Yeah. Are you walking to work?"

"I normally do."

Then he decided to test his powers to see if it was him or just weird luck. *Take the car. You might need it.*

His mother paused mid-step, then turned around. "But you know, I might need it, and given what happened to you . . . Yeah, I better take it to work."

Nick gaped at the fact that he *finally* had a working power. And it was a good one too!

"Let me let you in."

He waited until she'd unlocked the door and left before he summoned Kody and Caleb. Luckily, after Kody had talked to Brynna about Nick's plan, Kody had then explained everything to Caleb.

"And you're sure you saw a Trexian?" Caleb asked. "You were in the middle of another near-death experience. The chemicals in the brain can kick up all kinds of weirdness with that type of stress."

"I'm sure, Caleb. Since I've been on house arrest, I've taken your advice and have overcome my biblio-phobia. I've been doing a ton of research."

Caleb appeared shocked, then impressed. "Really?"

"Yeah, you know they have all kinds of information online."

Caleb passed an irritated smirk at Kody. "He can find more ways to navigate out of something he doesn't want to do than anyone I've ever met. Impressive. Ir-ritating, but impressive."

"So what's the plan?" Kody asked.

"I'm going to pick up Brynna and then we're going to pay the Trexian a visit."

Or Nick was going to jail for a really, really long time. . . .

Brynna was still protesting as they stood outside of Dina Quattlebaum's house. "Nick, I've known her most of my life. You're absolutely wrong about her. She didn't do this."

He refused to listen to her. "Then we can apologize. But I don't think I'm wrong. I know I'm right. Think about some of the things written on the site. The feelings of being invisible."

Brynna scoffed. "Everyone feels invisible at times. Dina's no different than anyone else. Believe me, she wouldn't hurt a flea. Never mind me, or anyone else."

"Bryn, *if* I'm wrong, we apologize and go home. But if I'm right . . ."

All of this would stop.

"Fine. Go on, then. Embarrass yourself. I'm right behind you."

Kody stopped them. "That might not be a good idea, since we don't know if she lied about her rape, or not. If she really was attacked, and she's not lying about that part, seeing Nick might unhinge her.— For all we know, her attacker really looked like him."

She had a point. A very good one.

"Nick, stay in the bushes and I'll check it out." Brynna went up the walkway.

Hoping for the best, Nick came in from the side of Dina's yard. He'd just ducked into the hedges that surrounded the ornate front porch, when Brynna knocked on the door.

No one answered.

Brynna glanced at him. "Maybe she's not home."

Nick knew better. He could sense people inside the house. Most of all, he could feel the deep sadness and hatred that fed the demon part of him. "Try again."

She did.

After a few seconds, the door opened slowly. Dina stood there in a pair of dingy sweats and an oversized gray sweatshirt. Her hair was in pigtails, and it was obvious she'd been crying. Her eyes were swollen and her nose red. Sniffing, she frowned at Brynna. "What are *you* doing here?" Could there be anymore hatred in that one single word?

"You haven't been in school for the last few days and you haven't returned my calls. I was worried about you."

"I'm fine. Just leave me alone, okay?" She started to close the door.

Brynna stopped her. "Why have you been crying?"

"I haven't been crying."

Yeah, right.

"Then that's one bad allergy you have. Have you been to a doctor about it?"

If looks could disintegrate people, Brynna would be porch dust. "Why don't you just go back to your perfect little life and leave me alone. I'm not your pet project, you know?"

Brynna scowled. "What are you talking about?"

Dina sneered at her. "You're such a bitch, Brynna. Go."

Brynna refused. "I'm not going anywhere. We're friends. And I don't understand where all of this animosity is coming from. What has happened to you?"

"You want to know? You *really* want to know?"

Brynna was aghast. "Of course."

Dina sniffed. "Who did you ask to be on your stupid committee? Huh?"

Brynna appeared stumped as she tried to remember.

"You're so pathetic," Dina snarled. "Okay, let me help you. Who did you *not* ask that you should have?"

Brynna's scowl deepened. "Well . . . Casey had cheerleading practice so I didn't ask her."

Screwing her face up, Dina grimaced at her, then tried to slam the door in Brynna's face.

Brynna caught it again. In that instant her eyes lit up as she finally understood what Dina was talking about. "*You?* You're mad at me because *I* didn't ask *you?*"

"Of course I'm mad at you. You slapped me in my face, in front of everyone."

"How?"

"We're supposed to be friends, remember? Everyone knows that except *you*. I waited and waited for you to ask me, but you didn't, did you? No. I'm not good enough to be part of the Brynna Addams posse. You didn't even bother to get the license plate number of the bus you threw me under, did you? No. Because you don't care. It's all about you, all the time. You couldn't care less about anyone else."

Brynna snapped her jaw shut and looked straight through Dina. "Have you lost every shred of sanity? Really? What are you thinking? I didn't ask you because you hate dances with a passion. You're always ranting and ranting about them and how lame you think they are. How you'd rather be set on fire than look like an idiot in public. No, wait, wait, wait, wait, *your* exact words . . . 'It's just an excuse for horny teenage boys to publicly grope girls and get away with it.' The last thing I want is to feel one of *those*"—she made air quotes with her hands—"disgusting things rub up against me while I'm dressed nice. Nor do I want to bump and grind on a girl. If I want to pay homage to Sappho, I'll write her a poem. Is that not verbatim your constant tirade?"

Now it was Dina's turn to sputter.

But Brynna gave her no reprieve. Not while she was on a roll. "*That* is why I didn't invite you. I didn't think you'd enjoy it, and given your most voiced negative feelings about dances, I thought it would make you mad if I asked. I figured you'd think *that* was an insult. Excuse me for trying to save *your* feelings. But no, it's not me, is it? You were looking for a reason to be angry at me, because I guarantee if I had asked, you would have been offended and you would have accused me of not paying attention to you or caring enough to really listen to your rants. Of not being a real friend because a real friend wouldn't have asked, knowing how you felt about dances."

As Dina became more flustered, her skin began to mottle. Her eyes turned glassy.

This wasn't good.

Terrified for Brynna, Nick jumped up on the porch. Just as he reached her, Dina lunged for Brynna and slammed into his broken arm. The pain from it was staggering. He clenched his fist against the cast, but not even that helped. For ten seconds, he feared he might pass out from it.

But after that, something peculiar happened. He felt a charge in his powers similar to what he'd experienced in jail. It was like they went into overdrive.

Dina's teeth elongated. Her eyes turned solid white as she snarled and hissed, trying to kill them.

From someplace deep inside, Nick tapped his inherited memories that came from his father and all the Malachai before him.

He caught Dina with his good arm and hauled her back from Brynna. When he spoke, it was in the Malachai's voice and in his native tongue. "You have no right to possess this girl. Let her go."

The demon protested its orders. "She invited me in. She wanted me."

"And you have used her against *me*. Have you *any* idea what I do to demons who come against me?"

The demon sniveled obsequiously. "Forgive me, Master. But remember, I have helped you grow stronger. You have learned from me."

Nick tightened his grip. "And there are much better ways to teach." With his powers and the words Xenon had taught him when they'd gone up against his coach, Nick forced the beast out of Dina.

As soon as she was free of the demon, she passed out in his arms. Nick laid her down on the porch at Brynna's feet.

"Watch her."

Eyes wide, Brynna nodded.

Nick went after the Trexian to keep it from jumping into someone else's body. But instead of fleeing, it went into attack mode. With a resounding cry, it spun on him.

Kody froze as she saw the Trexian tackle Nick. She took a step forward to help him, but Caleb caught her. "What are you doing? He has to learn to protect himself. We can't keep jumping in and helping him."

Kody didn't want to hear that. "But—"

"No, buts, Kody. If you want him to live and to thrive, he has to do this himself."

Easier said than done. "He's hurt."

"And it's strengthening him. Look."

She did, and he was right. Since the Malachai was born of the darkness, it was those negative emotions that fueled him.

Still, she cringed every time the demon got a punch in. It went low and swept Nick's feet out from under him. But instead of falling to the porch, Nick twisted his body and even with his arm in a sling, flipped to land on his feet.

The Trexian tried to bite him. He caught it in one hand and drove it back.

Nick felt his grip weakening. While he'd had the demon under control, he was fast losing it and he wasn't sure why.

"You are not the Malachai," it sneered, mocking him. "You don't have your full powers. You are *nothing*. Worthless spittle on the sidewalk. Trash."

That last word, instead of kicking him in the gut and making him feel less than human as it had in the past, fortified and angered him. For the first time in his life, he realized it wasn't true.

Nick Gautier was *not* trash. And he fully understood Grim's warning about how silkspeech and influence could backfire.

He smiled at the Trexian. "Baby, I ain't trash. Trash is something you throw away. My people keep me."

And with that, he felt his powers rise up and shoot out.

The Trexian screamed as Nick finally banished it back to the darkness that had birthed it.

Unfortunately, as it went, so did Nick's anger. And it left so fast that it zapped every bit of his strength. One moment, he was standing. The next . . .

Ow . . .

He hit the boards on the front porch face-first. Oh yeah, they definitely had to work on this. It was not dignified to kick butt and then hit dirt like a deflated balloon.

Kody came running to his side. "Nick? Nick?"

"I'm all right . . . well, all right is a stretch. I should say I'm breathing. Kind of." 'Cause breathing was really hurting right now. "And I'm really wishing I'd taken something for the pain." But unfortunately, he could never do that again. Bad things happened to him whenever he lost control of himself, and the last thing he needed was a painkiller knocking him out.

Gently, Kody rolled him over and held his head in her lap. "My poor baby, but you looked totally K-A!"

And she looked totally beautiful.

By the time Caleb double-checked that the demon was gone and made it up to the porch, Dina groaned from where she still lay at Brynna's feet. Pressing her hand to her head, she blinked open her eyes.

"Brynna?" she asked in disbelief. "What are you doing here?"

Brynna scowled. "Don't you remember?"

Dina's brow furrowed. Then she gasped. "The locket!" She snatched it off her neck and threw it into the bushes."

They all stared at her as if she'd been possessed again.

"What was that?" Brynna asked.

"Evil! I bought it in a store on St. Anne because I was feeling really bad. The man told me it would make me feel better about myself."

Caleb licked his lips. "When did you buy it?"

Dina blinked. "Yesterday, after school. Bryn and Shon were talking about what they were going to do for the dance and who they wanted for the committee." She sat up and glared at Brynna. "I kept waiting for one of you to invite me and *you* didn't! Instead you invited that geek and the trash and . . ." Her voice trailed off as she realized the trash was also on her front porch.

"W-w-what are you doing here?" Dina gasped.

Nick wanted to stand and do his tough guy strut. Unfortunately for his ego, his body was through listening to him. "Saving your butt, but now I'm thinking I should have fed you to it."

"Dina," Brynna said, her voice dropping an octave. "That wasn't yesterday. That was weeks ago."

"No, it was yesterday."

Brynna shook her head.

Nick's phone rang. And of course, it was in the pocket under his broken arm. He tried to reach it and couldn't. "Um, help, somebody."

Caleb backed up. "Ah, heck no, I ain't even groping in another guy's pants pocket. Forget it. That's your girlfriend's job."

Laughing, Kody reached in for it. For a full minute, Nick felt no pain whatsoever. All he felt was her hand sliding against his thigh. Yeah, he liked that. Definitely worth getting beaten with a bat to have her do that.

She pulled his phone out and answered it. "It's Madaug." She handed it to him.

"Hey, what's up?" he asked.

"Me and Mark *finally* cracked the site. It was weird. At first the code was like some living entity. Everything we tried, it deflected. I've never seen anything like it. Then a couple of minutes ago, bam. It opened right up. Go figure."

Because a few minutes ago was when Nick had banished the demon. "Let me guess, the site is owned by Dina Quattlebaum?"

"Close." Madaug sounded impressed. "Her father. How did you know that?"

Nick glanced over to her. "Really lucky guess. Tell Mark I said thanks, and Madaug . . ."

"Yeah?"

"Good job, buddy. You're the best."

"No problem. Talk to you later."

Nick hung up and sadly slid his phone into a pocket he could reach. "That was Madaug."

Caleb crossed his arms over his chest. "We heard."

Nick sat up slowly to meet Brynna's gaze. "We found out who posted those photos of you, and who's been running the trash site about our classmates."

Dina's face went white. "How do you know about my domain?"

"That was *you*!" Brynna shrieked. "You made photos of me . . . of me . . ."

The all-out panic on Dina's face said that part of the cruelty had been spawned purely out of her own jealousy and anger, not the demon's.

"Why would you do something like that?" Brynna yelled.

"It was a joke."

Brynna curled her lip. "No one laughed."

"Oh please . . . you and all your rich friends with your perfect Norman Rockwell lives . . . you all deserve to be knocked off your high horses."

Brynna screwed her face up. "My life isn't perfect, Dina. Good grief, my parents are divorced and they split us kids up like we're silverware. The one person in this world I love, loves someone else. I'm flunking math. I've flunked my learner's test four times now. I have a little brother who's a monster and my parents won't correct him. And I'm the only Addams in nine generations who can't cook. Believe me, there is nothing perfect about *my* life. And you don't see me maliciously attacking other people over it. I've read your aweful hate-filled postings. *You're* the one who thinks you're superior to us. And at the end of the day, what makes you angry isn't the money or the clothes or popularity. It's because you're jealous over the fact that even though our lives aren't perfect, even though life is doing its best to bring us to our knees, too, we still manage to be happy. In spite of everything, we don't attack other people and we laugh at things that are funny. And sister, no one worth a damn laughs at cruelty. That's what you're really jealous over. And *that* is what makes us better than you. We're compassionate human beings, not conniving, self-serving, bitter harpies spreading misery everywhere we go."

"You're an idiot. You don't know anything."

Brynna went to slap her, but Kody caught her hand.

"She's not worth it."

"Oh, trust me, she *so* is."

Nick shook his head. "Let her live, Bryn. The best revenge in the world? Let her face the people she's attacked at school. People like her think they're safe at home, making masked attacks on a glowing computer screen against people who've never harmed them. And while the anonymity seems to keep them safe, the Internet is the one place where you can be identified absolutely. Every IP is unique to the user and dedicated logs are kept. You *can* be found. And even if the person you attack doesn't retaliate, it doesn't matter. Karma will get you, and she's a nasty bugger once you rile her. Absolutely no one escapes her wrath." He looked at Dina. "I'm truly sorry for what you've brought on yourself. Right now, I'm so glad I'm not you."

Brynna lifted her chin with dignity as she stared Dina down. "I can't believe I almost let someone as petty as you drive me to suicide. What was I thinking? But you know what? I've learned who my friends are." Her gaze went to Nick, Kody, and Caleb. "And I've learned who they're not. As my mama used to say, sometimes you just have to run the snakes out of your garden. Have a nice life, Dina. But the saddest thing is I know you won't until you learn that when someone has something you don't it doesn't take anything away from you. Ever." And with those words spoken, she headed off the porch.

Nick made a Yoda gesture at Dina. "May the Force be with you."

They left Dina on her porch and made their way back to the sidewalk. Nick draped his arm around Kody's shoulders.

"So, how are you going to get her to apologize to everyone?" Kody asked.

Nick quirked a lopsided grin. "Trust me. Now, please," he whimpered, "get me home before I fall over. I am in pain. Lots and lots of pain. Giant, Malachai-sized pain."

Kody bit her bottom lip as she scanned him. "We'll get you there. And when we do, I'll kiss your boo-boos."

Yeah, she definitely had more power than he did. Because those last four words erased every bit of pain in his body.

EPILOGUE

Again, I want to apologize to everyone for what I did by setting up the Web site and telling lies about my fellow students. I am so incredibly sorry. It was wrong and cowardly, and I will never do it again."

Nick glanced over to Kody as Dina finished her public apology over the loudspeaker. Sadly, Dina was going to jail as soon as she finished her apology and left here. And he took no satisfaction from that knowledge whatsoever. It was too sad for any kind of victory celebration.

What had started out as a mean prank to get back at someone who had never meant to harm her in any way had caused her to commit a felony. Yeah, she could blame the Trexian for it. Or Brynna, and Dina was.

But in the end, she'd been the one who'd unleashed the demon from the necklace and allowed it to possess her. Nick was just grateful she'd admitted to lying about his raping her and that once the police had insisted she be examined, they'd found out she was as much a virgin as he was.

Still, there were no winners in this. As his mom so often said, in a fight, no one walks away unscathed. All participants get bloody. And even after all of this drama, people at school were still being mean to each other. Still mocking Nick over his arrest, and the other lies Dina had told.

Some things never changed. But even though he was a Malachai, Nick still had hope that people would learn and change.

The bell rang.

Caleb ran on to third period ahead of them, while Kody took his hand and walked him there. Dressed in that tight cream sweater, she was delicious. And best of all, she was wearing the pink heart necklace he'd given her once all the charges had been dropped. It was a celebration gift, and since she'd claimed his heart, it was a reminder that her life was much more important to him than his was.

Even though it was against the rules, Nick gave her a quick kiss before he went into the room, and stopped dead in his tracks.

Literally.

Grim was their substitute chemistry teacher. This had to be a bad idea.

"Are you planning to blow up the school?" Nick asked.

Grim snorted. "I'm not that lucky. Believe it or not, this is what I do for fun."

Yeah, he found that impossible to believe . . . unless the lab ended up exploding with lots of carnage.

Nick cleared his throat. "Well then, I'll take my seat. I am going to live through this. Right?"

"Have no fear, Gautier. *I* don't pose a threat to you."

A really bad feeling went through him. "What do you mean?"

"Is. English. Not. Your. Native. Language?" Grim spoke each word separately, and strung each syllable out.

Nick hated it when he did that.

"Oh, how silly of me," Grim continued. "I forgot Stupid is your native tongue. Fine. I'll spell it out for you. I'm not the one who is under orders to kill you."

He went cold with the news. "But someone here is?"

Grim inclined his head.

Nick's gaze instinctively went to Caleb.

Grim scoffed. "No, he's actually loyal."

"Then who?"

"You'll know instantly. You can't miss her. She's wearing a pink heart around her neck."